A NOVEL

Masks and Mirrors

Book Two: The Weir Chronicles

Sue Duff

CROSSWINDS PUBLISHING / DENVER

For Leah —
I hope you
enjoy the
"show" —
Best Wishes —
Sue Duff

CrossWinds Publishing
P.O. Box 630223
Littleton, Colorado 80163
www.sueduff.com

Publisher's Note: This is a work of fiction. Names, characters, places, and incidents are a product of the author's imagination. Locales and public names are sometimes used for atmospheric purposes. Any resemblance to actual people, living or dead, or to businesses, companies, events, institutions, or locales is completely coincidental.

Book Layout © 2014 BookDesignTemplates.com

Masks and Mirrors/ Sue Duff. -- 1st ed.
ISBN 978-0-9905628-4-9

For my sister Barbara
The distant thunder that refused to fade

Doubt

One of the most destructive tools an enemy can wield against a leader—a hero—a rebel. Delivered as a whisper, it creates a translucent fog that permeates trust and confidence. Time is its ally, transforming relationships like bursts of wind skimming across the dunes.

The strong become weak, the weak paralyzed—the adversary has struck a commanding blow without lifting a sword.

The Pur Heir, Book of the Weir, Vol. II

Part One

Those who walk in darkness can never be certain of
their destination.

{ 1 }

Troubled thoughts kept Jaered on the alert. Summoned in the middle of the night to meet his father, he shyfted to the texted coordinates and found himself in an office waiting room. He froze, not because Aeros had arrived ahead of him, it was the pharmaceutical company logo on the wall behind his father. This facility wasn't part of his father's network. It was part of Eve's.

Had Aeros stumbled upon Eve's interests in the company, or worse, discovered Jaered's collusion with the rebel leader?

An elaborate stretch and yawn slowed his erratic heartbeat. "What's so important it couldn't wait until morning?" Jaered said.

Aeros walked out of the waiting room without offering a response. The slight wasn't uncommon, but did nothing to ease Jaered's concern.

"You will see soon enough," said Cyphir, his father's most trusted guard.

Jaered lagged a few steps behind his father while the rest of their security detail followed at a short distance. The hallway was wide enough for the guards to flank his father, but no one kept abreast of Aeros. No one dared. The man commanded a presence that his inner circle respected and that those ignorant or outright suicidal, discovered soon enough.

They walked down the research lab's long antiseptic corridor with determined steps, headed toward a metal door. Its surface reflected abstract swirls from the overhead fluorescent lights. A tall, lean man stood next to it. He wore a custom-tailored suit and a silk tie that screamed position and wealth. His smug expression announced conceit.

The troubled thoughts gave way to a searing heat in the center of Jaered's chest. Eve had history with the CEO of the facility, but she would never say more. The midnight hour, coupled with Aeros's summons, brought a new revelation. Had the CEO betrayed Eve?

Cyphir pulled ahead the second Aeros's pace slowed. The waiting man's eyes widened and his lips parted, unable to conceal his horror at the guard's scarred and deformed jaw. Cyphir raised the man's arms and patted him down. A moment later, Cyphir's nod bespoke safe passage to the door.

The frisked man straightened an already aligned tie. He lowered his gaze in greeting. "Aeros, you humble us by your visit." He extended a hand in welcome. "I am Richard Donovan, CEO of Lux Pharmaceuticals."

Cyphir grabbed Donovan's hand and with the twist of the wrist dropped the pompous CEO to one knee. "Sire is the most powerful man in the universe." He bent low and paused next to Donovan's contorted face. "And the most feared for a reason. Show the respect he commands or you will replace today's test subject."

Donovan lowered his eyes and bowed his head, in pain or in reverence, Jaered couldn't guess. "Sire, I am your humble servant. I live only to serve you." Cyphir let go and took a step back. Donovan cradled his injured wrist against his chest and rose on unsteady legs.

Aeros remained silent, as though the man wasn't worth his breath. As powerful as Jaered's father was, he had but a single weakness. He had grown arrogant during his time on Earth. His swelling legion of Duach followers had infiltrated more than a thousand, carefully chosen laboratories around the world. Each one engaged in various forms of death and destruction on a global scale. Jaered's father had moved up his timetable since losing his lab in Oregon a couple months ago to the Syndrion and the Pur Heir. They had robbed him of his pet project.

A lone bead of sweat trickled down Donovan's otherwise cordial face. He turned away to enter a code on a keypad, then pressed his palm against the nearby screen. A muted buzz sounded and a blinking red dot turned to a steady green. He pushed the lever down and tugged. *Swish.* The airtight seal separated and he stepped into a small control room, then paused between two men wearing white lab coats, seated at a console. A larger, circular room lay beyond. A middle-aged man clothed in wrinkled street clothes lay strapped to a gurney in the center of the sparse, well-lit space. A rolled-up sleeve exposed one of his forearms. Thick glass separated the two rooms. Its curvature offered minimal distortion.

Donovan kept his hands to himself. Jaered questioned if he ever touched anything inside his labs. His facility secretly contained the types of viruses that brought nightmares to life and could change the course of history. Eve had commissioned the CEO to create such a weapon. Her interests often mirrored Jaered's father's as her rebel forces walked a precarious line between good and evil. Too often, Jaered found the line blurred—in the name of the greater good.

"This is Dr. Chang, head of the team that designed the weapon." Donovan indicated a man seated next to him.

The wiry man looked up at them with pride. Aeros discarded him with a glance.

"The test subject is a Sar?" Cyphir asked. "He has a powerful core?"

"A Duach, although I would have preferred to use a Pur scum," Donovan said. "This one commands animals."

Aeros scoffed. "You promised me a drug lethal enough to take out any Weir Sar, Pur or Duach." He turned to Donovan and the whites of his eyes turned a fiery crimson. "To convince me of its potency, I would expect it to be tested on the most powerful of Weir Sars, not the most common of them."

The deep tan flushed from Donovan's face. "I wasn't notified of your interest until yesterday, sire. The first trial wasn't scheduled for two more weeks." He stared down at Chang's bald head. "This is the best I could do on short notice."

"Cyphir will supply the next candidate," Aeros said. "For now, carry on with this inferior."

Donovan nodded, then cleared his throat. "Proceed."

Chang grasped the joystick and flipped a switch. A high-pitched screech from the other room pierced the window separating them. An overhead mechanical arm came alive and descended, then stopped inches above the man. A hypodermic rotated into view.

The prisoner turned his head toward them and his face contorted. The thick glass muted his shouts. The subject struggled against his bindings. The needle thrust into the port attached to his arm and an amber-tinted fluid drained from its vial.

Chang pressed the screen in front of him. Seconds counted off on the digital wall panel. Donovan regarded the clock, then turned toward the window.

Jaered hung back near the door, willing with everything he had for this trial to fail. Donovan and his research team would never leave this room alive, and the latest threat from his father will have been averted. If the trial was successful, would he be able to stop his father from using it, or discovering that Eve had a hand in creating it?

Seconds swelled into an eternity. The digital numbers on the wall rose with indifference to the suffocating tension in the room while Donovan's pungent sweat overwhelmed the airtight space. One of the scientists' coughed.

Aeros swept his arm. Donovan rose and hovered a few feet above the floor. "Wait! I have knowledge that you would want. I have a son—"

"What I *want* you did not deliver," Aeros snarled.

A scream from beyond the glass. Jaered stepped toward the window, aghast at the test subject's transformation. The center of the man's chest glowed crimson, bright enough to be seen through his shirt. Heated fumes emanated from every pore of his translucent skin. He pressed his head back and his mouth opened, releasing flames into the air. The man's core burned him alive from the inside out.

Aeros's hand dropped. Donovan crumpled to the floor, sputtering. "Delivered as promised, sire."

Jaered focused on his father's reflection in the glass. A smile parted Aeros's lips as he stared at the test subject's body engulfed in a brilliant blaze. The room filled with smoke. An alarm sounded. Overhead sprinklers kicked on and a torrential rain drenched the corpse. Aeros's entertainment was cut short. The disappointment on his father's face was palatable.

"I will require tremendous quantities," Aeros said. "My legions are vast. There are many Weir Sars scattered across Earth."

"I was under the impression there weren't that many Pur Sars left," Donovan said.

Cyphir grabbed the CEO by the arm and jerked him to his feet. Donovan's face twisted. "Dare to question the master again, and you will not draw another breath," the guard hissed.

Jaered clenched his fists at the man's naïveté. His father wouldn't limit its use to the Pur. All Weir Sars, Pur or Duach, were viewed as a threat to Aeros's global annihilation agenda.

"The serum is ready in its current form? Nothing further is required to mass-produce it?" Aeros said.

"No sire, unless you want to find a more suitable subject and test it further." Donovan rubbed his sore arm.

Aeros stared at the corpse through the glass. "It will be tested soon enough." He regarded Jaered for the first time. "You will see to it that the drug is ready for distribution within two weeks."

Jaered cautioned himself not to appear eager. He crossed his arms and threw the CEO a hateful glare, but the frightened expressions on the cowering scientists stole the edge from his voice. "I'm not babysitting him, or his pit crew."

"Who else knows of this?" Aeros asked.

"Only those in this room," Donovan said without the merest hint that it was a lie.

Aeros waved his hand.

"Ugh." Chang slumped down in his booth chair. His extremities contorted at unnatural angles. His eyes glassed over. The other scientist bolted from his seat. Cyphir reached out and grabbed his head. With a twist, the scientist's face lined up with his back and he slumped to the floor.

Aeros brushed past Jaered. "Now, it's manageable."

Jaered clenched his jaw, but hid any other reaction behind the mask he wore like a second skin in his father's presence.

A muted chime came from deep within Cyphir's pocket. He withdrew his cell and swiped the screen.

Movement under Jaered's feet. A ballpoint pen on the console rattled, then rolled off. One of the scientist's chairs moved a few inches but stalled next to the man's corpse. The puddles of water in the test room beyond sloshed in a rhythmic dance.

Donovan grabbed the edge of the control panel to steady himself. "These are common in San Francisco, but the tremors are occurring a lot more frequently."

Cyphir pocketed his cell and followed Aeros out of the control room.

Jaered stared at the pen on the floor until it stilled. His father's draining of Earth's core had triggered the mild quakes. Their frequency was on the rise across the globe, and soon, would begin to intensify. Jaered had lived through it before.

Once Aeros's legions killed every last Pur and Duach Sar, there would be no stopping him from sucking the life out of Earth.

{2}

Rayne jolted up in her bed. Awake in an instant, she held still, listening.

Whatever had roused her didn't repeat itself. A moment later she gasped, unaware that she'd been holding her breath. Her nerves prickled while unease settled across her shoulders. She checked her cell on the nightstand. No messages. If Tara had tried to reach her, she would have left one.

Did her friend's date end early? "Zoe?" she called. "Is that you?"

She slipped into a robe without bothering to cinch it and grabbed the first thing she could wrap her hand around, a tall, slender brass statue.

The cold hardwood floor numbed her feet as she wandered down the hall, and she rubbed her arm to erase a shiver. She knocked on Zoe's bedroom door. Silence.

Rayne inched herself down the stairs and, holding the statue like a baseball bat, she paused next to the kitchen threshold. The moon flickered in the windows. Swaying trees teased evening's natural light, compliments of a strong coastal breeze.

A metal chair scraped across the patio, then crashed into the gas grill. *Clang!*

Her bottled-up breath escaped in a sigh, and she lowered the statue. It's just noises from a storm, she tried to convince herself. Paranoia, fueled by Ian's ever-heightened concern for her safety, had held her prisoner for weeks.

Emerald sparkles formed over the kitchen counter, and she shielded her eyes as the glow intensified.

Ian appeared in the vortex stream and scooted off, but he didn't get far. The strap on his backpack caught on one of the burner grates and he bent over the counter. When he saw Rayne standing across the dimly lit room, his eyes grew big and he thrust out his hand. "Stay back!"

The backpack became animated and rose, towering above Ian's ebony hair. What Rayne had taken for straps were arms that extended like unfurled wings. A high-pitched screech filled the room.

Ian had a monkey on his back.

The animal leapt off and landed on the wooden dinette table then skidded across the slick surface, knocking a bowl of oranges to the floor. A second before reaching the table's edge, the animal vaulted in the air and grasped the cast iron curtain rod over the patio doors with a deafening screech.

"What the hell!" Rayne screamed over the animal's cries when Ian didn't intervene.

"Wait!" Ian shouted when she headed for the monkey. "I've got this." The animal gripped the curtain with its feet then sprang toward the dangling lights over the counter leaving ripped fabric in its wake.

"Clearly," Rayne snapped.

The monkey latched onto the light's narrow cable. It swayed under the weight, then gave way and crashed onto the counter. The shattering glass exploded like shrapnel, and Rayne shielded her face in the crook of her arm. The monkey clung to the remaining light fixture. It disconnected at the ceiling and dangled precariously by its wires.

"Ian!"

He spread his arms. *"Unapaswa kuwa kuja."*

The monkey hugged the swinging light pole and quelled it's squawking. Its eyes darted about the room.

"Since when do you speak monkey?" Rayne said.

"It's Swahili." Ian took a step toward the frightened animal. "I warned you that hitchhiking wasn't a good idea."

The monkey's chatter resounded off the stainless steel appliances. Rayne covered her ears as the animal argued its case to stay.

"Basi la kwenda nyumbani." Ian took a couple of steps toward the monkey. "You need to go home. I promise to come back and visit again."

The animal shook its head, then jumped into Ian's arms.

He stroked the animal's back and swayed, comforting it like a baby. He tossed an apologetic grimace at Rayne. "I'll be right back." Ian disappeared in a green puff.

Rayne's tension seeped out like water through a sieve. The bronze statue slipped out of her hand and bounced off her bare foot. "Ow!"

The garage door motor hummed, muted and low.

Zoe! Rayne's heart jumped out of her chest and she whirled around with thoughts racing faster than her legs. Rayne limped across the room and opened the sliding glass doors. A gale swept in depositing leaves and pine needles in the room. When Zoe stepped inside, she pushed the button to close the garage door.

"OMG, what the hell happened here?" Zoe cried. Her fuchsia pigtails danced as she took in the scene.

"The wind woke me up. I went outside to see about securing the patio furniture and a squirrel ran inside. I'm sorry, I was half asleep. I shouldn't have left the door open."

Zoe shook her head. "A squirrel did this? Is it still in the house?" She clutched her monstrous purse like a shield.

"I cornered it, and it took off across the lawn."

"Let's hope my aunt's insurance covers vermin." Zoe touched the dangling light fixture and it swayed.

"Zoe, I'll pay for it. I'm the one that screwed up."

"Hell, dents are a part of accidents. Get it, acci*dents*?" Zoe chuckled.

Rayne grinned. It was good to see the old Zoe peek out of the grumpy mood she'd wallowed in for the last few weeks.

"I'll get the broom." Her friend disappeared into the garage. The spring-loaded door banged shut behind her.

Emerald sparks formed next to the range top.

Rayne raced to the door leading to the garage and flipped the deadbolt latch.

Ian sat on the counter. "Don't get me wrong, I love that you have a vortex stream in your house. I just hate the fact it's in the middle of the kitchen." He hopped off. "Of course, Milo is envious as hell. He'd be in heaven if he could stir his pots and retrieve messages at the same time."

"Zoe's home," she hissed.

The door handle jiggled. Knocking followed. "Rayne?"

He froze. "Has she seen this?"

"You've been downgraded to a squirrel." The knocks turned to banging. Rayne braced herself, then opened it. "Sorry, the lock must have slipped."

"Deadbolts don't slip." The creases in Zoe's brow deepened the second she locked eyes on Ian. "Figures." She pushed past Rayne and shoved the broom and dustpan at him.

"A magic trick rehearsal gone sideways," Ian said. "I didn't take into account the wild animal variable."

"Zoe, I'm sorry," Rayne said.

"Zip it." Zoe looked between them and sighed. "At least one of us is scoring tonight." She pinched her nose and headed out of the kitchen. "I swear whenever you show up, it smells like a zoo."

Ian and Rayne poked their heads into the hall and watched Zoe make her way up the stairs. When she reached the topmost step, Ian turned back and extended his hand. Glass splinters scooted toward each other across the floor.

"That's what a broom is for," Rayne snapped. "How would I explain everything being fixed in the morning?"

The smirk she'd grown to love spread wide and the Pur Heir's dark eyes glistened with amusement. "Twenty-four-hour handyman. I'm sure we can Google one that can be bribed."

"You have an answer for everything." She couldn't muzzle the smile in spite of her best efforts to cling to her anger.

He approached, forcing her to back up and press against the wall oven. When he came to a halt, he was scant inches away.

"I thought you weren't coming back for another couple of days," she said.

"The Primary sent word to return as soon as possible."

"What does the head honcho of the Pur Syndrion want with you now?"

"I don't know. I didn't read the rest of the message." Ian hovered over her. "I finished what I had to and shyfted out of there."

"You should have taken Tara." The spark in his eyes vanished, and she regretted bringing up the painful topic.

"I had it covered," he mumbled.

"Were you able to stop the poachers?"

"You might say I solidified their belief in the supernatural." He glanced over his shoulder. "Am I interrupting something?"

"At eleven o'clock on a school night? Only my sleep."

His chest rose. Ian leaned in and blew his unique form of a kiss. It played across her lips. Rayne closed her eyes as nature's perfume engulfed her. It was lilac, her favorite.

"I've discovered a couple of rare African orchids I think you're going to like," he murmured. "God, I've missed you," came out in a hushed voice.

Rayne's breaths grew shallow and her body tingled the longer Ian was near. The Pur leaders—the Syndrion— hadn't bothered to hide their distain at Ian and Rayne's relationship, but it was her Duach scientist father and his experiments when she was still in her mother's womb that had created the chasm between her and the man she loved. Their inability to touch was torturous, yet exhilarating, like a forbidden, luscious fruit. What she would have given to feel his mouth pressed against hers, the stroke of his hand, the strength of his embrace.

Ian's breath warmed her cheek. "This world holds such beauty and wonders, Rayne. The sands of Qatar, Spotted Lake in Canada, the Perlemorskyer in the skies over Oslo. If only I could share them with you."

"Not everything you see is beautiful," Rayne said. The horrors he encountered, the dangers, invaded her dreams whenever he was gone. She turned her face and twitched her nose. The odors of Africa had followed him home. "Zoe's right, you smell like a zoo."

"You sound like Milo." Ian pushed away from the wall. "I have a present for you, well, hopefully for us." He spread into the killer smile that made her heart flutter, and grabbed something from his back pocket. "It was Dr. Mac's idea."

He held up an ostrich feather. Its wispy tips swayed in the bright moonlight. Barely touching her skin, he stroked the delicate edge down her face, across her jaw line and didn't stop until it reached the loose, top button of her nightshirt.

Rayne's toes curled. A stuttering shiver. His eyes didn't reveal discomfort. "Any pain?" she asked.

"No," he said, his breaths quickening.

She snatched it from him. "Then we test it further." Rayne slipped out from beneath his arm and tossed him a sultry glance from over her shoulder.

Ian growled, deep and throaty from behind a devilish grin.

A burst of subtle light. A silhouette splashed on the wall behind Ian, then disappeared. She looked outside, but only caught gentle dancing branches of trees. Beyond the property, lights of distant homes flickered on the hills at the horizon.

"What?" Ian said.

The drumbeat in Rayne's ears nearly swallowed his question. "You didn't see it?"

He followed her gaze out the sliding glass doors. "See what?"

"Something, a figure."

"Wait here." Ian stepped out onto the patio and gestured for her to close the door behind him, but Rayne followed. He gave her a disgruntled glance when she joined him at the edge of the back patio. He closed his eyes.

A milky blur appeared between the trees, moving rapidly. The wolf emerged at the opposite boundary of the backyard. Ian opened his eyes and smiled. "Glad to see you, too."

"How long has Saxon been here?" Rayne asked.

"You're rarely alone," Ian said, and stepped off the patio.

He headed for the tree line. Rayne followed. Saxon closed ranks at her side. She stroked the wolf when he brushed up against her and nuzzled her hand with a cool, moist snout.

They walked the perimeter of the backyard and the surrounding brush. Ian stopped now and then with a finger to his lips and cocked his head as if to listen. Saxon sniffed the air, wandered away for a few seconds, then returned. They found nothing out of the ordinary.

She followed Ian back into the kitchen and waited for Saxon to join them, but the wolf slipped around the side of the house.

"He'll keep watch." Ian leaned in and locked the door. "Did something happen while I was away?"

His fear for her safety hung over them like an ominous cloud. "Sometimes the house just gets to me."

His mouth pressed into a crease. "What do you want to do?"

The feather twisted between her fingers. What she wanted was to savor a few quiet hours exploring what intimacy they could before the Syndrion found another excuse to keep them apart. "Test this out."

Rayne exited the kitchen with the same unease that had brought her there in the first place.

Rayne chose her bedroom balcony with the light of the constellations sparkling above, a favorite spot whenever Ian returned from missions. She lay naked under a blanket, gazing into the night's sky while he shared his adventures with her the only way he could. The evening's breath drifted cool and moist. Ian lay on his side next to her, propped up with pillows, the comforter from her bed beneath them.

The recounting of his adventures came to an end, and he gazed at her with apprehension. The feather twitched between his fingers. She rolled over onto her stomach. If this didn't work, she couldn't bear to witness his pain. She closed her eyes in an attempt to block out the countless disappointments that came before. Would tonight hold the promise of something new?

He pushed the blanket down to below her knees. A cool breeze swept across her back and buttocks. The soft, feathery tip carved a path down her spine leaving a trail of goose bumps in its wake. Rayne stiffened. Her breaths turned shallow. Her head tilted at the brush of the feather at the same time her back arched.

Ian didn't jerk the feather away. There was no pain, no ache? Her power drain wasn't triggered by the feathery tips. He continued his strokes, and she allowed herself to savor the simple pleasure. Her body screamed for more than what he could give her, but this was a desirable start. "Ahh, that tickles." A jerk sent her honey-colored hair across the pillow beneath her. She gave him a sideways glance.

He grinned. "I won't forget that spot."

"You will if you want this evening to remain painless," she said.

He caressed up her arm, along her neck all the way, ever so slowly down her back. The sounds that emitted from her parted lips had no words to describe them when the feather found her inner thighs. Her breaths deepened, interrupted by occasional subtle gasps.

"What are the softest feathers?" she asked in a silky voice that drifted on the evening breeze.

"Down," he said.

Salt-laden air filled her nostrils and a gust of wind raised goose bumps along her arm. The feather twirled its way between her legs on an upward migration toward her buttocks. When it stalled, her gasp was more intense than before. Her breaths quickened as the feather stroked up and down in a teasing dance.

"Can we use the down feathers?" breeched her moan.

"No," Ian hushed, as if inviting her to remain quiet, no longer wanting words to pass between them, but something more.

"Ian."

"Rayne."

"Another kiss," she whispered.

"Choose," he murmured.

"Surprise me," faded into the night air as her sounds drifted to that place that only her dreams had ever taken her.

Ian leaned in. The perfumed heat of his breath gave her what she desired.

{ 3 }

Rayne pulled the car into the university parking lot, cut the engine and reached into the backseat to stroke Saxon. "Take Ian home. We didn't get much sleep last night." The wolf yawned as if to imply that Rayne and Ian weren't the only ones.

She slipped out of the car, then bent over and blew Ian a kiss through the car window. Rayne took off in the direction of the grounds with a carefree spring in her step, but a second later, stopped with a jolt. She turned and rushed back.

Ian pulled her backpack from the floor of the backseat and tossed it toward her when she opened the door. She grabbed it and hurried off.

He watched her walk across the lawn, wondering if memories of last night might distract her throughout the day. Ian lingered in the car and breathed deep. He swore her scent was more powerful, intoxicating than ever.

Caution told him to shyft out of there before the lot filled up. He hesitated. The vast college campus made it difficult to keep watch over her without being recognized, but the crowd of students and professors was in Rayne's favor. Weir law forbids Sars from using their powers where it might be witnessed by humans. But there were a growing number of Weir who scorned the old ways and thought themselves above all laws, human or Weir.

Ian shyfted Saxon home to the eastern vortex. He dropped to one knee and gave his beloved companion a playful scratch around the ears. Saxon pawed at him and wagged his tail. With a snort, he leapt over a log and vanished in the thick brush. The wolf preferred prowling the estate's grounds and forest to meandering inside the mansion now that spring had found its way to the Northern California coast.

Birds took flight from nearby trees with a shrill squawk. Ian pressed his hand against the cool earth. A low rumble. Pebbles bounced along the ground. Dirt wafted into the air. Saxon appeared at the edge of the clearing with a whine. A few seconds later, the earth's mantle settled. All grew still. The planet's outburst was no more than a yawn.

There had been too many outbursts of late. Several, too intense to ignore. When Ian had approached the Syndrion with his concerns, they reported that a large number of elderly Pur Sars had passed away in the last few weeks. The remaining Sars' hold on the planet was weaker than ever.

Ian had left the council meeting consumed with guilt. He was supposed to be Earth's savior. The handful of powers he'd been able to develop was a far cry from what was prophesied. He wasn't what the planet needed to survive. He'd never felt so helpless.

A scraping sensation deep in Ian's core confirmed that Milo had set the estate's energy jam at moderate. He set out on foot, unable to use his powers beyond the open vortex field.

He strolled along the path toward the mansion, but at the fork, turned onto the south path. The sun's energy seeped into Ian's shoulders, and he drew upon it. A soft breeze tickled the back of his neck. He paused in the small clearing and took stock of Mara and Galen's grave site. He'd only been gone a week, yet the early spring rains and warmer-than-usual weather had brought an abundance of wild flowers that filled the area with flecks of tangerine, lemon, indigo and jade reminiscent of a Monet painting.

It comforted him that the grave mounds, like his grief, were settling with time. Peace engulfed his soul whenever he visited. Not enough time had passed for their bodies to adequately decay and feed the earth, but their strength and wisdom had leached into the ground and enriched the soil. They spoke to him when he was near.

"Why is this your first stop whenever you return from assignments?"

Ian smiled. Tara's ability to approach without giving herself away developed soon after losing Mara, her identical twin. "I made them a promise that I would give their sacrifice meaning," he said. "I suppose it's my way of filling them in on my progress."

"As long as it's not to ask for forgiveness."

"I hope we are both beyond that." Ian turned to find her huddled down in a gray sweat shirt with exercise shorts peeking out below. Perspiration dampened the strands of hair closest to her face. Tara tirelessly strived to turn her half-self into a whole. With each passing week, bits of Mara emerged.

Eyes the color of fresh sage tinged in lavender came alive in greeting, and Tara's arms and face extended from the sweat shirt like a turtle emerging from a shell. They hugged tight and he kissed the crest of her snowy hair that trailed down her back in a loose braid.

"Rayne is hurting," Tara said softly.

Three words, and his newfound peace shattered. Regret twisted his gut. "If I could take her, I would."

"No, you wouldn't. You couldn't afford the distraction." Tara swiped her forehead with the back of her hand.

Ian turned onto the path with his arm around Tara's shoulders, and they strolled toward the mansion. He attempted to channel with her, but emptiness filled his head. Their most crucial skill remained elusive. He missed having Tara's thoughts blend with his and felt like a best friend had moved away, never to be heard from again.

"Drion Marcus is pissed at you."

"What'd I do this time?" Ian said.

"You can't keep dismissing the Syndrion's request."

"I have no intention of cooperating with new Channel trials. Mara can't be replaced, and I won't lose you, too."

"Your core strength isn't strong and you know it. The second you run into a Duach Sar you'll be incapacitated, without backup. Going solo on missions is insane. Last month proved it."

Ian's mission to relocate a group of black alligators in central Brazil had not gone as planned. He'd barely made it home alive.

Her voice lowered along with her face. "I should leave, Ian."

"Be patient, Tara. I still have faith we'll reconnect." He gave her a reassuring squeeze, but she pulled away and climbed the steps onto the back patio.

Milo's fresh-baked cinnamon rolls welcomed Ian as he stepped inside. The old grizzly caretaker stood at the kitchen counter, gave him a grunt in greeting, then topped off his mug of coffee. Any additional relief at Ian's safe return was masked by his growling yawn. "Discard your clothes in the laundry room before you head upstairs."

"You'd have me walk naked through the house?" Ian peeked inside the oven and earned a slap on the hand.

"I may not have diapered that bottom of yours," Milo said, "but thanks to your fiasco in Pantanal last month, it's nothing Tara and I haven't seen plenty of."

"I paid for it," he said. Patrick had crashed Ian's dirt bike to create a cover story for the storm that his injuries had unleashed. Ian lay unconscious for two days, recovering in bed with the healing powers of his boost. When he awoke, he recovered the remains of his pride and joy from the base of the cliff before the ocean claimed it. He then sat on the floor of the garage salvaging parts while Patrick dangled upside down from a nearby rafter defending his decision to wreck the only thing Ian had ever built for himself.

Milo and Tara's recounting of Patrick's elaborate press conference on the dangers of dirt biking brought a smile to Ian's face. It was good to be home.

The trio froze at the sound of a vacuum cleaner. Milo's smile vanished and he threw a concerned look in Tara's direction.

"What?" Ian said.

"It's Patrick." She pushed away from the counter. "He hasn't been himself this morning."

"Quirky is his middle name," Milo said. "But this is something else."

Ian took the steps two at a time up the winding staircase. The others followed. When they reached Patrick's room, all three squeezed into the open doorway.

Patrick had his back to them, vacuuming. The room was spotless, not a pile or piece of clothing in sight.

Something was wrong.

Milo nudged Tara. "Check the bathroom."

She slipped into the room unnoticed and peeked inside. Tara gave Milo a double thumbs-up. Patrick turned off the vacuum and rolled up the cord, oblivious to his audience.

"What the hell are you doing?" Milo said.

Patrick turned and gave them a puzzled look. "I'm cleaning, why?"

"Why is as good a place to start as any," Ian said.

"Do I need a reason?"

"Yes!" they blurted in unison.

Patrick sat on the chair with stooped shoulders. "I haven't known how to tell you. I got the message last night." He gave Ian a look reserved to announce a death. "We're about to have company."

"Who?" Milo asked.

Patrick sighed like it was his last breath on Earth. "My mother."

{4}

The blow came from behind. Jaered's keys flew out of his hand. Sprawled facedown on the floor, his thoughts whirled. Something connected with his ribs—hard— and he coughed deep and rough. A boot smashed his face into the floor. Something sharp pricked his neck. A second later, his body went limp. Rough hands rolled him onto his back.

Ning's chiseled front teeth sneered down at him. Jaered inwardly groaned. There'd been rumors that his father's assassin had survived.

"You lied to Aeros about me," Ning snarled. "If anyone betrayed your father it was that Syndrion traitor, Sebastian." His boot crashed into Jaered's ribs, fueling the sizzling nerve pain racking his body.

"It's suicide to come back," Jaered said. The warning came out breathy and forced.

"I'm cooking up a job, but will be throwing some revenge in for dessert." Ning's chuckle fell flat and he crouched next to Jaered. Ning rubbed the flaming tattoos covering his bald head as if fanning the flames. "It took some doing to find you," he said. "Why you would choose such a dump is beyond me."

Ning's spittle ran down Jaered's cheek.

"Look what I found." The assassin's gloat spread into a smile. A piece of paper came into view. Rayne's photo from the bathroom mirror. Shouts filled Jaered's head but never made it to his lips. Ning massaged his cheek with the photo and pressed it to his nose, inhaling deep. "Hmm, I remember the sweet aroma of her fear."

With every attempt to lift his head, stars erupted behind Jaered's eyes.

"I thought it was the Heir who drained my core that day on the cliff. It wasn't until I lay dying on the shore that I realized, I didn't lose my power until I grabbed *her*. It returned when she broke free." A circulating core blast formed in the assassin's open palm. It lit up his neck and cheeks in a fiery glow. "I don't blame you for keeping her all to yourself. I, too, like them feisty, but something so valuable could be my ticket back into your father's fold. Of course, she has to pay for stealing the Book of the Weir when my back was turned. Do you think she will smell as sweet when I barbecue a few choice pieces?" The core blast extinguished and Ning stood. He left the picture on Jaered's chest.

An attempt to speak resulted in a croak. Jaered drew what breath his lungs allowed. "You won't find her," came out harsh as he fought for every breath.

"What makes you think I don't already know where she is?"

Jaered's heartbeat stilled. "You'll have to get past the Heir, and me. And I know my father's orders. You can't touch either one of us."

Ning *tsk*ed and wagged his head. "You haven't been paying attention." His boot delivered another crushing strike. The last of Jaered's air burst out of him and the shooting stars turned to an erupting volcano. "Until I redeem myself in Aeros's eyes, I don't have anything to lose."

The door slammed.

It took a full minute for Jaered to suck in enough air to refill his lungs and several more to move a limb. Rayne's picture kept his beating heart company while the drug took its time to run its course.

{ 5 }

Ian stepped out of the shower and wrapped a towel around himself without drying off.

Milo had delivered lunch on a silver tray and left it on his bed, one of the old caretaker's rituals that Ian had never been able to discourage. He'd resigned himself to living in the mansion amidst the expansive, secure grounds, but the less everyone treated him like royalty, the more it felt like a home. It allowed him to embrace his human side.

A whiff of soy sauce tickled his taste buds, and he popped one of the marinated chicken bites into his mouth. Before he could sink his teeth into it, a knock barely registered and Patrick burst inside, then shut the door behind him. He was the color of chalk.

"This has disaster written all over it," Patrick said. "Why isn't she staying in a hotel in town like always?"

"Calm down. Milo spent the morning getting a room ready. He even gathered some pictures of you and your parents and scattered them around downstairs to make her feel welcome."

"This isn't about playing Martha Stewart, serving gourmet meals, or worrying whether this place will pass her white-glove scrutiny." He raked his fingers through his hair. "You know what can happen around here. There's no preparing for that." A muted doorbell sounded in the distance. Patrick looked like he would puke. He eyed Ian's towel. "For God's sake, it's my mother. Get some clothes on." He rushed out, leaving the bedroom door wide open.

Ian gulped. The piece of chicken left a bruise on the way down. An adrenaline rush swept over him, and he pulled on jeans and slipped into a black T-shirt. When he caught his reflection in the dresser mirror, the shirt was replaced with a black polo. Ian started out of the room, but a chill snaked through his damp hair. He conjured the towel from the bathroom floor and swished it across his head.

He reached the balcony and started downstairs. Patrick shut the front door and leaned against it with a dazed look. The foyer was empty. "Where is she?" Patrick stood mute and unmoving. Ian approached. "Who was at the door?"

"Merlin's clones," Patrick said as though not quite all there. "If we ignore them, maybe they'll just disappear." He sighed. "Do us both a favor and shyft me to a deserted island."

Ian opened the towering door. Four monks clothed in ankle-length brown robes stood on the landing. Long, thick white beards reached to their waists. They peered at Ian with the deep-creased faces of wisdom and age, yet eagerness painted their expressions. Marcus towered above them from behind.

"Distinguished scholars, I have the honor to introduce the Pur Heir," Marcus said when Ian failed to respond.

"Drion Marcus," Ian said. "What is this?"

Marcus's bushy eyebrows slammed together, and he regarded Ian as if he'd gone insane. "May we come in, sire?"

"Of course."

Milo and Tara emerged from the back hall. Their welcoming expressions wilted at the new arrivals.

The scholars shuffled in and looked around the expansive foyer, their multiple gazes pausing on everything from the cascading staircase to the hand-crafted round table in the center. One of the monks touched the stained glass of Ian's Weir crest flanking the doors.

"The Primary sent a message," Marcus said under his breath, his voice terse.

"I was summoned to return. That's all I knew." Regret at blowing off the message struck like a landslide. "What is this about?"

"The Primary has gathered a team of experts. We are here for the Book of the Weir."

"Why did he send so many of you to retrieve it?" Ian said.

"We're not here to retrieve it," Marcus said. "These men are here to study it."

It was then that Ian noticed the large cases and satchels the scholars carried. He glanced at Patrick and Milo. Their expressions left no margin of doubt. He was so screwed.

Patrick's homicidal grimace morphed into dread. "Mother."

JoAnna Langtree stood in the open doorway.

{6}

Patrick guided his mother into the house. "I hope your trip was pleasant."

"Where should I put these, madam?" the chauffeur asked in an exaggerated British accent that clashed with his California beach-bum glow.

"Right here is fine." Patrick gestured toward the foyer table, but the chauffeur placed her two gigantic designer suitcases just inside the doorway as if unwilling to lift another finger for her. He held out his hand.

"I've already added the tip on the bill for the charter service," Patrick said.

The chauffeur looked at him like he'd heard a cruel joke. "Will there be anything else, madam?"

"I'll take it from here." Patrick ushered him out the door, but paused and checked the front stoop. "I dare anyone else to show up today," he muttered under his breath and shut the door.

When he turned, his mother stood in the archway watching the scene unfolding in the great room beyond.

The monks bowed and kissed Ian's hand as Tara and Milo flanked him. Ian cringed with the formal gestures as Marcus made introductions. When Ian looked up, he smiled at Patrick's mother and raised his free hand in greeting. "Mrs. Langtree, we're so happy you decided to visit."

"Patrick, what's going on?" his mother said.

"Friars Club meeting." He grabbed her suitcases and grunted from the strain. "I think Ian is being inducted or something."

"Curious," JoAnna said. "I wouldn't have expected it."

"Ian is just full of surprises." He dragged the cases up the stairs. "Come, Mother, I'll show you to your room." She hesitated a second longer, then started up after him.

He led her down the south wing hall to the bedroom next to his and set the cases down near the door. "Where do you want them?"

"The largest one can go on the bed, dear." JoAnna ran her finger over the antique carving along the edge of the dresser. She panned the room. "What lovely accommodations."

"Milo worked fast to get everything ready." A moan escaped when he lifted the boulder of a suitcase onto the bed.

She opened the curtains. "Is that a pond or a lake?"

"They refer to it as a lake. Something about how deep it is." He grabbed his back and straightened. "Is everything all right?"

"Why do you ask?"

"You didn't give me much notice."

"I wasn't planning on coming for Isabel's soirée, but changed my mind at the last minute." She patted his chest. "When I stay in the city, we barely see each other. I wanted more of a chance to visit with my only child for once."

"So, you and Dad are okay?"

She primped herself in the mirror. "Why, don't I look all right?"

"You're as stunning as always." A pop came from his lower lumbar when he bent in to give her a peck on her cheek. He winced.

"You have your father's gift for telling white lies."

"I prefer to think of it as charm."

"As long as you don't abuse it like he does." She grew somber and stared at her reflection. "Not even the most expensive treatments can hide how I've aged of late."

"You're eternally beautiful, Mother." Patrick chuckled, whether from his own discomfort or to ease hers, he wasn't sure. With her pristine complexion, petite size six, and unnaturally blond hair; most people guessed she was at least a decade younger.

"I've been concerned about you." She opened the suitcase and set about unpacking. "Other than your call to give me the tragic news about Mara, we've had minimal correspondence."

"We've had a lot to deal with." He rubbed damp hands against his pants. "Where's Dad?"

"In Europe. He's been spending much of his time there. A hostile take-over, or someone, has been consuming him."

The edge in her voice was commonplace. His father deserved it. Rather than choose sides, Patrick had enrolled in college as far away from New York as he dared, without involving foreign language or currency.

Their conversation lapsed into silence. In the same room, only a few feet from each other, the chasm between them was unmistakable. She did her thing while he waited for something that never came.

"You've gained weight," she said.

Patrick rubbed his belly. "Not really." Compassionate one minute, hard as nails the next, his mother was a puzzle he'd spent years trying to piece together.

"It's understandable. All that downtime, with Ian taking a break from performances."

"Everyone is still mourning Mara's death," Patrick said, unable to give voice to the truth. The Syndrion's frequent assignments had made it difficult to restart the show's schedule, and momentum. Ian had a destiny far greater than the show, Patrick had accepted that. But how Fade to Black Productions could be a part of his life from this point on was anyone's guess.

"When we created the show, we both worked sixty-, eighty-hour weeks for the first three years. He's chosen to travel and regroup. I'm only too happy to support his decision," Patrick said. "Much of my time is spent managing the auditorium and booking performers and other functions in his absence."

"That's a great deal of explanation for something as trivial as your weight."

A spasm deep in the center of his chest denied him air. Patrick grabbed the doorknob with a fierce urge to escape. "I'll leave you to your unpacking," but caught his haste and paused. "Can I get you some tea?"

"Perhaps when I'm done here. I won't be much longer," she said. "I'll find you downstairs."

He shut the door behind him. It wasn't until he reached the balcony that oxygen once again fueled his thoughts. He focused on locating Ian.

Patrick needed to clear his head.

Nemautis hung back and fell into step with Ian at the rear of the group while Marcus led them on a tour of the inner mansion grounds. Ian recalled a few of Galen's stories about the revered Weir scholar and the joy that crept into Galen's voice whenever he reminisced about his old colleague. From the arch of Nemautis's back and his shuffling steps, Ian feared he'd keel over before they'd make it to the far side of the lake.

Nemautis put a firm hand on Ian's shoulder and paused with a wheezing exhale. The rest of the tour group ventured onward. "Galen was a good friend and is sorely missed among our academic kind. I would very much like to visit his grave site before these old legs seek cushioned elevation," Nemautis said.

"Of course." Ian gestured and Saxon ran ahead to block Marcus's path. The old general turned, and Ian pointed to let him know they were taking a different path. Marcus nodded and continued on with his diatribe about the water purification system connected to the lake.

Ian offered Nemautis an arm of support and led him down the south path with Saxon strolling beside the old scholar. It took a couple of stops for Nemautis to catch his breath, but they soon arrived at the small clearing.

Saxon lay on top of Mara's grave and rested his head on his paws. Ian held back in silence. Nemautis shuffled over and grabbed the edge of Galen's headstone. With a wince, he bent down and gathered a small handful of dirt, then sprinkled it over the mound. "May the energy of the earth sustain your spirit for all eternity, old friend." The grizzled scholar ran a gnarled finger over the word Father that Ian had carved into the stone.

Grief returned like a lightning strike, and Ian stifled the heave in his chest. He'd been so consumed with his own sorrow these past few weeks that he hadn't considered there would be countless others in Galen's life who mourned his loss.

"Galen was the youngest among us," Nemautis wheezed, pulling himself to his feet. "The only one who would have the energy to race after a young boy, destined to inherit the earth." The old scholar gazed at Ian with pride tinged in awe. "I am pleased to discover that such a strong young man grew out of his tutelage."

"Yet, not as powerful as the Prophecy claimed." Ian dropped his gaze. "As the Weir hoped."

"Galen never believed that to be in your control, although, knowing my old colleague, he may in part have blamed himself." Nemautis shuffled over and gave Ian's shoulder a reassuring squeeze. "Now that the Book of the Weir is in our possession, perhaps we will discover why, and have a chance to remedy that."

Ian, too, had held out hope that the Book of the Weir possessed the secrets to curing whatever ailed him. It's why he'd kept it hidden from everyone. The secrets to the Weir powers couldn't fall into the hands of those who might abuse it. Ian cautioned himself not to get his hopes up. "I'll help you back to the house and then retrieve it," he said.

"Sire, I may be crooked and sound like a spurting geyser, but nothing's wrong with my sense of direction. I'll make it back on my own, in due time." Nemautis settled on a fallen tree trunk and straightened his robes. "But first, I have some catching up to do with my old friend."

Watch over him. Make sure he returns safely, Ian channeled Saxon.

The wolf yawned, then closed his eyes.

Ian left the old scholar to his visit and headed for the eastern vortex. He shyfted to the base of the granite cliff in the national forest where he'd stashed the book far from the Pur and Duach. Ian stood listening from behind the thick brush. The only sounds came from the creatures that called the forest home. He felt along the wall with outstretched arms until he located handholds, then dug the toes of his boots against ripples in the face and scaled the rock wall.

He pulled himself onto the granite ledge several feet above the forest floor. The majestic bald eagle that had guarded the book for the last couple of months fed her squawking chicks and paid him no heed. He removed the stone he'd wedged into the vertical slit and grabbed the package from deep inside. Ian paused and stroked the eagle's back. "Thank you for your service," he said and climbed down as her ravenous offspring enjoyed their meal.

He returned to the mansion and removed the Book of the Weir from the waterproof wrap. Nemautis took it with gentle, reverent hands. The other scholars closed in.

"We've laid claim to the dining room," Marcus said, ushering Ian out. "Now that the book is here, no one enters that room without my permission.

"I'm shocked that Galen's old mentors are still alive. How did you convince them to leave their abbey stronghold?"

"The Primary promised them the opportunity to meet you and to study letters written by the Ancients. They took some time to deliberate but finally agreed and have been guarded by me ever since. I shyfted them here, taking several vortex routes so as not to be followed. No one else knows of this, Ian. It must be kept secret."

Ian pondered how he was going to keep JoAnna out of the dining room and tracked down Milo and Patrick. The second he stepped into the kitchen, Milo let loose an avalanche of frustration. Patrick chimed in and they closed ranks.

"How could you not read the Primary's message?" Milo hissed. The wooden spoon in his hand flailed about like a conductor's bow. "Feeding them is only part of the problem. We don't have enough beds."

Patrick grabbed a banana and aimed it at Ian like a pistol. "How do we explain them to my mother?"

"Milo, if anyone can do it, you can," Ian said. "This compound is self-sufficient. You have plenty of resources for meals. If you need me to shyft to retrieve anything else, I will. They can either share the remaining beds, or the cots in the escape tunnel can be brought up." Ian's phone buzzed in his pocket. He pulled it out and Rayne's picture smiled at him. He ignored it when the two men advanced. "Patrick, I'll handle this. Your mother's visit will go smooth."

"This isn't a monastery, Ian. What are you going to tell her?"

"I'll come up with something plausible. I swear." The insistent buzz tickled his hip again. Ian answered it. "Rayne, hold on. I'm in the middle of a crisis here." He waved his hand and three dozen long-stemmed yellow roses appeared on the counter. The two men startled. "For your mom" Ian said.

Patrick shook his head. "I thought you couldn't conjure anything you hadn't touched before."

"They're my prize Isabella Sprunts," Milo said. "Ian! Pull that stunt again and my greenhouse will be off-limits."

"You can grow them back with a flick of your hand," Ian said. Milo possessed the most common of Weir powers.

"You might as well have him conjure dinner," Patrick said to Milo.

"Not a chance. He'd serve chili on a bed of fries and think it a feast." Milo grabbed a knife and set about trimming the rose stems. Patrick grabbed a vase from under the cupboard.

Ian stepped out onto the patio and closed the door. Spruce from the surrounding redwood forest filled his lungs and nature's scent brought instant calm. He pressed the phone to his ear. "Hey."

"Crisis, huh?" she said.

"You won't believe what I came home to." Her laugh trimmed the last of his frayed nerves and brought warmth to his core. "Help create a credible story for why four monks are staying with us." Saxon trotted up and brushed against him. He stroked the wolf's thick coat.

"Patrick's PR side will kick in any minute," she said. "He'll come up with something."

"This is about his mother. Where she's concerned, he can't remember to tie his own shoes."

"How about, their nearby abbey caught fire and you offered to house them until other arrangements could be made."

Ian slumped back in the recliner. "It's scary how good you are at lying."

"Covering your screw-ups at my place has heightened my game. Zoe's working tonight. Come over after dinner."

He rubbed his face. "I doubt I can get away. Drion Marcus—"

"Don't bother. I get it. The Syndrion comes first." The call ended.

He sat up and checked his cell. He had service. He attempted to call Rayne back, but she didn't answer. Ian grabbed the back of his neck and hung his head. Guilt at not making more time for her had been eating away at him for weeks. Had Ian been avoiding her? As welcome as the feather had been, it was like a dangling carrot, a reminder of what was just beyond their reach.

Rayne believed the Syndrion deliberately kept them at a distance. *The Pur and Duach cannot unite, they must stay apart.* His childhood lessons about the sinister side of their race bounced around in his thoughts. Was she right? Had the Syndrion discovered more than her half-Duach blood? He wanted to believe that only those closest to him knew about her secret power. If that information ever leaked, he would be helpless to stop the Syndrion from killing her, if the Duach didn't get to her first.

Or was this something else? Had something happened to her? The urge to check on Rayne brought Ian to his feet and he drew the earth's energy into his core to shyft, but hesitated. The Journalism department was huge. She could be anywhere on campus. Saxon looked up at him. *She-wolf,* he channeled.

No. The tingling shyft energy dissipated in Ian's chest. Saxon lay down with a sigh and turned on his side to bask in the sun's rays. Ian returned to the house for what he feared would be round two, but stopped just inside the kitchen door. Milo's cheeks burned bright pink as JoAnna complimented him on the five-star accommodations. A warm smile lit up her face when she leaned in to smell the bouquet.

"They're beautiful, Patrick. How did you know that yellow are my favorite?"

Patrick gave Ian a grateful nod from behind his mother. By his relaxed shoulders, Ian had succeeded in avoiding at least one lynch party. "Mrs. Langtree, what brought you to the West Coast?" He closed the patio door.

"Isabel's charity gala is a favorite of mine every year. It's the social event of Northern California society, after all. And, it gives me a reason to come to town and spend time with you two boys every spring." She removed one of the stems and held it to her nose.

"We got word that you weren't going. We declined our invitations," Patrick said.

"When Isabel found out that Ian wouldn't be making an appearance and performing as always, she convinced me to change my mind, then threatened me to change yours. Naturally, I reassured her we would all be going and participating as usual. Sympathy shaded her face. "I know that Mara's death has hit all of you hard. But it's been two months. It's time to get back to work."

Patrick looked at Ian with unease. Ian kept a smile plastered on his face. He had secretly relished not having the charity performance added to his crazy-ass schedule.

"It's in two nights. Ian can't just pull something together at the last minute," Patrick said.

"Then do the same performance as last year."

"The guest list won't have changed that much, and liquored up or not, their memories aren't that poor."

"Pulling a trick out of a hat is what you two do, is it not?" She strolled out of the kitchen clutching the rose. "He's a magician, isn't he?"

"Illusionist," Patrick muttered as a crimson flush spread down his neck. "There's a difference."

Heat formed in the center of Ian's chest. He threw a panicked glance at Patrick and rushed out of the room with Patrick close behind. A message was about to arrive. JoAnna was headed for the foyer. He reached the front of the house in time to hear her gasp.

The message scroll spun on one tip above the silver platter at the center of the round entry able. Patrick's mother stood still, eyes wide.

Ian grabbed the scroll and with a flourish of his hands, bowed.

"I can't wait to see what you'll do for the event," she said with bright eyes. "That is quite the teaser."

When she started up the staircase, he uncurled the message. Meeting with the Primary. Northern vortex structure. One hour. He let the scroll spring back upon itself, then held it in the air. It burst into flame and turned to ash.

Applause came from the balcony. "Promise you'll treat me to more surprises before I leave." JoAnna turned a belittling gaze upon Patrick. "Why are you so worried? Ian can do the impossible."

Ian's muscles unwound. It wasn't because of JoAnna's enthusiasm or the averted disaster. A plan took shape that promised to solve so many things.

{ 8 }

The sensation prickled Rayne's arms. She twisted around in her chair, but the copier room that doubled as a teacher's assistant's office was empty other than her and Zoe. Someone in an oversized gray hoodie and jeans strolled down the hall in the opposite direction with hands in their pockets, slumped shoulders, and head bent low. It took a second to connect why she focused on the obscure figure in the crowded hall. Unlike the other students, this one didn't carry a backpack, books, or a laptop.

"What?" Zoe paused from spinning around in the chair. She draped her paperclip necklace around her neck, then peered out the open door.

"Nothing," Rayne said. She lost sight of the figure when a massive flower arrangement turned a corner and headed their way. Mrs. Wheeler, the Journalism department's secretary, parted the sea of bodies as she escorted whoever was carrying the bouquet. One look at the surface of Rayne's TA desk, and the woman waved her arms. "Make room!"

Rayne regarded the piles of papers she'd just spent the last two hours grading and organizing. Zoe swiped them onto her chair and wheeled it out of the way. The delivery girl placed the vase down and bent over to catch her breath.

Zoe whistled. "Someone killed a garden."

"I'm afraid I don't have anything on me for a tip," Rayne said.

"Taken care of," the delivery girl said in a hoarse voice. She turned and squeezed out between the onlookers.

"I'll be making lots of copies this afternoon," Mrs. Wheeler said. She fanned her hands, beckoning the perfume.

Rayne inhaled roses, lilacs, and a dozen other blossoms, then stepped back to admire the cascading rainbow.

"Who did you do to earn those?" Gary snickered as he stepped inside and leaned against his TA desk across the room.

"Don't you have somewhere else to loiter?" Mrs. Wheeler said.

The secretary hovered as Rayne cut a path through the jungle and located the card. She slipped a fingernail under the flap and opened it.

"Who's it from?" came from one of the students cramming in the doorway.

"It's from *him*, your secret admirer, isn't it?" Mrs. Wheeler's dreamy sigh set a fern swaying.

Zoe gave Rayne a conspirator's smirk. Rayne pulled a huge starburst mum out and handed it to the underappreciated secretary, then excused herself and headed down the hall to the women's bathroom. She settled into a stall and leaned against the closed door to read what came from Ian's heart.

You are the earth's most precious gem.

The bouquets grew larger with each assignment, but this one was extravagant, even for Ian. What had the Syndrion asked of him this time? She stared at a crack on the wall with a mixture of irritation and dread.

The restroom door burst open and banging on one stall door after another rang about the room. When the slap hit her latched door, Zoe rose on her tiptoes and peered over the top of the door. "Okay, it's just you and me, girl. Fess up. It's from Ian, isn't it?"

"You promised you wouldn't tell anyone about us." Rayne opened the stall door.

"Hey, I've kept mum for weeks about your famous magician love toy. Get it, *mum*?" Zoe snatched the card from Rayne. "I'm claiming half that florist shop in there. It's the least he could do for wrecking my half of the kitchen."

"Then do you want to be the precious, or the gem?" Rayne retrieved the card.

"I'm about as far from precious as you can get." Zoe turned and ran her fingers through her bangs in front of the mirror.

"Man, that bouquet was heavy." Tara stood in the doorway wearing the florist uniform. When she removed the cap, her snowy braid fell out.

Zoe's mouth sagged. "That was you?"

"Ian sent me on a mission," Tara said. "He has something up his sleeve, but it means playing hooky the rest of the day." She looked at Rayne. "Are you in?"

"Go with you, or sit in a cramped windowless room all afternoon grading papers," Rayne said. "Hmm, what do you think?"

Zoe cleared her throat and looked between Tara and Rayne with earnest. "Me, me, me, take me, too."

Tara hesitated. "You aren't part of the plan, Zoe."

Her face fell and she pushed away from the sink counter. "I've got better things to do, anyway."

"Zoe." Rayne started out after her. "Wait."

Zoe disappeared in the crowd.

Tara pulled the Hybrid SUV up to the concrete curb and killed the engine. The entire way there, Rayne hadn't been able to shake the injured look on Zoe's face as she stormed out of the bathroom. Had that been her roommate's problem these past few weeks? Did she see Tara as some kind of rival?

Rayne peered out the passenger's side window. Tara had brought her to a dilapidated warehouse on the edge of Chinatown. She rolled down her window and the intoxicating odors of oriental spices and heated oil filled the cab. "What's here?"

"This is Bazl's." Tara got out and walked to the rear of the car. She grabbed a suit bag and a long white box, then slammed the hatch. Rayne followed her to a dent-riddled door in the side of the building. Chipped paint along its surface curled like flower petals. Tara handed the suit bag to Rayne and rang a weathered brass bell. It bellowed with a clang. Rayne read the handwritten sign next to the doorway:

Packages accepted only if shipped, PAID IN FULL at the time of delivery. NO EXCEPTIONS

"Who's Bazl?" Rayne said.

"He creates all of our performance apparel and has been Ian's clothier since he started the show. Patrick's mother recommended him. From the moment they met, Ian and Bazl have been friends." Tara pounded on the door.

"I'm surprised Ian would let anyone near him, what with his scars and all," Rayne said, lowering her voice in spite of no one being nearby.

"The first time Ian had to strip for measurements, he shied away when Bazl walked around with his measuring tape and touched his back. But Bazl gripped Ian's shoulders and looked him in the eye. "Honey, he said to Ian, everybody has scars. Only a few are lucky enough to flaunt them in their own chosen way."

"And we're here, why?"

"For you, of course." Tara pounded on the door. "Like I said—"

"Ian has a plan." Rayne clanged the bell.

Metal scraped at the door and a deadbolt pulled back. The door inched open and a skinny, stoic face appeared. Tara addressed the young Asian girl in what sounded like Chinese. She didn't translate it for Rayne.

The girl nodded and led them up a narrow staircase while speaking rapidly to an old woman leaning over the railing above them. The inside of the place didn't look any more maintained than the outside. Worn patches of paint and stained concrete floors gave way to rickety wooden steps in a dark and otherwise dingy first floor.

At the top of the landing, Rayne's impression of the dilapidated surroundings transformed into awe. The upper floor screamed modern decor and opened onto the entire expanse of the warehouse. The towering floor-to-ceiling windows and bright sunlight lit up the place with oven-baked warmth as the sun's energy circulated in the room.

Long rolls of fabric lined the far wall arranged like the colors of a prism. Mannequin forms were scattered about, a couple fully dressed with most of the others bare. Large swatches of material were draped over a few in the back.

Metal scaffolding, which resembled upside-down metal bleachers, lined one side of the warehouse floor. The scaffold shifted in and out to the tune of a muted hum as though working some unknown dance of its own programming. Tara stopped and grabbed Rayne's arm. The scaffolding came to a halt with the uppermost platform extended beyond the lower levels.

A man's voice carried down, deep and resonant, addressing the women in Chinese. They paused and raised their voices back at him. Rayne wondered who was really in charge by their nonchalant indifference to him.

One of the women approached. Tara kicked her shoes off, then bent down and helped Rayne slip out of hers. "He's going to see us," she said. The younger woman handed them satin slippers. Tara donned her pair, then grabbed the box and suit bag from the floor.

Shadows moved across the upper platform. "Do you know how busy we are? No, of course you don't. But I do, I know exactly how busy we are." His flawless English switched back to Chinese and Rayne lost what came next.

When his diatribe ended the girl standing next to Tara nodded. "Yes, we are very, very busy," she said in English.

Tara smiled and stepped toward the scaffolding. Her sultry tone left Rayne stunned. "Bazl, let me show you what Ian has in mind."

The shadow's erratic movement stopped directly overhead. "I don't care what he has dreamed up this time. I'm busy. The gala is in two days. I have orders, many orders."

"Since when are you too busy for a challenge that promises to showcase your amazing talents?"

"My *awesome* talents have been showcased on his stage for three years."

"It's only one teeny, bitty dress."

"Now you're mocking me and my talents!" A stomp on the slats and a fine mist of dust rained overhead. "Nothing I do is miniscule."

"So you don't want to look at what Ian sent over in this box?" Tara held it out in front of her.

His tone smoothed. "What of it?"

"Just as you find inspiration in nature for your custom designs and one-of-a-kind masterpieces, Ian, too, is inspired by the wonders of this world." Tara stepped toward the bleachers. "Don't you want to see his latest?"

"You have closets of my work, why do you stress me so?"

"It's not for me." Tara motioned for Rayne to step closer. "It's for her."

The man's head poked between the railings like a bird from a nest. Dark, wide eyes peered at Rayne. An eyebrow raised under slicked-back hair that glistened in the bright light. His glare relaxed as he drank her in. His eyes darted up, then down, then up again. He brought a finger to his lips and tapped. "Bring me the box."

Tara handed the suit bag to Rayne then climbed the steps with a sway, all the while smiling at him as if taunting a lover. Rayne didn't know what to think. This was a side of Tara she'd never seen.

She paused in front of him and offered the box with a deep bow, then ceremoniously placed it at his feet. She removed the lid. From his shriek, Rayne couldn't tell if he was thrilled or offended. Bazl's eyes flew open and he clasped his hands. "I'm as much a genius as he is."

"A shared love of all that is natural," Tara said.

"These are exquisite."

Tara smiled. "Exquisite, yet, inspirational?"

He rushed past Tara, barking what sounded like orders in Chinese, and waved his arms at the women. They came alive.

Bazl entered a small wire cage at the far end of the structure and pressed a button. It descended to the bottom of the scaffolding with screeching gears and he stepped out, heading for Rayne. Curiosity trumped etiquette and Rayne stared at the man, not more than four feet high. His orange hair and freckled face clashed with his custom-tailored suit.

Tara returned the lid to the box and hurried down the stairs.

The man stopped an arm's length away and paced around Rayne. A sound much like humming blended with his steps. "How long?"

"Thirty-six hours." Tara removed an envelope taped to the suit bag that Rayne held. "There are some additional instructions for his tux."

He snatched it from her, ripped it open, and pulled out the handwritten sheet. He scoffed. "Ha! Impossible."

A sensuous smile laced Tara's lips and she cooed, "Bazl, have you not yourself claimed that the word *impossible* would never be a part of your lexicon? Your genius keeps you at the height of your game." She waved the box. "I know that look. You are inspired."

Bazl grunted. It must have been a signal because the girl reached out and took the box from Tara. The old woman stepped forward and thrust out her hand. Rayne passed her the suit bag. The two assistants scurried away.

"Get naked," Bazl commanded. He turned on the ball of his foot and stomped off. "He will pay dearly!" he shouted.

"He knows," Tara purred.

{9}

The Primary's image floated at the center of the vortex chamber. He wore a simple tunic that hung loose instead of his formal Grecian robe. The spider-web creases and dark circles surrounding his brown eyes had deepened in the past couple of months.

Ian stretched. "I retrieved the book. The scholars are settled and have begun to study it."

"They are the last of the Weir elders capable of deciphering the Ancient's dead language," the Primary said. "It took some negotiating. They never venture far from their abbey."

"I think they came to honor Galen," Ian said. "And to have a chance to say goodbye to their fallen colleague."

"I've requested that the Prophecy passages be translated first, to put an end to your nonsense about a looming Armageddon."

"Sebastian was very convincing," Ian said.

"Then you shouldn't have wielded your revenge and killed the traitor before he was interrogated."

The Primary was grouchier than usual. It put Ian on the alert. "Milo and Drion Marcus have the estate locked down tight. The jam is at full force." Ian rubbed his chest. He hated how the jam signal shut down his core powers, but even worse, at full force, the irritating grinding was like an itch that couldn't be scratched. "Why did you send Marcus without his troops? There's not many of us to protect the book."

"The less involved the better." His tone adopted an edge, "The Duach and the human are your responsibility."

Ian didn't reward the slight with a response. There wasn't anything he could do to change the Primary's attitude about Rayne and Patrick. He'd always view them as outsiders, and a threat.

"You are to remain at the mansion and guard it until their initial review is completed."

Ian nodded but averted his eyes. The Primary wouldn't approve of him attending the charity event. "I'm looking forward to being home. The assignments were becoming tedious."

"Your assignments have been carefully chosen to help you gain knowledge, Ian, to provide firsthand experience of what the Weir have dealt with for centuries. We hoped you would develop additional powers in the process."

"My hearing, sight, and smell have heightened," Ian said. "The ability to recall what my senses experience is new. I can replicate bird and animal sounds, natural scents. I've also learned to draw and direct the core blasts better."

"Nothing else?"

"I'm not sure. Maybe. I'm testing a theory. It would help if you would give me a heads up about what to nurture. Why do you continue to keep information about Weir powers from me?"

"They cannot be forced but must be discovered naturally. It is our way."

Well, it's stupid, Ian kept to himself. "The Weir's laws about hiding our powers, even from each other, may have been necessary for survival for hundreds of years, but I would think I'd be an exception."

"Being born the Last Sar guarantees your safeguard and sanctuary, but no one is above Weir law. Your twentieth-year milestone is next month. Additional powers could surface during your ceremony." The Primary's image faded. "If the Ancients' Prophecy holds true, you will discover all that you need to protect the earth. No more, no less, and in your own time." The room darkened.

"I hate it when you hang up on me," Ian muttered in the pitch-black room.

Ian stepped into the vortex stream at the center of the chamber and appeared in Rayne's kitchen. He let himself outside and walked the edge of the property. The erratic beat of her heart the previous night had given her away. Something had her scared.

He crouched next to a pine tree and listened. Nature hummed in harmony. A change in molecular energy from behind. Ian bolted upright. Arms wrapped him in a vice.

Ian struggled for a foothold, but whoever the Sar was, he was strong. He pulled Ian off the ground, twisting him around. Unable to loosen the man's grip, Ian kicked against the tree and rammed the back of his head into the assailant's face.

"Ugh." The man managed to stay on his feet but heaved Ian off to the side.

Ian hit the steep slope, rolling over and over, then slid several yards farther downhill. "Shit!" He grasped a passing limb of a bush to steady himself and shyfted. Ian leapt to his feet at the top of the hill.

The Sar was gone.

A gale whipped through the trees spraying leaves and pine needles into the air. Ian searched the grounds while struggling to control his anger. The wind eased but failed to come to a complete stop. A Sar was at Rayne's house. Who? Why?

The clouds rolled in like a looming wave. A small rectangular shadow rocked across the lawn, then melted into the graying overcast. Ian looked up. A thin object dangled a few yards overhead in the sparsely branched tree. He grasped a sturdy limb and swung himself up.

He climbed the rest of the way and grabbed the object.

Scuffs in the bark along the thick limb told Ian the wind hadn't displaced it. Why would anyone be up here? he wondered. The location offered a partial view of the dining room, the east end of the patio and backyard lawn, and directly ahead—Ian gritted his teeth—Rayne's bedroom and balcony. The curtains were drawn and obscured any details inside her room. He started to climb down, then dropped the rest of the way.

The hanging object was a company visitor tag clipped to a lanyard. Lux Pharmaceuticals. Ian traced the logo with his finger, certain that he'd never seen it before. He pulled out his cell and pressed Tara's contact. She answered on the first ring. "We need to talk. I don't want Rayne to hear." Muffled voices. A minute later, traffic noises.

"What's up?" she said.

"Rayne has a stalker. A shyftor. He must be Pur because the Curse wasn't triggered."

"Why would a Pur Sar be stalking her? The Syndrion?"

"Stick with her and don't let her out of your sight until I figure out what's going on." Ian hung up and leaned against the tree with a heavy heart. Wind kicked up the nearby debris. The clouds grew ominous.

{10}

Jaered dabbed at the blood on his lip. It wouldn't stop seeping, and it throbbed like hell. The bedroom's privacy curtains allowed one-way views of the outside. The Heir sat in the tree and looked right at him. Jaered didn't flinch. It was the same spot Jaered had sat guarding Rayne on many nights. Once she found her father in Oregon and discovered who she was, it was only a matter of time before others discovered *what* she was. Ning turning up alive, and here, had sent Jaered's concern into hyperdrive.

A couple of minutes later, the Heir climbed down.

An alarm went off in Jaered's head. The Heir had Jaered's visitor tag from Donovan's facility. Unable to find it that morning, Jaered had retraced his steps—and accidently appeared behind the Heir.

He touched his lip and winced. He needed ice.

Jaered reached the bottom step of the staircase, but froze. Someone was in the kitchen. He pressed against the wall and stole a glance around the corner.

The Heir had his back to the doorway. He tore off a piece of tape and pressed a note to the oven door, then hopped up onto the counter, taking the ID with him. He shyfted in an emerald cloud.

Jaered grabbed an ice cube from the freezer and held it against his lip while he read the note.

Rayne and Zoe,

Pack some things and feel free to either hang out at the mansion or let Tara check you into a hotel in town. My treat. I've arranged for the kitchen repairs and insist on putting you up for the next couple of days to avoid the hassle and mess. Hope all is forgiven, Ian.

Jaered's core ignited and icy water moistened his shirt. He grabbed the pen and drew a line through the mansion option on the note. Like hell he was going to place her in the same location as the book. His cell vibrated in his pocket. It was Eve. He hesitated, then answered.

"You're not where you're supposed to be," she said.

"I'm tying up some loose ends," he said. "I'm headed to the hotel now."

"You're the only one in a position to keep that formula out of Aeros's hands."

He massaged his temple to ease the pounding headache. He needed to refocus, but first he needed some aspirin.

"What time is the meeting?" she asked.

"Tomorrow, during the party."

"Everyone has a price, Jaered. It's your job to find out what Donovan's is."

It was the way she said his name that gave Jaered pause. What was her history with the CEO?

"Are you prepared?" she asked.

"All but the clothes on my back," he said.

"Off-the-rack will get you noticed in this crowd. There's a tux in your hotel room along with the invitation."

He didn't bother to ask how she knew his size. Jaered measured the damage with the tip of his tongue. He wasn't going to be as invisible as Eve hoped. "Ning's here," he said. Silence. She didn't know. Jaered pressed his hand against his bruised ribs. "He paid me a visit. He's been hired to kill someone in town."

"Who?" Eve asked.

"Didn't get that far. He knows Rayne can drain core power. He'll grab her if he can."

"Your priority is to keep the formula out of your father's hands and get a sample to me. Leave the Heir to protect what's his." She hung up.

That last bit stung worse than his lip. Jaered shyfted and appeared inside his car at the bottom of the hill. There was no sign of Ning. As far as Jaered could tell, he hadn't been followed. He settled against the headrest and surveyed the quiet neighborhood, wallowing in memories that refused to stay suppressed whenever Rayne Bevan invaded his world.

The sun's rays baked the inside of the cab and the warmed air morphed into searing flames, peeling the skin away from Jaered's hands as his vivid memories took hold. He let go of the heated steering wheel and rubbed his face to erase the nightmare. He started the car and mulled over options. How could he protect Rayne in the days ahead?

{11}

Rayne stared at the ceiling, afraid to move her head. Whatever they spread over her had hardened, and the itch under her breast was torturous. "Does he create casts for everyone he designs for?"

"Bazl prefers them over live clients." Tara said. "He works fast." She hesitated. "A little *too* fast. Ian suspects that he has a Weir partner behind the scenes."

"A Sar?" Rayne furrowed her brow, confused why a powerful Weir would choose to use his gift to create clothes.

"It explains why Bazl won't use anything but natural materials," Tara said.

"Have you ever heard of such a power?" Rayne asked.

"There's a lot about the Sars that us common Weir don't know. They've always been a secretive bunch."

"And the fat mannequins?"

Tara chuckled. "Not all of Bazl's clients are as tiny as you." She leaned on the edge of the vat and rested her chin on her arm. She stared ahead.

"You and Mara must have spent a lot of time here," Rayne said.

Tara bit her lip. "I miss her every day, with every breath."

"I get why Ian can't take me on his assignments," Rayne said. "But why you? It's what you and Mara had trained for."

"He blames himself for what happened to Mara and Galen. He's afraid of losing anyone else he cares about." Tara tilted her head and gave Rayne a gentle smile. "But there's more to it."

"What?"

"I think he keeps me home to guard who he cherishes the most."

Rayne had consciously been reaching out, to be there for Tara ever since her sister's death. It hadn't occurred to her that it could be the other way around.

"Ian needs to lighten up," Rayne said. Heat spread across her skin and beads of sweat tickled in too many places to count. "His paranoia makes me feel like a victim."

"Ian would die if anything happened to you. He loves you more than the world itself."

"He's never said it."

"He's afraid of how he feels," Tara said. "He'll always be forced to put the earth's needs above everything, everyone else. Even at the cost of his own heart."

The warehouse doorbell rang in the distance. The older Asian woman shuffled past.

Rayne closed her eyes. "I hunger for him when he's away. I ache when he's near. I never thought that love could be so painful."

"It would be different if he could take you with him. Be able to share the best of what the world has to offer," Tara said.

"There's still a chance for you to go with him on his assignments and help him protect Earth. I will always be left behind." Rayne's throat tightened. "He can't even kiss me goodbye."

A door slammed. Loud voices. Angry footsteps carried up the wooden stairs.

"What the hell is going on here?" The familiar voice came from the top of the landing.

Tara pushed away from the vat. Her expression morphed from startled to guarded in an instant.

Rayne moved to look, but the hardened plaster around her neck made twisting impossible. "Zoe? What are you doing here?"

"Humph." Zoe stepped into view. Rayne blinked. Her roommate's fuchsia pigtails were gone. From the looks of it, Zoe had cropped her hair close to her scalp and colored it blacker than a witch's cat. "Why do you look like you're covered in my brother's dried snot?" Zoe asked. She fingered the *Kiss Me, I Voted* button on her jean jacket lapel.

"They're making a cast of her to create a custom gown. Ian's taking her to a charity masquerade ball," Tara said. Zoe poked the cast, then knocked on it. "You followed us?" Tara's relaxed smile did little to deflect the tension in her voice.

Zoe pursed her lips and lifted her chin. "Maybe."

Tara's jaw bulged. "Aren't you the resourceful spy."

A revelation struck like a tidal wave and Rayne bit her lip. Did Tara consider Zoe a threat?

"Subtract two place settings for you. No wingman for me." Patrick tilted the cell phone for Milo to see Ian's text. The old caretaker grunted and returned to kneading his dough, but with louder slaps and deeper punches.

JoAnna wandered in from the back patio with her finger stuck in the middle of a closed book. "Where are Ian and Tara? I haven't seen them since breakfast?"

Patrick poked the mound of dough and thought fast. "At the auditorium, working on the routine for the gala. I'm not sure how much we'll be seeing them between now and then."

"I have the utmost confidence he'll throw something memorable together." She patted Patrick's hand. "After all, he is the one with the talent." She wandered out of the room.

Patrick sunk his fist into the dough. "Now I remember why I moved away." Milo hid his grin by taking a sip from his mug.

"Patrick!" Marcus shouted.

Patrick rushed into the dining room. Marcus and his mother were squared off. "But I insist," JoAnna said.

The Drion waved what looked like a check in the air. "The damages to the abbey were covered by insurance. Please, take it back."

JoAnna ignored his outstretched hand. "Insurance never covers everything. They can use it toward their deductible, to buy new furniture or a fountain. They like fountains, don't they? They're so relaxing and serene."

His mother's philanthropy had kicked in at the worst possible moment. Patrick glanced at the Book of the Weir, opened on the table, and in plain view. "Where are the scholars?"

"They took a break and went for a stroll." Marcus's tone was casual enough but the Drion's brows were jammed together into one long, bushy gray caterpillar. "Here, take care of it." Marcus passed off the check, and the dilemma, to Patrick. The Drion straightened a stack of papers on the dining table. "Are you enjoying your visit, madam?"

"Oh, yes. It's been too long. Patrick and I never see each other anymore."

"We are powerless to stop them from growing up, but it doesn't make it any less painful when they move on and leave us behind," Marcus said.

JoAnna looked surprised. "I thought monks were celibate."

"I am not of their order. Simply helping them."

"How many children do you have?" JoAnna asked.

"Just the one boy." Marcus followed the length of the table, pushing chairs in. A sense of melancholy stooped the Drion's shoulders, and his typical hardened features softened behind a soulful mask. JoAnna broke into stories about Patrick as a baby, following behind Marcus and readjusting each chair.

The setting sun cast Patrick's shadow on the wall. It was as if the boy appeared in the room, summoned by his father's pensive brooding. Patrick couldn't help but wonder what had happened to Marcus's son.

{12}

I an emerged from his bathroom to discover his tux hanging on the closet door with a note pinned to the jacket.

Will I ever find out why? Of course not! After all, you are the man of mystery are you not? I would have it no other way.
Bazl

The additional thickness to Ian's jacket confirmed that Bazl had followed the directions. He got dressed.

A knock on the door. Ian opened it. JoAnna stood in a beautiful crimson gown that accentuated her slender frame. She clutched one of the yellow roses.

"I'm almost ready," he said.

"I'm not here to rush you. I wanted to thank you for my flowers."

Ian returned to his dresser and concentrated on tying his tie with the aid of the mirror. "They were from Patrick."

"Of course they were." She eyed his attempt at a bowknot. "I've had lots of practice," she said. He stuck his hands in his pockets and turned toward her with a raised chin. She placed the rose on the dresser and set about tying it. "Whenever we get together, I can't help but remember that day we met at the park."

Ian stiffened, wary of the open bedroom door. A glance and a keen ear verified the hallway was empty. "It's been, what, four years?"

"That long?" She scrutinized her work, scrunched her face in disapproval, then loosened the knot and started over. "You were but a young teenager, yet sat on that bench like you had the weight of the world on your shoulders."

The day Ian had finished assembling his dirt bike, he'd syphoned gas from the Jeep, jumped on the cycle and took off before Milo noticed. The closest he ever came to running away.

Ian pushed the bike to its limits and didn't stop until deep in the city. He found a park bench that overlooked the ocean. Laughter from children playing ball. Parents pushing their toddlers on swings. Others encouraging little ones to let go at the top of the slides. For the first time in his life, Ian got a taste of normal, family life. The sting of what he had missed festered in the pit of his stomach long after Milo's punishment had come and gone.

"You were so sweet," JoAnna said. "Sliding over to make room for me when I approached." She tugged on the edges of the bow, then stepped back to admire her handiwork. "How I must have talked your ear off."

Ian had clung to her every word and scooted closer when she brought out her cell phone to show him a picture of Patrick in his cap and gown, clutching a diploma. Ian stared at it and found himself envying a young man he'd never met.

"It must have been hard on you that he moved to California for school and ended up staying to pursue being an entertainment agent."

"We had lost Patrick long before he went to college. He needed to be on his own." A dark look crept into JoAnna's face. "Not live in his father's shadow." A curtain dropped on her dark mood and JoAnna grinned up at him. "Little did I know I was spilling my heart to a budding magician."

"Whatever I've become, is as much Patrick's doing." Ian turned away to step into his shoes. "You should give him more credit, JoAnna."

"But I do."

Ian's objection lodged in his throat. He'd kept his distance from their conflict, unsure how to help mend a battle that had waged long before he came into their lives.

"You're a good friend, Ian. A loyal friend. Patrick didn't have anyone like you growing up."

"I never had any close friends, either," Ian said.

She picked up the flower and held it to her nose.

Curiosity had driven Ian to shadow JoAnna as she left the park that fateful afternoon. She'd strolled by several flower beds without giving them a second glance, but bent down and admired the yellow roses before crossing the street, heading for her hotel.

He'd come close to telling Patrick about that meeting while salvaging what he could of his wrecked bike, wanting Patrick to understand why he reacted the way he did, what the bike had meant to their friendship. Of all the secrets Ian ever kept from Patrick, finding out that his mother served a part in his success would be the most painful of them all.

Ian offered her his arm. "Let's have a night to remember." He escorted her downstairs.

Marcus and Nemautis were discussing something in hushed tones next to the front door. Marcus pulled back when he saw Ian with JoAnna. He opened the door at their approach.

"Patrick took your suitcase and things out to the limo. You're not returning with them?" Nemautis asked JoAnna.

"She has a morning flight and is staying at the hotel where the event is being held," Ian said.

"My social calendar keeps me quite busy. Please let me know if I can help the abbey in any way. I simply adore throwing parties that squeeze money out of my friends." JoAnna offered her hand. "I'm glad we had a chance to break bread together."

Nemautis cupped her hand in his. "I as well, madam."

Marcus grabbed Ian's elbow. "A word before you go?"

JoAnna raised a finger at Marcus. "Don't be long, or I won't be responsible for my son's meltdown."

"Heaven forbid there's another one," Marcus said. He closed the door behind her.

"Has your research found something?" Ian asked Nemautis.

The old scholar's face lifted. "We've finished separating the manuscript into sections."

"They've discovered it was written by five different Ancients," Marcus said.

"We've always suspected there were five originals," Nemautis said sounding every bit the teacher. "We'll go page by page tomorrow, starting with prophecies pertaining to you." Nemautis removed his glasses and rubbed his eyes. "It's a shame the Ancients didn't have the forethought to write in larger script and in an ink that wouldn't have faded so much over time." He put them back on. "I envy you and your youth. Enjoy your special night."

"I'll have more time to visit and share stories about Galen tomorrow," Ian said.

Nemautis brightened. "I would enjoy that very much, sire."

"Dinner's ready!" Milo shouted from the kitchen.

"Compared to the modest meals we prepare for ourselves, Milo's culinary skills are a touch of heaven," Nemautis said. He shuffled off toward the kitchen.

Marcus eyed Ian's tux. "If the Primary found out that you were leaving like this, his blood pressure would be off the charts."

"Marcus, please—" Ian said.

"I'll guard your secret about slipping away tonight, but keep your cell phone handy. I know that the Primary wants this book to be hush-hush, but with you gone, that's one less security measure in place."

"You can alert me if anything comes up," Ian said. "I'm just a shyft away."

{13}

Dozens of flashes blinded Ian the second he stepped out of the limo. A swarm of paparazzi leaned over the barricades. TV news cameras were hefted onto broad shoulders, every one of them directed at Ian. Someone stuck a microphone in his face. Patrick stepped in with waving arms. "Please, let us just have an enjoyable evening."

An attractive female newscaster raised a microphone to her chin. "Ian, this is the first public appearance you've made since losing your assistant in that horrific fire on your property. Are you here to attend the charity event, or to perform?"

"Both," Patrick said.

A man pressed closer and stuck a microphone toward Patrick. "You claimed his dirt bike incident an accident, but rumors still circulate that it was a suicide attempt at losing Mara."

"How absurd!" JoAnna blurted. Ian kept a protective arm around her, but she broke away and stood next to Patrick.

An entertainment personality strolled toward them dressed to the hilt. The microphone in her hand clashed with the million-dollar rented jewelry. "Does this appearance mean that you will return to the stage soon?" she asked. "That your fans can expect future performances?"

Patrick hesitated at her question. "That remains to be seen."

"The fans are losing their patience," she said and tried to maneuver around Patrick with Ian in her sights. "Do you really expect them to wait much longer, Ian?"

JoAnna stepped in front of Patrick. "Fade to Black Productions has always been a valued supporter of Isabel Stanton's charity events. We are thrilled and honored that Ian has chosen this event to return to the public spotlight."

"Mother," Patrick hissed under his breath. He pressed a firm hand against her back and ushered her toward the hotel entrance.

"This is not the time to be cautious." JoAnna dug in her heels, turned and waved toward the flashing cameras like a beauty queen.

Patrick intercepted a couple more network reporters camped out in the public lobby, but thankfully Isabel's steroid-fed security guards blocked the entrance to the banquet hall and they couldn't follow.

Raised in secluded Weir villages in the most remote areas of Europe and Asia hadn't prepared Ian for American society. This event was the only one he had ever cooperated with, but it never stopped Patrick from trying to add to the list with claims it would benefit the show.

The closer they drew to the waiting hostess, the tighter Ian's shirt collar grew, like a boa constrictor entrapping its prey. He stuck a finger inside and tugged, but he failed to loosen JoAnna's noose. He closed his eyes and drew a deep breath in an attempt to erase his sour mood.

Mrs. Isabel Stanton, reigning dominion of charitable acts and purveyor of contributions for her favorite charities, stood at the door dressed like Scarlett O'Hara.

"Mrs. Stanton, it's wonderful to see you as always." Patrick planted air kisses on each cheek.

Isabel gripped Patrick's shoulders. "My boy, I swear you're taller every time I see you." The moment she spied Ian, she clapped with lace-gloved hands. "Ian Black, our most treasured sponsor!"

"As promised, Isabel." JoAnna winked at Ian.

Isabel latched onto his arm. "My boy, you arrive unattached, making yourself an instant magnet for half the ladies in this room." She leaned in closer. "With or without escorts."

"Mrs. Stanton, you look as elegant as ever." Ian held his breath against her pungent perfume.

A waiter approached with a black mask and a clear plastic bag. "Check your phones, everyone," Isabel chirped.

Patrick stiffened. "What?" A bag was thrust at him. He dangled his phone over the opened bag with a grimace. It took a disgruntled glare from JoAnna for him to let go. One of the waitstaff handed him a ticket. "Why?" Patrick bemoaned.

"With all the effort I put into my parties, I'm done with guests ignoring one another, or stepping away at the whim of a chime, too often right in the middle of conversation." Isabel adjusted her ringlet wig. "I can't stand the abominations with their intrusive, unflattering candid photos broadcast to thousands."

"But darling, your husband makes his millions in the industry," JoAnna said.

"Who better to appreciate their nefarious side?" Isabel patted Ian's arm. "I'm not going to apologize for being greedy; those closest to me accept me as the bitch that I am. Those who don't can kiss their TV-dinner derrieres. But, Ian, I understand you've canceled the past two shows at the Children's Hospital. I hope your appearance tonight won't take the place of your monthly show this week. You uplift my little ones, so."

"Count on it," Patrick said. "It's one of Ian's favorite engagements."

Patrick's response was the magical password. Isabel disengaged her clamp from Ian's arm.

"Masks, everyone, after all it is a masquerade ball!" Isabel clapped and costumed footmen opened the main doors.

Patrick and Ian donned their masks. JoAnna held up one that matched her gown. They stepped into the ballroom.

Artificial weeping willows strung with strands of natural moss towered above the guests at the perimeter while a life-sized replica of a steamboat, complete with flowing water turning its wheel, sat at the opposite end of the hall. Moss swayed in a gentle breeze thanks to camouflaged fans circulating air from the trunks.

Creole seasoning, crawfish and mint filled the room. Banjo music came from a strolling Cajun dressed as if plucked from the bayou.

"You have outdone yourself," JoAnna said. "Each year the gala becomes more and more extravagant."

"I have wonderful friends and even more generous sponsors. Speaking of which," Isabel locked elbows with Ian and Patrick, and ushered them ahead, "I must thank you for the contribution of your show tickets for our silent auction. An entire orchestra section this year was simply magnanimous."

Patrick's choking fit sent Isabel in search of a waiter with water. "You donated an entire floor section?" he croaked.

"Don't look at me," Ian said.

JoAnna patted his back. "You two were so busy. I took it upon myself to help out in a small way these past couple of days."

"Mother."

"Oh Patrick, you'll thank me next spring with the tax write-off."

Patrick mumbled something incoherent under his breath and grabbed a glass of champagne from a waiter's tray. He polished it off in a drawn-out gulp, then snatched a fresh one at the next pass.

The low grumble under Ian's shoes was his first warning. He grabbed JoAnna around the waist as the room absorbed the earth's quake. The hanging moss jerked and the artificial trees creaked. The musicians skipped a note.

"Oh my," JoAnna said.

"These have been coming more frequently," Patrick said, holding his champagne glass out in front of him.

The subtle tremor subsided. Ian's apprehension kicked up a notch. There was something unnatural about the quakes. They were more like aftershocks, but if so, from what?

"Oh my god, the old crone is still breathing." JoAnna seized the fresh glass of champagne from Patrick as her other hand swept into the air. "Beatrice, darling." And with that, she disappeared into the crowd.

Patrick stopped a waiter and helped himself to another glass. "I'd grab you one, but at nineteen, you're not old enough to drink yet."

"Would you really want me out of control?" Ian said.

Patrick winced. "Good point."

Ian stuck his hand in his pocket and conjured his confiscated cell phone. He was groping for the on button when nearby voices faded. The music fell into a hum. It was as if time held its breath. He turned around.

Rayne's hand was upon Bazl's shoulder. Energy emitting from her aura shone bright and alive. Her smile ignited his core and he savored the afterburn.

"It cost you," Bazl said, leading the way through the parting crowd.

"She's worth it," Ian responded, unable to peel himself away.

"She is, isn't she?" Bazl took Rayne's hand in his and kissed it. "My work here is done. Enjoy your ball, Cinderella." The designer blended into the crowd.

Peacock feathers covered Rayne's bodice and sleeves. Just as Ian had imagined, their color was the perfect shade to match her incredible eyes. Bazl and his partner had done their magic, creating a flow with the feathers and the cut to complement every one of her curves and features. The back of her slender neck was outlined in scalloped tufts. The feathers draped forward, framing her bosom. The peacock pattern drew in at her waist and down over her hips. The feather's colorful tips ran the length of her forearm sleeves and ended in a V at the back of her hand. Bazl had gone so far as to lace one of the feathers through her upswept, sunlit hair. Flowing, pearlescent blue silk lay underneath, a shade lighter than the feathers that adorned it. The gown cascaded to the floor reminiscent of a waterfall.

Her eyes sparkled like Mediterranean waters from beneath the matching mask. The pounding in his chest was the only sign that Ian hadn't died and gone to a blissful heaven.

"I don't know what to say," she said softly.

He leaned in and gave her an aromatic kiss, a rare blossom he'd discovered in the heart of the Brazilian rainforest. "No words could thank me more than the way you look at this moment," he murmured. Tara approached. Ian drew back, stunned at how amazing she looked in a creamy silk evening gown. "Wow, you look—"

"Drop-dead gorgeous," Patrick said. "Since when do you dress like that?"

Tara beamed. "Bazl convinced me that even working girls can look—"

"Incredible!" JoAnna cried. She appeared with the designer and other chirping women in tow. "You are an artist above all others, Bazl." A deep rose lit up Rayne's cheeks as JoAnna stepped up. The gaggle of women closed in asking Bazl questions about his inspiration, where he found the exquisite, striking model.

Ian would have shyfted them both out of there if he could. He wanted Rayne all to himself.

"I suppose you're getting a taste of what she goes through with your fans," Tara said, brushing shoulders with him.

"I only want the night to be special for her."

"You did good, Ian. Real good."

"How can I repay you, Tara?"

"Silly. You bought me this dress." She accepted a glass of champagne from Patrick and they clinked glasses. "By the way, Zoe tagged along. She showed up at his shop and it was impossible not to involve her, too."

"Do you still have suspicions about her?" Ian said.

"I'm on the fence."

"Wow, three gowns is going to put a hole in your wallet." Patrick grabbed a snack from a passing tray.

"I put Zoe's on your tab, Patrick." Tara leaned closer to Ian and lowered her voice. "I think you're right. Bazl must have a Weir partner. Only someone with powers could have created three gowns in two days, and made the alterations to your tux."

"Where's Zoe?" Patrick asked.

Tara rose on tiptoes looking out across the crowd. "I lost track of her when we arrived. She mentioned something about going shopping the second we stepped in the room."

"She'll turn up. She always does," Ian said.

"So I've noticed," Tara said.

Bazl cupped Rayne's elbow and twirled his finger, directing her to show off the back of the dress. Rayne complied and laughed over her shoulder at something JoAnna said.

Warmth filled Ian's chest. Cinderella had stepped into the ball, leaving her concerns at the door. If he knew what was good for them both, he'd do the same.

JoAnna gestured for Ian to join them. "My boy, you have been holding out on me. Who is this startling creature?"

"Rayne, I'd like to introduce Isabel Stanton, the hostess of this gala. And this is Patrick's mother, JoAnna Langtree."

"The hall is amazing, Mrs. Stanton," Rayne said. "Mrs. Langtree, I couldn't wait to meet you."

"How ever did you two meet?" Isabel said.

Rayne hesitated and looked to Ian. "She's a student at one of the local universities," Ian said. "She interviewed me for the school's website."

"Ian, you will break hundreds of hearts when this hits the news." Isabel fanned herself.

"I'm counting on the discretion you offer all of your patrons," Ian said. "It is a masquerade ball for a reason, is it not?"

JoAnna chuckled. "You do stress anonymity, Isabel."

"And not a cell phone to sneak a picture. Dear boy, I may not forgive you for denying me the gossip of the year," Isabel said.

"Your event rules have come back to bite you. No doubt what Ian counted on, all along." JoAnna clasped Isabel's hand. "Come, let's you and I mingle and enjoy everyone else's gossip. The room is swimming with it, darling." JoAnna led Isabel away.

"Time to blend into the crowd," Ian said, and offered Rayne his arm. She hesitated. "Bazl made some modifications to my tux," he said. He took her feathered cuff and placed her hand on his sleeve. A slight energy drain tickled from deep in his core, but the debilitating pressure remained at large. He led them into the crowd.

Tara broke into a wide smile. "Feathers."

"It's about time you found something other than the air-freshener kisses," Patrick said.

They stepped out onto the dance floor. Ian's confidence wavered when Rayne faced him.

"Are you sure?" She looked at the other dancers around them.

"There's only one way to find out," he said.

She placed her hands at his shoulders. Her power drain gripped his core in a tight fist, but didn't squeeze. He pressed his hands across the feathers at her back waist and clenched his jaw when the draining force tugged on his core. It stopped short at crushing it. Ian managed to keep his features relaxed and turned them onto the dance floor, counting off the seconds before the pressure, or the core energy drain, grew too great and he'd have to let her go.

Rayne's beating heart thrummed in rhythm with his. Her perfume swirled in his head. Intoxicated, he hungered to pull her against his chest and kiss those forbidden lips.

"I never dreamed that one day I'd be in your arms." She studied his face. "You're in pain." She tried to pull away, but he tightened his grip on her back.

"It's nothing," he lied.

"Ian, please. I love you for trying, but don't make me hurt you."

"I can handle a bit of discomfort now and then, testing our limits, if it means moving a step closer to you."

Her eyes glistened. "I love you," she whispered.

It balanced on the tip of his tongue. A sliver of effort was all it would take to give it a voice. Ian's mouth postured to spill the words, but a need to hold back, like countless times before, put a stop to it before he could release those three simple words in return. He gave her a heartfelt smile and leaned in close while inwardly chastising himself for giving into his fear that they'd never be closer than this.

"Here's to an unforgettable night," he murmured.

{14}

Milo and Nemautis finished the last of the dinner dishes and put them away. "Would you like some dessert?" Milo asked.

"Your wonderful meal has more than satisfied my needs for tonight," Nemautis said.

Milo opened the freezer and removed the stack of frozen meats. He pulled out his hidden contraband. If Dr. Mac found out he'd ignored the prescribed diet restrictions, there'd be hell to pay. He scooped a generous amount of ice cream into a bowl and settled on the barstool.

Nemautis eyed the sugary mounds.

Milo scooted the bowl toward him, then got up from the barstool and walked around the kitchen island to fix himself another. "Should I scoop out a few more?"

"The others went to retrieve their coats to head out for an evening stroll."

"Will you be joining them?" Milo asked.

"My legs prefer to be raised rather than lowered by the end of the day. I hope to decipher a few more pages in the book before I retire." Nemautis stuck a generous scoop in his mouth. "Hmm, I don't believe I've ever had this flavor. What is it called?"

"Heart disease. But I prefer to think of it as heaven on a spoon." Milo stood on the opposite side of the island and savored every mouthful. He debated starting a load of laundry before an early bedtime with his latest cop thriller.

Shadows flitted across the shiny surface of the refrigerator. A flash of light brighter than the sun robbed Milo of his sight. A deafening explosion knocked Nemautis off the stool and he landed hard on the kitchen floor with a groan. The room shuddered. The last thing Milo remembered was shattering glass . . .

{ 15 }

Jaered found the conference room and stepped inside. There were a dozen round tables surrounded by empty chairs. A podium stood at one end. The room was bathed in a warm light. Buffered music and muted sounds drifted down from the masquerade ball overhead.

Yannis stood next to a table with his arms crossed over his chest. A sheen of sweat came off his bald head. It clashed with the expensive suit. He peered at Jaered with impatience. "You're late."

"I'm here now. Where's Donovan?"

"Hopefully on his way," Yannis said. "I haven't heard to the contrary."

Jaered pulled out a chair one table over and sat down. Yannis had arrived a week ago as Donovan's new executive assistant, sent by Aeros to keep an eye on the serum production. His father's spy hadn't wasted any time infiltrating the company records. It was only a matter of time before Eve's connection to Donovan and the company was discovered. Jaered had insisted on tonight's meeting. He was running out of time to get his hands on a sample and to sabotage the rest without getting caught.

A child's squeal came from down the hall. The door opened a second later. Kurt, Donovan's goon, looked between Yannis and Jaered then stepped to the side. Donovan entered. He wore a tux and carried a small child on his shoulders. The smiling boy wore Spiderman pajamas and clung to the CEO's head by his ears.

"What's with the kid?" Jaered said.

Donovan set the child on a nearby chair and handed the boy a stuffed dinosaur. "My business," was the man's only response.

Donovan's smug expression put Jaered on the alert. Something wasn't right. He looked at the boy with brewing questions.

"Pee-pee, Daddy," the child said before Donovan could sit down. He slid off the chair, clutching the dinosaur and reached toward his father with wide arms.

Donovan scooped him up and turned toward the door. "Looks like nature calls," he tossed over his shoulder. "I'll be back in a minute."

Kurt remained next to the door as if daring us to leave.

Yannis and Jaered exchanged glances. Jaered's concern morphed into irritation. The CEO had delayed handing over a sample for more than a week. Jaered's patience was running thin.

{16}

The banquet table offered bite-sized hush puppies, andouille sausage, and massive shrimp. Rayne didn't know where to reach first. A waiter offered her a mint julep, but she declined.

"Well?" Tara asked from beside her. "Was it worth it?"

Rayne would never forget the love she'd found in Ian's eyes. "And then some."

Tara popped a black olive in her mouth. "I want to bring some of this back to Milo," she said, grabbing a plate.

"They have plenty of plastic bags at the entrance," Zoe said from across the serving table. The pile on her plate resembled a pyramid. She ran her hand down her black, silky hip. The formfitting dress was striking, and showcased her ample bosom, but Zoe's awkward movements spoke how out of place she felt in it. "I keep reaching for my cell. Hell, even if they'd let me keep it, no pockets in this nightgown."

One of the party guests cut into the banquet line next to Zoe. He didn't have a plate with him. "Where have you been all my life?" The deep voice was directed at Zoe, but the face aimed at her chest. The smirk on his face spoke conceited, and his silver head of hair screamed old enough to be her father.

A wicked smile spread across her roommate's face. "Really? You think that old cliché will work on my generation? Get some new material, or start shopping in the right decade."

Tara's snicker ballooned into laughter. It earned more than a few stares. Rayne and Zoe ushered her away from the table when it verged on the hysterical. Milo's collected treats rolled off Tara's plate like breadcrumbs dropped in the forest.

Tara quieted and brushed at a tear worming its way down her cheek. "You sounded like my sister." She swiped at her nose with the back of her hand.

"Wow, the ice queen thawed," Zoe said.

Someone tapped a microphone and blew into it.

"Is it time for your performance?" Rayne asked.

"I think the auction is first, then us." Tara dabbed at her face with Zoe's napkin. But we should find the guys."

With the sea of black tuxes and satin masks, Rayne knew better than to lead the way. Tara and Ian might not have rekindled their channeling ability, but Tara was still connected to him in other ways. They soon caught up with the men. Patrick was getting cozy with a striking woman dressed as a Grecian warrior.

Ian abandoned him and joined the girls. He brushed Tara's cheek affectionately. "It's nothing. Patrick's drunk," he said.

"Why would I care?" Tara stuck Milo's sole surviving appetizer in her mouth and vigorously chewed.

JoAnna grabbed Rayne's arm from behind. A young woman, not much older than her midtwenties, accompanied Patrick's mother. "Everyone, I'd like you to meet my godchild. Carlene Donovan, this is the lovely Rayne, Tara, Ian, and—" Her lips pursed upon spying Patrick's conquest. "— my son, Patrick."

Carlene leaned in and offered her hand. "It's wonderful to meet you all."

"This is my roommate, Zoe," Rayne said.

"Who?" JoAnna asked.

Rayne turned. Zoe was a few yards back, flirting with a waiter. Zoe wasn't used to her short hair. She kept twisting her finger around an imaginary strand and broke into a snorting laugh at something he said.

"Carlene's mother and I go all the way back to my college days," JoAnna said. "Alise and I were best of friends at Yale."

"Is she here?" Rayne asked.

"In spirit only," JoAnna said and clasped Carlene's hand.

"She passed away last year," the young woman offered.

"I'm sorry. I lost mine a couple years ago." Rayne felt an instant solidarity through shared sorrow.

"Carlene has the most precious son. How old is Bryant now?"

"Almost three."

"Where did Richard wander off to?" JoAnna glanced about.

Carlene's tone turned guarded. "A business meeting. I don't expect him back for another hour."

"Men can't seem to separate work and pleasure." JoAnna regarded Patrick with scowl. "While others . . ."

"JoAnna," Carlene grabbed the woman's arm. "Let's find that quiet spot to catch up, shall we?"

JoAnna patted her hand. "Of course. We won't want to miss Ian's performance later." The two women excused themselves and headed for the main doors.

"How about one more dance?" Ian extended his elbow to Rayne.

She shook her head. "Ian, you're still pale from the first dance. You might be able to hide the pain, but I know I'm draining you."

"The feathers in my jacket are acting like insulation. My core is overheating. That's all."

"You're a terrible liar, Ian." She gazed at the couples on the dance floor, touching, many entwined in an intimate embrace while moving as one to the slow melody playing from the stage.

Ian leaned in, gesturing to give her a kiss. With a moan, he pulled away and pressed a clenched fist to the center of his chest. Rayne stepped back. "It's not you," Ian said through gritted teeth.

Tara pushed in and threw an arm around him. She ushered Ian toward the open doors and onto the outside deck. They didn't stop until they were deep in the shadows at the end of the patio. Ian leaned heavily against the stone railing and shed his jacket while Tara loosened his tie.

Rayne hung a couple feet back. "What happened?"

"The Curse," Ian said. He handed Tara his mask.

Patrick caught up to them. "I knew you'd go solar with all that feather insulation." He grabbed the nearby stone lion's snout and steadied himself. "Boy, do I need to clear my head. Bubbles and I don't mix."

"Patrick, it was the Curse," Tara hissed.

It took a full second for his stupor to lift. His eyes flew open. "That means—"

"A Duach Sar is here," Ian said. "Someone, at the party."

"Did you see anyone having a reaction in there?" Rayne asked.

"There's hundreds of people," Patrick said.

"The Curse lifted when I came outside. He must still be in there." Ian rubbed his chest.

"Not tonight. Not here." Patrick raked his fingers through his hair. "What are the odds the Duach will just ignore the Curse and go away quietly?"

Ian didn't respond. He didn't know if he could.

{17}

Ian made up his mind. He headed for the ballroom doors.
"Wait, if you go in there, you could trigger the Curse." Patrick blocked his path.

"I'm counting on it," Ian said. "Tara, go on stage and scan the crowd from there while I walk through the room. I need you to be my eyes." He squeezed her arm when she gestured in protest. "Go."

"What can I do?" Rayne said.

"I want you and Patrick to wander around the crowd. If anyone reacts, signal Tara on stage."

"Every man in here is wearing the same thing. How are we going to identify him?" Patrick said.

"He'll be in as much pain as me."

"What if he's not alone?" Patrick said. He looked at Tara. "Most Weir Sars have guards with them, right?"

"Ian, they'll come after you," Rayne said.

"I should be far enough away and lost in the crowd. Tara will come to my rescue."

Rayne didn't look any more convinced than Patrick. "I'll be all right, go," Ian said. "Go."

Ian acknowledged Tara when she made it to the stage. She went about like she was helping to set up for the auction. He walked the room like a grid, eliminating sections as he went. The fluid crowd was a challenge. Many of the guests hung together while others wandered toward the dance floor or the food line. Isabel diverted his attention for a couple of minutes to ask about last-minute details for his performance.

Several minutes in, Patrick signaled, but Ian hadn't felt any symptoms. Patrick had found a man choking on a piece of food. Ian went to help but a guest announced he was a doctor and pushed in. He stopped the man's agony with the Heimlich maneuver.

Zoe fell in with Rayne. On their first pass, Ian caught Zoe mutter, "Lose something, like your date?" She nudged Rayne when she and Ian ignored each other for the second time. "Lover's quarrels are a bitch, aren't they?"

Ian ended up at the entrance to the room without further incident. Patrick found him and Tara. Rayne joined them after giving Zoe the slip.

"Maybe they took off," Patrick said.

Ian perused the room. "We're thinking two dimensional."

"Of course." Tara turned around. "The range of the Curse can be—"

"Any direction." Ian looked up. "He wasn't above me." The room towered more than two stories high with stained-glass windows in the rotunda.

"We've ruled out around you," Patrick said. Everyone's eyes fell to their feet. Patrick groaned. "You aren't going to let this go, are you?"

Ian rushed out and headed down the hall with the others following. He paused with his hand on the stairwell doorknob. "Patrick, take Rayne back inside. Tara and I will go from here.

"Don't shut me out, Ian. I can help," Rayne said.

"He'll likely have a guard, maybe two with him," Ian said. "It's one thing to be lost in a crowd. I won't be able to protect all of you in an empty hallway."

"It's about time you see me as an asset," Rayne snapped. "Not someone to be protected."

"She is the Sar zapper," Tara said.

"Or, we can just drop this," Patrick said. "Maybe it was a false alarm, a short in your chest hairs or something."

"You know I can melt your kneecaps," Ian said.

Patrick grimaced. "It's the champagne."

Ian took a second to judge Patrick's sobriety. "You should return and cover for us."

"Be saddled with my mother and Isabel when you don't show up for your performance? I'll stick with the superhero squad."

"Then everyone take a deep breath and relax. We're just checking this out." Ian led them down the stairwell and slowly opened the door to the floor below. He peered down the hall. It was empty. "These aren't hotel rooms."

"Looks like they're small conference rooms," Patrick said.

"The room on the left, about midway, would be about where I stood in the ballroom."

"If he's still around, you can't go any farther," Rayne said.

"I'll go." Tara pushed ahead.

Patrick stopped her. "If the Curse triggers, you'll need to be with him. Rayne and I should check it out."

Patrick's right, Ian realized. He needed to take a step back from react mode and think this through. He could be walking into a trap. "Intel only. Be careful."

Patrick threw his arm across Rayne's shoulders. "Follow my lead, I have an idea." He led them toward the room. A tray piled with discarded dishes sat on a small round table in the hall. Patrick paused long enough to grab an empty wine bottle.

"You don't need a weapon," Ian said.

Patrick waved him off from over his shoulder and stopped at the door. A moment later, he opened it and they entered.

{18}

"Hey, sweetie," the man slurred.

Jaered's face shot up at the familiar voice. Patrick stood in the doorway, waving a wine bottle. Unsteady on his feet, he twisted about, playing out some kind of drunken act. Jaered's heart clawed at the inside of his chest. *She* was in his arms.

"I think we gave everyone the slip." Patrick raised the bottle to his lips.

"Not everyone," Rayne said.

Why? Jaered's thoughts spun out of control. What made them come in here?

"I claim this room for the intent of defiling this woman." Patrick thrust the bottle at Yannis. Kurt slipped his hand under his jacket and took a sideways step, blocking the door.

"Uh, I didn't sign up for an audience," Rayne said.

Jaered should have turned away, but looking like she did, he couldn't peel his eyes from her. Voices blended into the background as Jaered was transported back to when his life offered immeasurable happiness as long as he was in Kyre's arms. He looked down and pinched the bridge of his nose, hard. She didn't just rise from the grave and walk into the room. Her paral, Rayne Bevan, did.

His mask was in his hands.

She tilted her face from Patrick's puckered lips—and froze. The second her attention locked on Jaered, her throat lifted and bulged with a swallow.

Jaered shook his head, ever so slightly. With everything he had, he willed her not to show recognition—not to address him—not to approach him.

Both of their lives depended on it.

{19}

The mysterious Sar, the one that had rescued Ian in Oregon, sat off to one side hunched over with his forearms resting on his thighs. He wore a tux and a mask was dangling from his fingers. Rayne's heart skipped a beat, and her chest denied her air. *I'm a ghost who was never here,* he had said, and swore her to secrecy. The price for saving Ian's life.

Warning flashed in his eyes. She turned her face, and focused on everywhere else but him.

A bald-headed man wearing an expensive gray suit got up from the table. "I suggest you take your partying elsewhere."

Rayne took note. Zoe's grandmother spoke in the same dialect.

The bald man gestured to someone behind them. "Kurt."

Rayne glanced in the ghost's direction. He gazed down at his mask with indifference. Large hands gripped their shoulders from behind and shoved them out the open door.

"Hey, watch it, buddy," Patrick shouted to the man the size of a boulder. The door shut in their faces. Patrick grabbed her arm and they hurried down the hall to join the others.

"Anything?" Ian said.

"Two guys at different tables, one of them hunched over looking bored. A King Kong of a brute standing guard at the door." Patrick said. "There was a lot of tension in the room."

Ian brushed his finger across Rayne's feathered sleeve. "You okay, you look like you've seen a ghost."

"Fine." She cradled her arm. She didn't dare look him in the eye.

"Anything we can go on?" Ian asked while giving her a curious stare. "Names, tattoos, accents?"

"One of them spoke with a Baltic accent. Ukrainian maybe," Rayne said. "He was at the table. The big guy at the door was named Kurt. He took orders from the Ukrainian," Rayne added. "I didn't see anything else."

"How could you miss the lip on that other guy?" Patrick said.

Ian stiffened. "What did you say?"

"I think the bored guy came from the party. He wore a tux and had a mask," Patrick said. "But he sported a lip like he'd been in a fight. Someone nailed him, and good."

Ian stared at Patrick, then took off down the hall. Confusion delayed Rayne from following. By the time she caught up to him, he was almost to the door. "Ian, wait!"

Click. The door opened a crack. Rayne ducked into the woman's bathroom across from the room, and the others rushed in behind her.

Ian pushed open the door, giving them a slim view of the conference room doorway. Voices emerged in the middle of a conversation. ". . . fed up with the delays. Kurt, where the hell is Donovan?"

"I'll check the bathroom," Kurt said. He crossed the hall and opened the door next to the woman's bathroom. He disappeared inside. A second later he returned. "They're not in there. Maybe he took the boy to his suite upstairs."

"Yannis, track down Donovan so we can finish this," the ghost said. He returned to the room and shut the door as if irritated.

"Kurt, check upstairs. I'll cover the main floor." Yannis and Kurt separated. The bald man walked down the hall in the direction of the stairwell. A second later, the door banged shut. In the opposite direction, a *ding* and then the *swish* of an elevator door in the distance.

Ian opened the bathroom door and headed for the conference room.

Rayne bolted out and grabbed his feather-insulated sleeve. "Ian what's gotten into you? The Curse wasn't triggered by anyone here. There's no Duach," she hushed.

He hesitated with concern splashed across his face. "Rayne, I think you have a stalker. Whoever it was jumped me when I went to check out your house yesterday. I never got a good look at him, but he took a blow to the face."

Patrick and Tara joined them. "The purple-lip guy?" Patrick asked.

Rayne's head spun. What was the ghost doing at her place?

"Stay here, I'm going to check it out." Ian opened the door and burst into the room.

{20}

The room was empty. "Where is he?" Ian said.

Patrick shrugged. "He must have gone out the service entrance."

"Or shyfted," Ian said, remembering the surprise attack at Rayne's.

"What are you all doing in here?" JoAnna stood in the open doorway clutching Carlene Donovan's hand. Patrick's mother appeared to have shed her festive self. The woman's shoulders were rigid. Concern erased whatever youthful glow her makeup had given her. Her voice held an edge.

"Ian was stretching his legs before his performance," Patrick said. "What are you doing here?"

"We found a quiet place nearby to visit and catch up. Come, return before Isabel tears out her wig. The auction will wind down soon and you need to get prepared." JoAnna left with Carlene.

Ian grabbed Patrick's arm. "What do you know about Carlene Donovan?"

"Not much. My mom talked more about her mother, Alise. I know Mom was devastated when Alise died."

"Why, Ian?" Tara asked.

"Because she's Carlene *Donovan*, and her husband wasn't at the party because of a business meeting—"

"And this Donovan disappeared on them," Rayne said.

"About the same time the Curse was triggered." Patrick looked like he'd taken a blow to the gut. "This can't be happening. Not someone my mother knows."

"We need to get back," Ian said. "Keep an eye out for lip guy. He might have returned to the party."

"Ian, if Donovan's the Duach Sar," Rayne said, "And he joins the party, you'll be a sitting duck up on stage. If the Curse strikes, no way can we hide you from that."

"I know," Ian said, fighting to keep his panic in check. "I know."

{21}

Music rose from the speakers, and the tables closest to the stage quieted. The rest of the room soon followed suit.

Tara pirouetted on stage holding rods trailing long silk fabric. The material matched the pearl-colored gown that Bazl designed for her.

"Did you create something new for the act?" Patrick asked Bazl from across the table.

"I don't snip and tell," Bazl snapped his fingers.

"You will if I'm writing the check," Patrick said.

Tara swung the poles. The fabric lifted as if kites caught in the wind. They swept across the stage like billowing clouds while she danced in rhythm to the music. A hush fell over the room.

Patrick scooted his chair closer to Rayne. "Do you know what they have planned?"

She shook her head, focused on Tara's graceful ballet with her silk partners. "Relax, Patrick, or your mother's bound to notice."

"Brand-new illusions with no rehearsals, half of Northern California high society in the room and," he reached for his champagne glass, "my mother has a front-row seat for when Ian crashes from the Curse at any minute."

"Where is he?" Rayne glanced around. "You'd think Donovan would have shown by now."

The music built to a crescendo as Tara's dance brought her to the center of the stage. She turned around; slow at first, then faster and faster. The material spun overhead like two sweeping helicopter blades. When she came to a stop, the fabric settled, swirling around her and covering her from head to toe.

"Isn't she breathtaking," Bazl said.

The last of the sweeping material came to a rest on the stage. A second later, it unfurled at her feet as though caught in a circular wind. The shimmering cream fabric pulled away revealing black silk underneath. To Rayne's astonishment, black shoes and tuxedo pants emerged.

The audience erupted into thunderous applause when the final piece of fabric fell away and Ian stood holding the poles out at his sides. He spread into his killer smile. Whistles and shrieks drowned out the fading music. Ian bowed.

"Now that's what I call an entrance," Isabel said, clapping wildly. "Bravo!" she shouted.

"Genius," Bazl said and fanned himself.

"Wow, where'd that one come from?" Patrick slowly clapped.

Rayne recognized nature's influence on Ian. It was a cocoon.

Ian shot a fleeting glance in Rayne's direction. She shook her head. He addressed the crowd. "It's been a while since I took the stage. Hopefully, I'm not too rusty."

The music grew upbeat. He held up one of the poles and draped the material like a curtain. He turned it to the ivory side. When he flicked it with his finger, it grew stiff. He let go and took a step back. The material stood as erect as a painter's canvas.

Bazl shrieked in delight and clapped.

"I'm going to need some help tonight," Ian announced.

He pulled a thick black marker out of his inside pocket and quickly sketched an outline of a life-sized body on the surface. Ian spun the canvas around displaying the dark silk side, then turned the drawn image back to face the audience. He stepped to the side and extended his hand toward the canvas.

The crowd gasped when the drawn arm moved like an animated cartoon and its hand reached toward Ian. The moment they touched, the canvas turned to loose cloth and collapsed onto the stage floor. Tara stood grasping Ian's hand. The room swelled with applause.

"I give you the lovely, Tara." The audience applauded. Ian tossed another glance at the empty chair between Rayne and Carlene.

"If only it were so simple," Carlene said. "To just . . . vanish."

JoAnna clasped her hand. "But it is, darling. You simply need the right person to ask for help." Patrick's mother gazed at Ian on stage as if deep in thought.

Neither woman had been themselves since they'd left to talk about whatever concerned Carlene. Rayne sat brooding, wondering if she could find out more about their conversation, without coming across as rude or prying.

A shout came from the back of the room. Ian cracked a joke at the inebriated man's expense. The crowd laughed. Rayne looked over her shoulder at the group choosing to stand behind the tables. She scanned the faces for any sign of a man headed their way.

Behind the crowd, someone in a tux was walking toward the ballroom doors. Rayne stared, focused on getting a good look each time his profile bobbed in and out between heads. Her throat tightened. He had a swollen lip.

Rayne's common sense screamed for her to stay put. She bolted from her seat.

Patrick threw panicked eyes at her. "He's here?"

"I'm just checking. I'll be back." She navigated chairs and tables, then pushed her way through the wall of people.

The ghost exited the crowd and headed for the main door, but paused and tilted his face to the side. Rayne hesitated, certain that he would turn and see her, but a heartbeat later he continued. When he reached the door, he exited without looking back.

By the time she stepped out, the hall was deserted. Her heart sank. Laughter and loud applause rose behind her.

Click. A door closed at the end of the hall. Rayne sensed someone watching her. She looked over her shoulder. A tuxedoed man wearing a devil's mask and red cape had his back to the stage. He leaned against the portable bar counter with a drink in his hand and appeared to be watching her. The costume's facial expression sent a shiver across her arms. She hurried down the hall and approached the door, but stole a peek from over her shoulder. Whoever the devil was, he didn't follow. Rayne pushed down on the handle and stepped inside a dimly lit room.

The ghost stood facing her as if waiting. He thrust out his hand. The door shut behind her. "Why are you following me?" he said in a harsh voice.

"I'm not," she retorted.

The snicker on his lips ruffled her temper. "You *intended* to come into the men's bathroom."

Too late, she saw the commodes along the wall behind him.

"Why are you here?" he asked.

"Isn't it obvious? I'm attending the party," she said.

"You're here, with *him*."

The grievous tone piqued her curiosity. "Who are you?" His silence riled her. "Why did you attack Ian?"

"I didn't." His smug expression bordered on amusement. "I was searching for something. He was in my way. I moved him."

"You're the one who's been following me." She took a step toward him. "Did the Syndrion send you?"

"I'm neither Pur, nor Duach," he snarled.

Rayne shook her head. "All Weir are one or the other."

"Only those born on Earth," he said.

She took a step back, and then another. "But if you're not from—"

He was on her in an instant. Rayne pressed up against the wall. The ghost hovered, keeping a few inches distance. Brilliant blue eyes softened behind his mask. His fingertips floated down the length of her arm on an invisible current of air. "He touched you . . . here." His fingers lightly brushed her forearm. He stared at her with interest. "I'll be damned, feathers. You touched him. How?" When she didn't answer, he ventured a guess. "His jacket, something inside, a lining."

His breaths heated the air. Her inner voice screamed to shove him away at being so bold, but silence filled the space between them as her emotions ran amuck and stilled her tongue. Rayne's head spun, her pulse quickened the longer he was near. Who was he? Where'd he come from?

He groaned and pushed away from the wall, then stepped to the opposite side of the room. "Is he going to be in town?"

"Who?"

"The Heir. Is he going to be around for the next few days?"

"I don't know." She shook her head. "He doesn't always know himself."

"Make sure he is."

Her hackles rose. Rayne didn't know if it was his demanding tone, or the painful reminder. "What if I can't?"

He turned hardened eyes to her. "*Convince* him."

"Why?"

"I can't . . ." He hesitated. "I can't stand watch over you anymore."

"I can take care of myself," she said.

"You're far from safe."

"Who are you?" she said, but bit her tongue when it sounded like pleading.

"A ghost," he hushed. "I'm nobody."

"At least tell me your name," she said louder—insistent—needy.

The handle moved and the bathroom door opened. He reached out. It slammed shut. The handle jiggled. A muffled voice came from the other side.

"Please," she said gently and took a step toward him.

He met her halfway and paused in the middle of the room, under the light. The mask couldn't conceal it. Rayne knew a tortured soul when she saw one.

Anguish spilled from his eyes. "Jaered." He spoke the name so soft, Rayne didn't know if she had imagined it. His hand waved. The bathroom door burst open.

A man fell into the room and stumbled between them. He startled when he saw Rayne. "You must be drunker than me," he slurred.

She ignored him and stepped to the side. Jaered was gone.

Rayne rushed out and returned to the table with Jaered's name haunting her thoughts. She discovered a man seated in the chair next to her vacant one. Her steps slowed and she looked at Ian on stage, engaging a woman from the audience in a sleight-of-hand trick.

Richard Donovan sat with his arm slung across the top of his wife's chair. He squeezed her shoulder and leaned in to whisper something to her. Carlene nodded.

Rayne sat down and stole a sideways glance. The man had rugged features and an honest tan as if he spent time outdoors. Donovan didn't acknowledge her and appeared engrossed in Ian's performance.

Patrick grasped Rayne's arm and pulled her close. "No Curse."

Richard Donovan might still be of Weir heritage, perhaps a Duach, she thought, but no Curse meant he wasn't born with a core. He wasn't a powerful Sar. Rayne slumped against the back of the chair releasing the pent-up tension as best she could.

Ian believed Jaered to be an enemy. How could she convince him otherwise, without breaking her promise to the ghost and disclosing the secret that she'd carried around for months?

And who—where—was the Duach Sar that set off the Curse?

o

{22}

Jaered stepped up and got the bartender's attention with the wave of a twenty. "Whatever you have on tap," he said, laying the bill down on the counter. The hotel bar had emptied when someone propped open the banquet hall door. The patrons were all taking advantage of the free show.

"ID," the bartender said while drying out a glass.

Jaered pulled out his wallet and held up his driver's license. The bartender scrutinized it, then turned away. Jaered stared at the ID. Eve's connections had created the necessary documents for him to blend in on Earth. The worst part was having his picture taken. Not one showed him smiling. His home world of Thrae had no such petty rituals in their daily struggle for survival.

A foaming beer was set down in front of him. Jaered returned the wallet to his back pocket. Yannis entered the bar area with a disgruntled Donovan in tow.

Kurt hung back near the entrance to the bar. Yannis settled at a table within earshot. Aeros had Jaered babysitting the pompous CEO, but there was no love lost—only the illusion of trust—between Jaered and his father. It dawned on Jaered that the serum production wasn't the only thing Yannis had been sent to keep an eye on.

"I have to keep up appearances. What couldn't wait?" Donovan stepped up to the counter without making eye contact.

"You blew me off." Jaered grabbed the brew and took a swig. "You wasted my time."

"A Pur Sar showed up." Donovan snapped his fingers and pointed to a bottle of Scotch. The bartender grabbed it. "I'm surprised you didn't go after him when you felt the Curse."

"Unlike you, I can prioritize." Jaered took a swig of the beer. Not being born on Earth had one advantage. He was immune to the anomaly that incapacitated the Pur and Duach Sars when in close proximity to each other. The disadvantage was that Jaered had a difficult time telling the rival factions apart.

He positioned his hand below the counter, directly under Donovan's. Jaered drew magnetic power into his core, using the metal in Donovan's wedding ring to pin the man's hand against the counter. Jaered increased the energy draw, just enough for Donovan to get a painful message but not so bad that he couldn't hide his reaction from the bartender.

"No more games," Jaered said for only Donovan's ears. "You promised to give me a vial of the serum tonight to test on a powerful Pur Sar. Where is it?"

The grimace on Donovan's face twisted into a ferocious scowl. His free hand slipped inside his tux jacket and he removed something from the inside pocket. He handed Jaered a small vial of liquid under the counter.

Jaered cut the power draw and pocketed the vial. His relief at obtaining Eve's prize was short-lived.

"It's the formula. Almost." Donovan sneered.

"What do you mean, almost?"

"There's a missing key ingredient in the one I gave you." Donovan rubbed his sore hand. "If I was to give you a viable sample, what would stop you from duplicating it in another lab and squeezing me out altogether? I'm not turning over the only bargaining chip I've got to join Aeros."

Jaered had misjudged Donovan. The man was no fool.

"I've got a problem." Donovan slid his bruised hand into his pocket and downed his drink in one gulp. The colliding ice cubes *clinked.* "You're waiting around for the formula to be ready. You have time on your hands and can take care of it for me." Donovan lowered his voice. "My wife, her family, offered business connections that were otherwise beyond my reach. Those days have come and gone. She's no longer an asset. She's a human, not one of us."

"Sic your lapdog, Kurt, on it."

"Too close to home. I hired someone to take care of her, but the fool has proven to be unreliable and reckless. Her accident was to happen earlier this evening, but he skipped out to take care of his own agenda."

Was that why he had dragged the child to the meeting? Jaered wondered. "Your domestic woes are your own." He grasped his glass in both hands. It was either that or toss the man into the stacked liquor bottles behind the bartender.

"If you're half as ruthless as your father, I would think you'd jump at a chance to kill a human," Donovan said. "Take care of my problem, and I'll hand over the missing ingredient

●

a few days early, when it's too late to duplicate." He left without paying for his drink. The bartender kept a steady eye on the twenty lying on the counter.

Jaered sighed. Eve said everyone had a price.

{23}

Richard Donovan was a Duach. Ian knew the second they shook hands. The man's irises were fringed in red. Like Rayne's. Thanks to his keen sight, Ian didn't need one of the Pur guard's prism lights to detect it.

"Sorry I arrived late for your performance," Donovan said.

JoAnna hung onto Carlene's arm. "That's what happens when you're the one in charge. How is business, by the way?"

Donovan appeared to be looking for someone while he massaged the ring finger on his hand. "Couldn't be better."

Ian erased the Duach stench on his trousers and studied the room. A few dozen people lingered in the ballroom. Hotel staff were dismantling the steamboat and tugging on the moss in the trees. Rayne's supposed stalker never reappeared, but could still be nearby.

Ian excused himself and left JoAnna and Carlene with Donovan. A compulsion to get Rayne out of there grew fierce. He found the others near the entrance to the ballroom. Their numbers were short by one. "Where's Zoe?"

"She hooked up with some guy in a devil mask and cape," Rayne said.

"Hellish tattoos," Patrick chuckled. "He took off his gloves on the way out."

"She said not to wait up." Rayne yawned.

"Time to go," Ian announced.

"What now?" Tara asked.

"We're headed home. We've got to get back to the book, but first thing tomorrow our attention focuses on Richard Donovan. He's connected to the stalker, and maybe to the Duach Sar."

JoAnna approached. She cast wary eyes at Donovan as he escorted his wife to the door. Ian's core ignited and his chest blistered from deep within when the CEO put a firm hand on his wife's back and forced her to keep walking without stopping to acknowledge them.

"I can't believe I stayed up this late," JoAnna said. "Tara, it was wonderful seeing you again. Rayne, I have high hopes we'll see more of each other." She grabbed Ian's and Patrick's arm and headed out into the hall. "Breakfast in my hotel room tomorrow morning. Both of you. Eight o'clock sharp. No excuses about being hung over. Who knows when I'll return to town again." She gave Patrick a peck on his cheek and left.

Patrick groaned. "Did she not see how far a drive we have?"

"You can always crash with her in her suite," Ian said.

"What am I, twelve?"

The limo turned the corner and headed for the main gate. A rush of adrenaline flushed Ian's exhaustion and he sprang upright in his seat. Floodlights lit up the inner compound. A regiment of Pur guards patrolled the outer perimeter of the mansion grounds. One of them held up a hand as the car approached. A couple of unmarked dark vans were parked in the circular drive beyond the front gate.

"Oh no," Tara said.

"What?" Rayne opened her eyes and sat up in the backseat. Patrick snorted, deep in slumber with his head resting against the limo door.

Ian threw a panicked glance at Tara. "I've gotta—"

"Go," she said.

He jumped out of the car and ran into the inner compound. Not one guard attempted to stop him. They dropped their faces in reverence and remained silent as he passed.

Squeaks came from a stretcher being wheeled toward the back of one of the vans. Its doors were propped wide in wait. The body bag bulged from the sides of the gurney. Two Pur guards eased another stretcher out the front door.

Ian approached the closest stretcher, and the guards stopped. With trembling fingers, he pulled back the zipper. The odor of burnt flesh rushed up to greet him. It was one of the scholars. A core blast had stripped away one side of the man's face revealing charred strands of flesh and bits of splintered cheekbone beneath. Stomach contents rushed up and blistered Ian's throat. He unzipped the other bag. Nemautis's dull, lifeless eyes stared past Ian.

What Ian would have given to hear the strident breath coming from those still lips. He pulled further on the zipper. He'd been murdered by a core blast to the center of his chest. Galen's colleague had died instantly.

Ian rushed inside and nearly collided with a Pur guard releasing a message scroll at the foyer table. It spun on one tip over the silver platter, then vanished in a green burst.

A sheet of paper blew past the soldier's shoulder. A blast had left a gaping hole in the outside wall of the dining room. The cool, ocean breeze sent what was left of the scholar's notes blowing into the foyer. Some of the Pur soldiers were clearing the debris and gathering them up.

"Were there any survivors?" Ian twisted around. "Drion Marcus? Milo!"

"Here," came from the great room. The old caretaker sat on the couch with his back to the foyer. The drooped head and sorrowful tone dammed the flow in Ian's veins.

Ian slowly approached. A thick bandage surrounded the old caretaker's upper arm. Scrapes covered one cheek. Red, swollen eyes, as if he'd gazed directly at the sun for too long, locked on Ian. His sweater was coated with plaster dust.

Ian's knees threatened to buckle. "Marcus . . ."

"Upstairs, in your boost."

"How serious?" Ian asked.

"Dr. Mac removed some shrapnel from his leg. A nasty concussion. He shouldn't be in there but a couple of hours."

"Saxon?" The look on Milo's face stopped the beat of Ian's heart.

"He took a core blast. Dr. Mac's working on him in the kitchen." He looked up at Ian through a veil of moisture. "They got the scholars. I couldn't save Nemautis. I was blinded by one of the blasts. I couldn't see a thing."

Ian threw his arms around the grizzly caretaker and buried his face in the man's shoulder. The day they had laid Galen and Mara to rest, Ian had promised them that he'd never put himself above the needs of the earth. A selfish desire to please loved ones in his life had taken him away from the mansion tonight. It had cost Galen's friends their lives.

Milo's steeled frame melted and he patted Ian's back. "I'm okay, boy," he said. "It'll take a lot more than what they threw at me to put me six feet under."

Ian leaned back. "Why didn't you call me?"

"By the time I woke up and found Marcus, the Pur guards were responding to the alarm. There wasn't anything you could do." Milo swiped his nose on his grimy sleeve. "Ian, the book. They got it."

Ian's nightmare went viral. "How did they get into the safe?"

"It wasn't in there. They attacked right after dinner, before it was put away for the night."

Tara dashed into the house. A Pur soldier stuck an arm out to stop her, but she darted around it and ran into the room. She threw her arms around Milo from behind. The guard detained Rayne and Patrick at the front door.

"Let them through," Ian ordered. They started into the great room, but Ian shook his head. "See if Dr. Mac needs any help. He's working on Saxon in the kitchen. You too, Tara."

"Milo?" Tara asked.

He patted her arm. "I'm fine. Check on Saxon."

They disappeared down the hallway.

"A Duach Sar with core blast powers attacked Saxon outside. That much is certain." A twinge of fear clouded Milo's features. "But that's not who killed the scholars. Ian, I might not have been able to see, but I still have my nose. I think it was a Pur Sar who killed them."

Stunned, Ian recalled the body bags. The overwhelming odor of burnt flesh. Shock at the injuries. He'd never noticed what was missing. The smell of sulfur.

"Everyone's to stay put," Milo said. "Primary's orders."

Thoughts swelled so fast, Ian's head threatened to explode. "But I can help."

"There's no fixing this, Ian. Only damage control." With a grunt, Milo scooted to the edge of the couch. Ian helped pull him to his feet and didn't let go until the old caretaker's rickety legs stopped quivering. Milo didn't protest.

"Why am I not dead?" Milo said.

"You're too stubborn to die," Ian said without a lick of amusement in his voice.

"They slaughtered the scholars, but spared Marcus and me. Why?"

Saxon lay on his side. The large wolf covered much of the table. The odor of sulfur slammed into Ian when he entered the kitchen. Duach core blasts reeked of it. Ian had been hit by a few. The smell triggered a twinge of nausea.

Dr. Mac had a stethoscope pressed to the wolf's chest and he was bent over, listening. The girls stroked Saxon while avoiding a bandaged patch. It stretched from the wolf's ribs and stopped short of his hip.

Patrick was pouring a cup of coffee. More than a few drops spilt. The tremor in his hand wasn't all alcohol withdrawals.

A lump formed in Ian's throat at the thought of how close they'd come to losing Milo, Saxon and Marcus. His back bent with guilt for the murdered scholars, for failing to protect Galen's colleagues. Despair at the loss of the book cemented it in place.

Dr. Mac righted up and patted Saxon's head. "He'll recover. It didn't penetrate too deep thanks to his thick coat. He's one lucky dog." Saxon lifted his snout and directed a weak growl at Dr. Mac. "Sorry ol' boy, wolf." Dr. Mac slung his stethoscope around his neck.

"Can we try putting him in my boost when Marcus is done healing?" Ian asked.

"The boost works entirely off a core," Dr. Mac said. "Since he doesn't have one, the healing powers wouldn't be triggered. He's tough. He'll recover quickly on his own." Dr. Mac shuffled toward the sink in his soiled pink bunny slippers. "If you wouldn't mind cleaning up, I'm in need of a hot shower."

Tara grabbed a trash can and swiped the bloody rags into it. Rayne helped gather up the surgical instruments.

Dr. Mac regarded Ian. "You look like hell. How long has it been since you got a full night's sleep?"

"I don't know," Ian said. "A few days." If the elders only knew about the level of power drain he'd endured for the sake of love.

"Then get some rest. You're no good to anyone like this."

"I can't sleep with what's going on. Marcus might need me."

"His squad is a well-oiled machine, with or without him." Dr. Mac yawned. "Catch a few winks, Ian. You've got some explaining to do." He left the room.

"What did he mean?" Rayne asked.

"The book was my responsibility. This is my disaster," Ian said.

"But you successfully kept it hidden from everyone for months."

"Once the scholars arrived, it was vulnerable. I lost focus," he said and avoided looking at Rayne's gown, a reminder of where his priorities had been. The sleepless nights staking out her house for a Pur Sar that never returned. Heat escaped from his core at the resulting train wreck.

Ian stroked Saxon and scratched him behind the ear. *I'm sorry I wasn't here,* he channeled. *You fought bravely.*

Duach. Saxon whimpered.

The trash can slipped from Tara's grasp. She twisted around and stared at Saxon.

I know the one that attacked you was a Duach Sar, Ian channeled. Fatigue dug its claws in him and wouldn't let go. Tara took a step toward them, her mouth fell open, tears pooled in her eyes.

QualSton. Saxon channeled. *QualSton Duach.*

Tara laid a gentle hand on the wolf. *The same QualSton Duach that killed Mara?* she channeled.

Ian stared at Tara. Her voice was in his head. *It can't be,* Ian channeled. *He's dead.* His thoughts backpedaled. Rayne survived the fall, but they had assumed the ocean current claimed the Duach. A tremendous gust slammed into the sliding glass door. A ruthless enemy had returned from the grave.

Rayne gave him a puzzled stare. "Ian, what is it?"

Saxon whimpered. *Not dead.*

{24}

Ian no sooner had stepped out of the vortex building than a frigid blast slammed into him. Spring came early in Northern California. Not so in the Black Forest of Germany. He pushed his exposed hands deep into the pockets of his thin jacket and followed Marcus across the courtyard. The revelation that Ian and Tara could channel through Saxon, coupled with the resurrection of Mara and Galen's murderer, was cut short by the Primary's summons to meet in the Syndrion chambers within the hour.

A shared melancholy linked Marcus and Ian while ominous clouds hung heavy overhead. With every crunch of the icy snow beneath his boots, Ian's despair grew more and more unbearable. A slight mist formed, laden with moisture. They stepped into the chamber hallway and Marcus lit a torch.

"I allowed you to leave. I take the responsibility, Ian."

"I left you alone. The blame is mine."

"A blame to be shared, then," Marcus said.

More than anything, Ian didn't want to step through that door. Every muscle ached, screaming for his feet to stay planted in place. He steeled his jaw, grabbed the torch from Marcus, and turned the handle.

The chamber door swung wide, and he stopped. The dreariness outside heightened the gray of the ancient hand-carved walls in the room. Streaks of gold and crimson spit across the polished stone floor, a dying fire the only warmth and light in an otherwise lifeless room.

"I thought we were supposed to meet here?"

"That was the message," Marcus said.

Motion next to the fireplace. The Primary stepped from the shadows and stuck his hands in his sleeves.

Ian struggled to read the old man's eyes, but the exhaustion he found there camouflaged everything else. Marcus nudged Ian's back to keep him moving.

"Where's the rest of the Syndrion?" Ian glanced at the vacant Drion thrones around the massive oak table, carved in the image of the earth. "I thought we were being summoned to explain ourselves to the council?"

"Knowledge about the Pur having the Book of the Weir has been a closely guarded secret," Marcus said. "Even from the Syndrion."

"They'll never know what slipped between the Pur's fingers," the Primary said. "Before you hid the book, did you make copies of it, Ian?"

He'd been so quick to hide it, that it hadn't occurred to him. He shook his head.

Marcus stepped next to the Primary and warmed his hands at the fire. Ian held back and doused the torch, choosing to shiver. He counted on it to mask his trembling nerves.

"Report," the Primary said.

"The compound security has been fully restored," Marcus said. He rubbed the back of his neck. "Whatever good that does against assault rifles and an expert tactical team."

"What of the book?" the Primary asked. "Why was it not in the safe?"

"Nemautis had intended to return to it after dinner," Marcus said.

"What of the outsiders?" the Primary snarled. "Could they have been involved in this?"

"No!" Ian stepped forward. "Not a chance."

"Except for those closest to you, Ian, no one else even knew about the book being in your possession," the Primary said. "Someone must have leaked the information at some time or another."

The implication sent Ian's pulse racing. The Primary could use this as an excuse to throw Ian back into isolation, and what would be Rayne and Patrick's fate? He stepped forward. "It was my—"

"My fault," Marcus blurted.

"No, Drion, I was the one who left you alone."

"I knew Ian had plans that took him away from the estate. I chose to keep it to myself without bringing undue attention to the compound. My troops were told I was visiting Ian for a few days. If I pulled in some of my guards, the true nature of my visit might have been questioned.

"But—" Ian said.

"Enough!" the Primary smashed his fist on the table. "I don't want should-haves or could-haves. I don't want confessions, and I certainly don't want blame." He faced them. His eyes reflected the flames of nearby torches. "I want my book!" His roar echoed in the vast chamber, building upon itself and engulfing the room. Ian held his breath. The Primary's choice of words caught him off guard. "Neither of you will pursue this. I have put others more experienced with treachery on this."

"Primary, I understand your reluctance to send Ian, but let me lead a team."

Marcus's words stung Ian to his core. Sleet struck the windows outside. "Don't shut me out," he said. "I've grown stronger over the past few months, with or without my powers."

"Silence!" The Primary gestured toward the windows. "Get control of yourself." Ian took deep breaths in an attempt to calm. The sleet eased, then came to a halt. The Primary pressed upon Ian. "I *forbid* you to search for the book. For all we know, that's exactly what their endgame is."

"But Aeros murdered four defenseless men to keep us from knowing what was in that book," Ian said. "The answers to my weak powers."

"What proof do you have that it was Aeros?" the Primary asked Marcus.

"What makes you think it wasn't?" Marcus said.

"He's not the only one who would be so brazen," the Primary said. "There's someone else who has coveted it, who will stop at nothing to keep its secrets to herself."

"Who?" Ian said.

"She is known as Eve. A cunning manipulator of Pur and Duach alike. The last thing I want is to have Ian anywhere near her." He headed for the door.

A powerful female Weir working with both Pur and Duach? Milo's concerns rang in Ian's thoughts. The scholars were struck down by Pur core blasts. Questions billowed and swirled in Ian's head. Who was this mysterious enemy? Why would the Primary keep them in the dark? Ian focused on his breathing, the only way to stop himself from rushing after the Primary. The man's decision to keep him at a distance gouged out a chunk of Ian's self-esteem, but it was the Primary's parting words that sent him into a tailspin.

"Ian, you are to return home and remain until further notice. Your Syndrion assignments will cease until you make a decision. You either embrace your destiny and live among us as the Weir that you are, or be banned and live the rest of your days among the humans. You can't have it both ways. Not anymore." The door slammed with a resounding echo.

{25}

JoAnna dabbed at the corners of her mouth with her napkin. "You'll have my full financial backing, of course. It must be as soon as possible."

Patrick's mother had dropped the bomb of the decade in their laps, right in the middle of French toast. Ian sat in stunned silence. Carlene twisted her napkin in her hands and gazed at the untouched breakfast in front of her.

"You can't be serious," Patrick said. "Ian can't help Carlene and her son disappear."

JoAnna gave him a perplexed stare. "Why not?"

"I can't imagine how many laws that would break. What you're asking would make him vulnerable to possible criminal charges."

"Carlene, why haven't you gone to the police?" Ian said.

"I have no tangible proof that my husband is dealing with criminals. Only suspicions, bits and pieces of overheard conversations over the past few months. He's too smart to keep something like that out in the open. I know Richard has a safe at the house in addition to the one at his office. I haven't been able to locate either one, much less know what their combinations are. If there's proof, it would be in one of them."

"If you can throw the show together that you did last night with just two days' preparation, you can do this and keep your culpability out of it." JoAnna stabbed the last strawberry on her plate and gave Ian a reassuring smile. "I have complete faith in you."

"Ian is in control on stage," Patrick said. "Every detail worked out to the finest point. What you're asking—"

"Could save my son's life." Carlene looked between Patrick and Ian with a mixture of sadness and desperation. She twisted the napkin tighter.

"Tell them what you told me last night," JoAnna coaxed.

"Bryant had spilled juice on his father's suit the other morning. Richard set his cell phone on the counter and grabbed a towel, but it had soaked through. He was headed upstairs to change when an airline confirmation text flashed on his cell's screen. I checked the flight after he left for work. Two first-class seats to Brazil, at the end of the week."

"Naturally, I thought it was a business trip," JoAnna said. "But—"

"One of the tickets is in Bryant's name." Carlene swiped at a tear. "He's never mentioned wanting to take Bryant anywhere before. I spoke to a lawyer. I can't stop Richard from taking Bryant. But I know in my heart if he gets on that plane, I'll never see my son again."

"Who better to help Carlene and Bryant disappear than a magician?" JoAnna said.

"What makes you believe that Richard is dealing with criminals?" Ian asked.

"He has locked himself in his office at the house on several occasions over the past few weeks. One night, he sounded upset. I listened in at the door. He was arguing with whoever was on the phone with him. From what I could tell, he's created a lethal drug for someone."

"Terrorists would be my guess." JoAnna leaned back in her seat.

"Whatever Richard created for this person, he said that it had turned out better than expected. That he didn't want to limit its use. That he could kill every last one with it."

"Every last what?" Patrick asked.

"Someone called the Pure."

Ian and Patrick froze.

"A drug cartel, maybe. Pure cocaine, heroine?" JoAnna's pulse skipped a few beats. Ian looked at Patrick's mother. The color flushed from her face. She grabbed Carlene's hand and squeezed it. "Sweetheart, did you at least hear anything else, a name, something the authorities could investigate?"

Carlene shook her head. "I'm not sure, but I think I heard him call her Eve."

Ian's fork clattered on his plate. JoAnna startled. She gave him a curious stare.

"I've got to get back. I don't dare leave Bryant alone with Richard for long." Carlene pushed back and got up from the table. She grabbed her purse and rummaged around in it, then withdrew something and handed it to Ian.

It was her husband's business card. Ian did a double take at the company name and logo.

"I wrote my cell phone number on the back. Please, help me," Carlene said. JoAnna walked her to the door and they hugged. Carlene hurried out.

"I didn't sleep a wink last night after Carlene told me about the plane tickets," JoAnna said.

"JoAnna, what do you know about Richard?" Ian asked.

"His company has been in his family for generations and is a leader in drug research. Richard travels the globe in search of rare or unusual plants for new breakthroughs in medicines. It's been said that he's a natural, has a gift for it, like his father before him. They live in his childhood home, a secluded mansion a few miles from town, much like you, Ian. I know that Alise never fully trusted Richard."

"Why?" Patrick asked.

"She believed his business was the only thing he truly loved, but Carlene was devoted to him. Then, Alise fell terminally ill." JoAnna turned away. "I'm just thankful she lived long enough to see her grandson born." JoAnna's back straightened and her shoulders squared. She gave Ian a piercing stare. "I owe this to Alise. Carlene has no one else to turn to."

A rap on the door. Patrick opened it. A porter dragged the towering cart in and loaded JoAnna's things. She kissed Ian on the cheek, then turned and spread her arms with a step toward Patrick. "We might live on separate coasts," she said, embracing him. "But that doesn't mean we have to live at a distance."

"I'll try harder to stay in touch," Patrick said.

She grabbed her napkin and dabbed at her cheek. "Let me know how I can help." She led the porter out of the room.

The door swung shut behind them. "I'm sorry. You've got enough on your plate. I'll think of something to tell her," Patrick said.

Ian opened his palm and conjured the visitor's tag he found in Rayne's tree. He held it up next to the card. The company names and logos matched.

"Where did that come from?" Patrick said.

"I found it at Rayne's house." Ian stuck both items in his back pocket. "This is confirmation that her stalker and Donovan are connected." He rushed out of the room and took off for the elevators. "JoAnna!" he shouted. "Wait!"

Her petite hand stopped the doors from shutting.

"We'll help Carlene," Ian said. "But I may not be able to do it without you."

Her expression morphed from gratitude to conviction. "Anything, just name it."

Ian and Patrick returned to the mansion and found Milo, Rayne and Tara in the kitchen. The group huddled close together at the island, the only way to be heard over the construction noise. Marcus had a crew repairing the damage to the mansion.

Between the previous night's attack and the commotion of the day, Milo looked on the verge of losing it. The old caretaker stood punching and kneading his dough, taking out his frustrations the best he could.

Patrick filled everyone in on the events from breakfast between shrill bursts from a power saw on the other side of the kitchen wall.

Ian held up the visitor's pass from Lux Pharmaceuticals. "Rayne, have you seen this before?"

She slid off the barstool and took a closer look. "No. Why?"

"It was stuck in a tree, directly across from your bedroom. I think it was what your stalker was after when he attacked me." Ian caught Rayne's quickening heartbeat in spite of the racket.

The old caretaker slammed the ball of dough down on the counter with a *whop.* "You can't seriously be considering this! If I could, I'd lock you in your room."

"This might be a chance to right some wrongs of the last few days," Ian said.

"Or put you in an even hotter seat with the Primary than you already are." Milo swiped at his nose with the back of his hand. It left a snowy smudge behind.

"If I get intel on this Eve and whatever this drug is that Donovan is going to use on the Pur, then I can prove to the Primary that living between the human and Weir worlds has its advantages. It may be my best chance to stop him from making me choose sides."

"You didn't see how scared Carlene was," Patrick said.

"She's got a three-year-old son, Milo," Tara added.

"You can't convince me that this will turn out okay," Milo said.

"If the Primary has his way, what happens to Rayne, or Patrick? He won't protect them, and you know it," Ian said. "This may be the only solution to saving us all." He swept his hand across his torso. Sweats replaced his jeans and T-shirt. A finger to his bare feet. Athletic shoes appeared.

"What are you doing?" Rayne said.

She hadn't been herself since the gala. Ian hoped his decision would be reassuring, but her heart had yet to stop pounding in her chest. "I need to think. I'm going for a run." He lowered his voice. "I won't stop until I get to the bottom of who's after you. I promise."

The woe in her eyes was hard to walk away from.

Ian let himself out the back and ran around the lake, then cut over and disappeared into the woods. He passed a handful of Pur guards patrolling the grounds. They had all but surrounded the estate. If the Primary prevailed, Ian feared they might never leave.

He sought to rid himself of the draining, suffocating self-doubts created by his recent mistakes and turned toward the ocean cliffside, welcoming cramped muscles and burning lungs as his act of penance, seeking forgiveness from no one but himself. Nature offered solace as the sun beat down on his troubled soul. The longer he ran, Ian managed to stifle the guilt at the loss of the book, but he couldn't erase the image of Nemautis's face when Ian had pulled back the zipper on the body bag. Every time his thoughts fell to the Primary's ultimatum, his heart slammed into his chest. Could he live as a human and turn his back on his Weir destiny, knowing that the earth and everything and everyone who roamed across it would suffer for his selfishness? Did he have it in him to forfeit everything, everyone in his life and embrace his role and duties to the Weir? To Earth?

For the past few years, he'd fought to live life on his terms, believing that he could have the best and thus give his best, to both worlds. In so doing, had he ultimately failed?

An hour later, he stopped and sat on an outcropping in the cliff's edge. The weight lifted, and he cleared his head with each gulp of air. Mesmerized by the sparks of sun teasing the ocean waves, the roar of the crashing surf below proved to be the perfect canvas. His thoughts fell to the one thing he could control.

By the time the sun leaned toward the ocean and the energy of the earth replenished Ian's core, confidence filled him with peace.

Part Two

Illusion is the art of creating the impossible.
David Copperfield

{26}

Patrick left the coffee shop and chose a patio table next to the sidewalk as instructed. It gave Tara a clear view from the roof. He panned the buildings across the street, trying to locate which spot she'd chosen.

"Stop looking for me," Tara said in his earpiece.

"Sorry." He lowered his face to his cell screen. "I just wanted to verify you were where you said you'd be."

"Focus on what you need to be doing and don't worry about me," Tara said.

He swiped the screen. "You're used to this, I'm not."

"You've begged Ian to let you be more involved. This is an opportunity to prove yourself."

"Right. No pressure there, whatsoever."

Tara cleared her throat. "Here she comes."

Carlene crossed the street with a small boy in her arms. Patrick rose and pulled the chair out for her when she entered the café's patio by the street gate.

She settled in the seat with an appreciative smile. "Bry don't you want your own chair?"

The boy dug himself deeper in his mother's lap and peered at Patrick like he was an unwanted nap.

"Bry, this is my friend, Patrick."

"Hey, sport. Your mommy's told me a lot about you."

Bryant Donovan closely resembled Carlene with matching brown eyes and hair that shimmered auburn in the bright afternoon sun. His innocence dispelled the last of Patrick's resistance at getting involved.

"I never realized how close our mothers were. She really enjoyed seeing you again."

"I'm sorry she never got a chance to see how much Bry has grown." Carlene wrapped her arms around her son.

He melted into his mother's embrace, and his eyes smiled at Patrick. A sheepish grin crept up his face. Patrick winked at him.

"Mommy, I'm twirsty."

Patrick got up. "I'll get it. What would you like?"

"Duce," he said.

"Juice," Carlene translated. "Apple if they have it."

"Coming right up, sport." Patrick stepped inside and stood in line. He tilted his head and scratched behind his ear. "Does it look like anyone's tailing her?"

"Not yet," Tara said. "Stick to the plan, Patrick."

Patrick rubbed his sweaty palms together. He got the apple juice and brought it outside. He pulled a napkin out of his pocket and set the drink down on it in front of Bryant. "Here you go."

"What do you say?" Carlene said.

"Tank you." Bryant grabbed the cup with both hands and slumped back against his mother, sipping through the straw with loud slurps. The slurps soon turned to bubbles.

"Here's Ian's autograph that you asked for." Patrick slid a small book toward her with a picture of Mickey Mouse on the cover.

"Thank Ian for me," she said. "I hope Bry can see one of his shows someday. He's amazing."

"Ian's just full of surprises," Patrick said.

"Stop improvising," Tara snapped in his ear.

Patrick cringed. He smiled at Carlene when she threw him a puzzled expression.

They chatted until Bryant drained the glass. Carlene pushed away from the table. "I'm sorry, but we need to run. Thank Ian again for the autograph. Give your mother my best the next time you talk to her." She picked up Bryant and settled him on her hip. "What do you say, Bry?"

He hid his face in her shoulder.

"Sorry, he's like this with strangers." She grabbed her purse and slung it over her shoulder. "Let's try and keep in touch."

"Let's." Patrick remained standing while she walked to her car. Bryant peeked at him from over her shoulder. When he waved, the boy grinned and hid his face, then looked again a second later. He played the game all the way to their car.

"Sit down and finish your coffee," Tara said.

Patrick plopped down in his chair and watched Carlene climb into her car to secure Bryant in his car seat. "Anything?" Patrick said behind his coffee cup.

"Nothing that screams she's being followed."

"Then we should head back." He tossed his empty cup in a nearby trash can.

"I'll meet you at the car," Tara said.

Patrick strolled along the sidewalk feeling pretty smug. This cloak-and-dagger stuff was fun. When he entered the parking lot, he hit the remote. The car beeped and the lights flashed. He got in and shut the door.

"How'd it go?"

Startled, Patrick grabbed the steering wheel with both hands. He found Ian's reflection in the rearview mirror. "I thought you weren't coming?"

Ian passed one of his sleight-of-hand performance balls between his fingers. "Just checking."

"You coached the hell out of us, Ian. We all know what to do."

"Props and equipment are predictable," he said. "People aren't. The stalker is the wild card. I don't know anything about him. He could turn this entire thing sideways without a moment's notice."

Patrick half turned in his seat and regarded Ian. There was something bothering him. He would often get moody, brooding, right before doing a new illusion. But this was different. "You okay?" Patrick asked.

"Something's been bothering me, like an itch that I can't scratch."

"What?" Patrick asked.

"Carlene told me they'd arranged for a babysitter in their suite. But from what we overheard in the hallway the other night, Donovan chose to take Bryant to that business meeting. Why?"

Ian's question gave Patrick pause. If Donovan was conducting business with a powerful Sar, why risk endangering the boy? "What do you think it means?" Patrick said.

"Maybe nothing. Perhaps everything." Ian stared out the side window. "Tell me about the child."

{27}

Jaered watched Carlene Donovan exit the hotel.

He left the lobby a few steps behind her and crossed to the opposite side of the street. The woman often glanced over her shoulder and paused in front of shop windows while studying her surroundings. Did she suspect her husband was having her followed?

It wasn't difficult to stay off her radar. Jaered spent his life living that way. Born Aeros's son, forever linked to the man who destroyed an entire planet's ecosystem, had dictated it. Surviving his childhood had been a challenge.

She lingered next to a bus stop cubicle and pulled a small book out of her purse with a picture of a mouse on the cover. She flipped through the pages and then paused as if reading.

Jaered raised his face to the sun. Even after a year and a half of living on Earth, its gentle rays continued to fascinate him. Its ability to nourish a thriving planet, instead of devastating everything it touched, remained a foreign concept to him. Everyone on Earth, the Weir and humans alike, took so much for granted.

Whenever he brooded like this, his thoughts dwelled on the souls he couldn't forget, forever lost in the struggle to save their dying planet. Those still alive on Thrae were the fuel that drove him to follow a young mother caught in the middle of a battle she knew nothing about, and to do the unthinkable.

She entered a shop. He stepped off the curb and crossed the street. Dressing rooms and back alleys were opportunities.

Carlene was sorting through piles of shirts on a table when Jaered entered. She didn't look up at the tinkling bell announcing his arrival.

"Welcome," the young woman said from behind the counter. "Let me know if you have any questions, or if I can help you find something."

Jaered glanced about the shop. To his dismay, it was a children's boutique. Scratch the dressing room. Two women walked in and brushed past him. They stopped at the sale table and took a break from texting to check out some garments next to Donovan's wife. Jaered turned to escape before suffocating from the whimsical décor and candy-colored garments. It was as if the tinkling bell snickered on his way out the door.

He slipped into the bus stop cubicle at the curb and leaned against the glass-paneled wall. He closed his eyes. *For the greater good,* he recited over and over, but there was nothing great, or good, about any of this.

"I don't want excuses, I want assurances." Donovan's voice came from behind. "If you can't have the shipment ready on time, I'll find someone who can."

Jaered gazed beyond the cubicle partition. Donovan strolled toward the shop. He had his cell pressed to one ear while a small boy trailed from his other hand.

His wife stepped out of the boutique with a shopping bag.

"Mommy!" The child let go and hopped on his toes the rest of the way. She gathered him up into her arms. They touched foreheads in greeting. He held up a dinosaur. "This finger got ate by the dino." He held out his pinky on the same hand that clutched the toy.

"There's not much missing. He wasn't too hungry." She kissed it.

"How much more?" Donovan pursed his lips. "But you will guarantee it'll be ready? Very well. Add the personnel that you need. I'll approve it."

"Problems at work?" she asked.

"I have a lot riding on this project. Everything, in fact." Donovan looked up from his cell screen and tapped his son's nose. "But some things are worth the outcome." He eyed the shopping bag. "What's that?"

"Something for Bry."

Donovan shook his head. "Women and shopping."

"It's in our genes." She gave him a relaxed smile.

"Park, park, park," Bryant said and hugged his mother.

"Looks like you've got your hands full," she said to Donovan. "I'll take him so you can go to the office."

"Here's the car key." He dangled it in front of her. When she reached for it, he grabbed her hand in a tight fist. "Wait, on second thought." Her eyes widened. Her lips parted. He kissed her, not affectionately, but rough, wielding power over her. Donovan let go. She pulled her son tighter to her chest. He rubbed the boy's head affectionately. "Going to the park sounds like a great way to spend the afternoon as a family."

Fear flickered across her face. She regained her composure. "I thought you had a lot on your plate?"

"Family time is what's important in life. Am I right?" He waved his cell phone. "I'm only a call or text away if they need me."

When Donovan turned, he glanced at Jaered through the smoky glass partition. If he was surprised to find Jaered there, he didn't show it. The young family strolled back toward their hotel. Carlene Donovan hugged her son close to her chest.

When they reached the parking garage, Jaered headed for his car. A sleepless night and a lengthy phone call with Eve hadn't yielded any alternatives. Getting Donovan to hand over the formula, and stopping his father's shipment, took precedent over any obstacle.

Even if it meant that a young mother had to die.

{28}

The park bustled with activity thanks to the warm, sunny afternoon. Patrick leaned against the car, stretching his calf muscles. "The fickle finger of fate has rammed up our butts."

"I'm sure if she could have slipped away as planned, she would have." Tara sat inside the car with the small binoculars up to her face.

"What other glitches are on the horizon?" Patrick said.

"Welcome to Ian's world," Tara said. "If you want to be a part of it, you'll learn to go with the obstacles life throws at you."

"Obstacles I can dodge. Train wrecks are something else."

"Stop with the drama," Tara said, but the edge in her voice gave away her concern. Carlene was supposed to rendezvous with Tara and Patrick at the park. Donovan hadn't been in this part of the equation. They were waiting for Ian to contact them with a revision.

Patrick dried his sweaty palms on his pants. "Why couldn't Ian just shyft them to some secret hideaway halfway across the world and have this done by dinner?"

"One. Carlene is human. Ian's not about to violate Weir law and disclose his powers to her. He's in enough hot water with the Primary as it is. Two. Carlene and your mother are expecting Ian to use his skills as an illusionist to pull this off. He needs to keep up the ruse for their benefit." Tara lowered the binoculars. "But it'll also buy us time."

Patrick paused in the middle of his stretch. "Time for what?" What hadn't Ian shared with him?"

"Ian intends to infiltrate Donovan's company. And this way—"

"Donovan will be too busy trying to find his wife and kid to pay attention to what's going on at the office." Patrick's strained muscles started to unwind.

"Carlene's hoisting Bryant up on the monkey bars," Tara said. "Patrick, go. He's climbed to the top."

"But we haven't heard back from Ian, yet."

"Carlene doesn't know that. She's sticking to the original plan," Tara said.

"Donovan could recognize me from the masquerade ball." Patrick hesitated.

"You've got a hood. Use it." Tara gestured. "Go!"

Patrick pulled up the hood on his sweat shirt. He took off at a jog and kept one eye on the boy and his mother. Donovan had settled on the bench with his nose in his cell phone. Patrick navigated the path while silently pleading for him to stay there. Caution dragged his pace. It took only a second for him to realize he was taking too long. Bryant was halfway down the bars. Patrick picked up his speed and clenched his teeth as he approached the play area, dreading what he was about to do.

Something slammed into Patrick's back. He landed on all fours. No! He couldn't screw up before he got started.

Shrieks filled the playground. Patrick jolted to his feet. Saxon wore a seeing-eye-dog vest that covered most of the scorch mark. Something was wrong. It was as if the animal had gone rabid, jumping around and snarling at the scrambling bodies of children on the equipment.

Bryant fell through the middle of the bars and landed on the rubbery gravel. He screamed in terror at Saxon's snapping jowls.

Patrick stared, dumbfounded.

"Get away from him!" Carlene rushed at the wolf, swinging her jacket at him.

Saxon turned and snapped at a girl clinging to the edges of the slide. The wolf turned and leapt at shoes racing toward him from the swings.

Donovan took off toward Saxon. His hand reached under his coat.

Alarms shrilled in Patrick's head. Did Donovan carry a gun? He looked at Saxon, still focused on wreaking havoc. Patrick headed for the melee. He had to stop Donovan without bringing attention to himself.

Parents shouted with waving arms. Others rolled up magazines or newspapers and brandished them in the wolf's direction. A couple of women threw handfuls of the rubbery pebbles from under the playground equipment. A dozen phones were whipped out of pockets—a couple were thrown at the animal, most snapped pictures. Donovan reached the monkey bars but paused at the social media blitz going on around them. He slowly withdrew his hand from under his coat. Saxon took off cutting in and out between bushes and trees. Brave fathers ran after him but held up at the edge of the park.

"Mommy," Bryant whimpered.

"I'm here, sweetie," Carlene said pulling him out between the bars and wrapping her jacket around him. A second later, he cried out in pain.

"What's wrong?" Donovan said.

"I don't know. I think it's his arm."

"Let me see," Donovan said. He reached toward Bryant.

Patrick's breath caught in his throat. Everything hinged on what would happen next.

"No, Mommy," Bryant cried and buried himself in his mother's shoulder. Carlene turned away from her husband and held him tight.

A young father grabbed his squealing son off the monkey bars. "I've never seen a dog that big."

"It looked more like a wolf than a dog," a grandpa said dragging an empty stroller across the rubbery gravel, headed for a white-haired woman clutching a toddler.

Donovan punched a button, then held his phone to his ear. "Come on, come on, answer."

"Who are you calling?" Carlene said.

"His doctor's office, who do you think?" Donovan snapped. He pulled the phone away. "Blast! I got a recording."

"It's Sunday," Carlene said. "They wouldn't be open. Besides, he's halfway across town." She turned for the parking lot. "The Children's Hospital is nearby. We'll take him there."

Donovan blocked her path. "He only gets seen by his pediatrician. No one else. You know how I feel about that."

"Really, Richard? When are you going to realize that your octogenarian pediatrician isn't the only doctor in San Francisco?"

"Our Children's Hospital is the best in the state." A young mother said, brushing dirt off her little girl. "Celia broke her ankle last year. They were wonderful."

"Good luck," another mother called out, carrying her child away from the equipment. "I hope it's not too serious."

Carlene stepped around Donovan and paused when she reached their car. With a disgruntled expression, he opened the car door and Carlene slipped into the backseat with Bryant. A moment later, they drove off.

Patrick retraced his steps and got in the car. Tara shifted into reverse. "Where did Saxon come from?" he asked.

Tara held up her cell. "Ian used my GPS. He deposited Saxon in the backseat a second after you took off."

She drove to the far end of the parking lot and opened the back door. Saxon leapt inside, and they sped off.

"Oscar material," Patrick said and rubbed the wolf behind the ears. "That rabid dog act had me fooled."

Saxon snorted.

"Get Ian on the phone," Tara said, dropping a few car lengths behind Donovan's Mercedes. "Tell him about the newest snag."

"Other than Donovan showing up, what else is there?" Patrick said, pulling out his phone.

"That Donovan might be carrying a gun."

{29}

What are they up to? Jaered had pondered the possibilities ever since spying Patrick and Tara hanging out in the parking lot at the children's playground. When they followed Donovan's car, the questions swelled.

Donovan pulled up to the entrance to the emergency room. The small interior parking lot was packed with cars. He swerved back around and stopped across from the doors. His wife got out and gathered the boy into her arms, but not before grabbing a shopping bag. Donovan yelled something to her and took off with squealing tires.

The second he pulled out of the inner lot and entered the multilevel parking garage across the street, the young mother disappeared inside the hospital.

Jaered swerved in ahead of another car and grabbed a choice parking spot along the curb. Fingers shot into the air, compliments of the elderly couple waiting with their blinker flashing. Jaered ignored them when he got out. He crossed the street and followed Donovan's wife inside.

Carlene Donovan stopped at the reception counter and set her shopping bag down. She attempted to get the nurse's attention. From over her shoulder, the boy turned his face toward Jaered.

There wasn't any sign of pain in the child's expression. Jaered's curiosity heightened. If he wasn't injured, what brought them here?

His mother leaned in and whispered something to him. Bryant buried his face in her shoulder.

The packed waiting room harbored coughing, anxious whispers and bored or irritated expressions. A couple of boys with bloody bandages held to their noses were being escorted down a back hall. Playground brawl, Jaered mused.

Too late, the harried staff had underestimated another child in crisis. Retching set the waiting room into chaos mode. The nurses rushed to deal with the spewing lunch.

"I was told to ask for Margaret," Donovan's wife said.

The frantic nurse paused. "Oh, right. She's been expecting someone. The nurse peered at the mess in the middle of the waiting room and bit her lip. "I should escort you back, but I'm shorthanded at the moment. If you would, just go through the double doors behind me and head all the way to the back examination booth on the left. I'll let Margaret know you're here.

A raven-haired woman in a nurse's smock walked past Jaered. She grabbed the bag's stiff handle and took Donovan's wife by the elbow. "Here, I'll take you back." They disappeared through the double-wide doors.

The wife entered a curtained booth. The raven-haired nurse stepped in behind her and shut the curtain.

He glanced over his shoulder at the sound of frantic steps. Donovan burst into the waiting room and looked about. Jaered turned back and focused on pinpointing into which booth the young mother and boy had gone, when three other nurses dressed in identical smocks entered or exited the nearby curtained exam areas. Their identical raven-colored hair brought his thoughts to an abrupt halt.

"Hey!" Donovan grabbed the receptionist by the arm when she didn't look up. "I don't see my wife and son. They came in here a couple of minutes ago. He hurt his arm."

"I'll help you in a minute. Let me finish taking care of this first," she said, cupping the sick child's chin. He opened his mouth and gagged as if he was gearing up for round two.

Donovan gave a rough jerk to her arm. "You'll help me now. Where did they go?"

"Sir I understand you're worried, but no one's come in with serious injuries in the past several minutes. As soon as housekeeping gets here, I'll find out where they are."

"My wife's name is Carlene Donovan, my son's name is Bryant. He's wearing jeans and a T-shirt with red, white, and blue stripes. He's not quite three."

The nurse paused. "No one's been admitted by that name." She pulled her arm out of his grasp and returned to the child.

Donovan stared as though confused. He wandered the room. When he spied Jaered next to the doors, Donovan settled within earshot. "Did you see her come in?" he said under his breath.

"They're in one of the examination booths just ahead." Jaered stepped away from the doors.

Donovan sauntered over and stole a glance through the window. "I don't want you pulling anything in front of my son. I'll see if I can separate them, send her to retrieve something in the car. The second you get the opportunity, you take care of her. This place will give me the alibi I need."

Tara gave Bryant a wink. "Carlene, you can keep him on your lap." Tara removed the neon green gauze from its packaging, then pushed the cart closer and sat on the stool across from them.

Carlene put headphones on her son and let him play with an app on her phone. She bounced Bryant on her knees. "I didn't know what to do when he insisted on coming to the park."

Tara gave her a relaxed smile. "You've done great so far."

"He's going to storm back here any second. How can Ian pull this off with Richard this close?"

"There was always a chance he might be having you followed. Ian's allowed for that."

"You don't know my husband. His son is his world. Richard controls everything where Bryant's concerned, even choosing our pediatrician. He's never let me take Bryant to any medical appointments without him coming, too." Carlene startled when a child cried out across the way.

"Have faith in Ian." Tara placed a gentle hand on Carlene's leg. The bouncing came to a halt.

"I all better," Bryant insisted, louder than necessary. He waved his arm. "See?"

"I'm sorry I pinched you so hard, Bry," Carlene said and gave Tara a knowing look.

Tara removed one of Bryant's earbuds. "I know you're not hurt, but my face is." She made a silly face. He smiled. He pushed away from his mother's chest and sat up straight when Tara held up a sucker. "Bry, do you know how to disappear?"

He nodded and held his hands in front of his eyes. When he pulled them away, he giggled.

"Good job." Tara unwrapped the promised sucker. "Now, I'm going to show you a new way."

{30}

Jaered put some distance between him and Donovan. He didn't believe anything could exceed the man's ego, but the longer the nurse kept him waiting, rage was about to top the list. If Donovan didn't pull himself together, he'd be shown the door. Housekeeping arrived and took over in the waiting room. Security joined the party. The nurse nodded in Donovan's direction, then sat at her computer, scrolling as if searching for something.

It had struck Jaered that Donovan might want to be remembered, to solidify his alibi. Whatever unnerved the man, felt like something more.

The nurse looked up at the security guards and shook her head.

"What the hell?" Donovan pushed through the double doors and rushed down the emergency exam room hall.

"Stop, you don't have authorization," the nurse yelled. Security took off after Donovan. Jaered lent a hand and held the door open, then slipped in behind them.

"Bryant!" Donovan called out. "Carlene, where are you?"

A raven-haired nurse stepped out of a stall halfway down, and headed in the opposite direction. She cradled a boy. Bryant's striped sleeve and forearm drooped over her shoulder. A bright green cast covered it.

Security grabbed Donovan. "Wait!" He yelled. But the nurse exited through a far door without turning around. "That's my son. Where is she taking him?"

"Look, calm down, buddy. Let's find your wife. I'm sure she knows," one of the guards said.

Donovan stopped struggling. When they let go, he pulled the curtain to the side. The stall was empty. "What the hell? Where's my wife?"

Jaered stopped a passing nurse. "Where does that lead?" He pointed at the far door where the nurse took the child.

"The auditorium," she replied. "There's a magic show if you're interested."

{31}

Ian revealed the coin to the boy, then held it high for all to see. Applause from the audience drowned out the child's squeal.

A pale girl, no more than six, leaned heavily on a metal walker beside the boy. Ian's heart leapt out to the frail child, and he crouched down. He looked past the emaciated cheeks and dark tones around her eyes and was touched by her aura. It revealed incredible, inner strength. "What is your favorite color?"

"Blue," she said, but then giggled. "No, yellow."

He tapped her nose affectionately, then reached into his closed fist. "Since you can't decide, how about both?" Ian pulled out a baby-blue scarf with yellow polka dots.

Gasps and applause filled the small auditorium.

Rayne tied the girl's dark hair back with the scarf. She helped the child to her front-row seat, but first caught Ian's attention with a tilt of her head.

He hardly recognized Tara with her snowy hair tucked up inside the ebony wig. The loose nurse's uniform hid her petite frame. She walked down the aisle heading toward the stage with the boy in her arms. Donovan appeared a couple of minutes later, trailing a couple of security guards. He paused at the sight of the nearly full crowd then followed the nurse, but the security guard held out his arm to block him. Donovan crossed his arms and stood at the rear of the auditorium.

"Our time is almost up," Ian announced. He cued Rayne and she lowered the stage lights.

"Wait, what about my phone?" One of the teen volunteers stood in the second row. "You made it disappear, remember? I'd like it back."

"Ah, yes, you broke the rules and brought it in with you."

She looked coy. "I just wanted a picture of you for my Instagram."

Ian held his chin in mock contemplation. "Where did it go?"

A musical ring tone played from the person sitting directly in front of her. The startled man held up an empty water bottle. The phone rested inside.

She grabbed the bottle. "Oh my god, how did you—"

Thunderous applause erupted from the crowd. "I'm sure maintenance can help you extract it." Ian stepped to the edge of the stage.

Tara handed off the boy and disappeared behind the curtain at the back of the stage.

"I have a helper for my next trick," he said. "Let's give him a round of applause." Ian held the microphone to him. "How did you hurt your arm?"

He shied away at first and looked out at the crowd, then leaned in and touched his lips to the microphone. "I fall down." In spite of the microphone, his voice was barely above a whisper.

Ian lifted his casted arm and turned it back and forth as though examining it. "Does it hurt?"

The boy didn't respond.

He set the boy down on the stage and knocked on the cast. "You may not need it. I'll take it off."

"No!" screamed a few of the children in the audience, and they shook their heads at the thought.

"Perhaps you're right. I should get a second opinion. Dr. Bailey," Ian gestured to the pediatrician, "would you be so kind as to come and examine the cast for me?"

She approached and ran her finger across the hard surface. "Is it really broken?" she asked under her breath.

"No," Ian hushed.

"It can be removed," Dr. Bailey proclaimed.

Ian grasped the cast in both hands. "What do we say?"

"Abracadabra!" screamed the crowd.

"Abracadabra!" Ian shouted. A blinding burst of light. He stepped back holding the solid cast up high for all to see. The boy's arm was bare.

Squeals and laughter filled the room.

"Dr. Bailey," Ian held the cast toward her. "Would you make sure I removed it correctly?"

The woman shook her head in disbelief as she confirmed the cast was still intact. "I could use you in my clinic," she said and handed it back to him.

Ian tossed the cast to Rayne and grabbed the boy's hand. Ian bent over in an elaborate bow at the drawn-out applause. When the child didn't join in, Ian bent him over and over in a comical gesture. Boisterous laughter rose from the seats. The curtain opened behind them and Tara wheeled a gurney to the center of the stage. A large rectangular box rested on top of it.

"For my final trick of the afternoon, I will require my young helper one last time." Ian grabbed the boy's hand. "Let's make sure it's sturdy," he said and knocked on the side panel. The boy slapped it with his hand. They continued all around the box, their knocks and slaps falling into rhythm.

He opened the lid. "Are you ready?" Ian asked. The child didn't respond but raised his hands to be picked up. Ian helped him climb inside. "Say good-bye," Ian waved at the audience.

"Good-bye," the crowd responded with a sea of waving hands.

The boy bent down and Ian closed the lid, latching its lever. He turned the gurney around in a circle, then stopped.

"Audience, help me out here," he said.

"Abracadabra!" the children screamed.

Ian waved his hands toward the box. "Abracadabra!"

In a bright, green flash, the box collapsed. Its panels and the gurney folded in upon itself at his feet.

The crowd went wild.

Ian bowed. "You've been a great audience! Be safe and get well soon." Ian smiled and stepped down into the pooling crowd.

Donovan headed for the stage. "Where is he?" he hollered. The security guards were on his heels, but Ian raised his hand and they held back.

"Do I know you?" Ian said. Rayne paused at collecting prop pieces on stage.

"I'm Richard Donovan. We met at the charity event the other night," he said. "JoAnna Langtree introduced us. What have you done with my son?"

"How should I know?" Ian said. "I've never met him."

Donovan got in Ian's face. "Don't play games with me. You just made him disappear!"

"Who's missing?" Rayne asked.

"My son, Bryant," he snarled. "And Carlene."

"I'm here doing my monthly show," Ian said. A door banged open at the rear of the auditorium. Ian paused at Margaret, the hospital liaison, stomping toward them. By the look on her face, she had no qualms about getting in the middle.

"What is the meaning of this?" She approached the stage and gestured for the security guards to close ranks.

"My son and his mother are missing," Donovan said. "And he made them disappear."

"I'm afraid you don't know what you saw." Ian backed up toward the rear curtain. "No one's disappeared." He pulled the fabric aside to reveal Tara, still wearing the nurse's uniform and wig. She bounced a young boy, similar to Bryant's size and hair color, on her lap. He wore the same jeans and striped T-shirt as Bryant. Tara's and the boy's smile wilted at their grumpy audience.

The fury in Donovan's eyes remained. He regarded Ian with seething interest.

Ian grew cautious at perhaps underestimating Donovan.

"If you follow me, we'll start back at the beginning," Margaret said. "Let's see exactly where they were admitted and who might have examined the child."

"Can I return him to his mother? She's waiting over there." Tara indicated an anxious-looking woman sitting in the front row.

"Yes, of course," Margaret said.

Ian turned away. "Rayne, the rest of these go in the crate." He indicated the last two panels. She picked them up from the stage and carried them to a large wooden box. She froze when Donovan stepped closer to Ian.

"I don't believe in coincidences," Donovan said for Ian's ears only. "You'll regret getting involved." He stared at Rayne. "Everyone has something to lose."

{32}

Jaered gripped Ning's neck from behind and leaned in. "Are you insane?" he hissed in the assassin's ear. He'd found Ning seated in the farthest row from the stage, watching from the shadows. "Get the fuck out of here."

"I'm here on business." Ning tilted his face to the side. "What are you doing here, son of Aeros?"

Jaered watched the stage below and focused on cooling the center of his chest. Rayne held the side door open. Once Ian pushed the dolly through, she followed. The door slammed with a *clang*.

Jaered had gone ballistic after receiving Eve's late-night text. The book had been taken from the Heir's estate and the rebels hadn't reached the mansion in time to save the scholars. With the book out of the equation, Jaered wondered when Ning would show up to claim the only bargaining chip he had left. This bold move, even for Ning, was Jaered's answer. The assassin would snag the slightest opening.

"One phone call and my father's wrath will swoop down on you," Jaered said.

"But you won't make that call. You don't dare." Ning twisted in his seat and gave Jaered a shark tooth grin. "If you do, it might bring attention to her. You don't want your father finding out about her. Why is that Jaered? Saving her for yourself? Or is there another reason you're keeping her and her ability a secret?"

Stunned, a retort didn't make it to Jaered's lips.

Ning closed his eyes and breathed deep. "I can already hear the sizzle of her skin as it bubbles and blisters." He pulled out his cell and swiped at the screen. "The friend has a naughty side to her. A shame, really, that she's a human, and disposable." Ning tilted the screen for Jaered.

It was a picture of Rayne's roommate, Zoe—her hair black as coal, with the college campus in the background.

Donovan followed the woman from the hospital up the aisle, headed for the doors at the back of the auditorium. The CEO gave them a sideways glance, but kept walking. Jaered stiffened. Donovan didn't look at him. He looked at Ning.

"The powerless Duach still believes he's in control. Said my head isn't in it. The bottom-feeder Weir doesn't wield one of Earth's greatest powers. How can someone so common, so meager, appreciate the game . . . ," Ning lifted his face and breathed deep, ". . . the hunt. The ultimate power that comes from knowing you can take a life any time it suits you." Ning stood and watched Donovan exit behind the hospital liaison. "I understand he's pitted us against each other. Whatever he's promised you, don't get your hopes up." Ning left a few steps behind Donovan.

Jaered shadowed the assassin. Ning hung back near the emergency room entrance smoking a cigarette. When Donovan walked out several minutes later, Ning followed him across the street, but they didn't enter the parking garage. They stood off to one side, talking. Jaered couldn't get close enough to hear without being detected.

He cautioned himself on the way to his car not to overreact and give Donovan reason to question him. For now Rayne was safe as long as she stuck with the Heir. If Jaered was going to get the serum sample for Eve, he had to get to the wife before Ning.

He sat behind the steering wheel, gazing at the hospital and calculating what could have happened to Carlene Donovan and her son. There was little doubt that the Heir was behind their disappearance. "Fuck!" He slammed his fist into the car door. What made them get involved?

{33}

Patrick rapped twice, paused, then once. The door opened. Carlene shielded her eyes at the glare.

"Your chariot awaits." Patrick said.

She unlatched the metal cart doors and swung them open. Bryant grinned from ear to ear. "I do good hiding Mommy?" he asked with the sucker stick twitching between his lips.

Carlene gathered him into her arms and gave him a cocoon of a hug. "The best ever."

"I like hide and squeak. Let's play again, Mommy."

"Hide and squeak?" Patrick asked.

"The metal cart had a squeaky wheel," Carlene said. "Maybe another time, okay, Bry? We have somewhere we need to go."

"I transferred the car seat." Patrick opened the back door of the SUV. Carlene took a step out, but froze at the security camera overhead. "No worries," Patrick said. "This whole wing is shut down—electricity, everything, because of the construction."

Carlene strapped Bryant in and climbed in the back with him. She grabbed the change of clothes on the seat.

Patrick got in and closed the door.

"I hungry, Mommy."

"It's been a while since he ate. Can we stop somewhere or is that not okay?" Carlene asked.

"Let's get closer to our destination and then we'll see what we find," Patrick said, and buckled his seat belt. He drove through the maze of the hospital complex while she shed the nurse's smock and changed. She exchanged Bryant's sticky striped shirt for a fresh one from her purse. When Patrick pulled out onto the main street, a sigh from the depths of her soul escaped.

"You okay?" Patrick asked. When she didn't respond, he let it go, but kept stealing glances at them in the rearview mirror.

She brushed Bryant's cheek with the back of her hand. "There was something about Richard that was different from anyone else I'd ever met," Carlene said softly. "Confidence, charisma. He opened up my world, helped me see the wonders of nature. He had such a love of plants and knew amazing things about them."

Welcome to the Weir, Patrick kept to himself. He grew pensive. There was something about their race that attracted you to them. It wasn't only their dedication to the survival of the planet, it was how connected they were to the wonders of all things natural. It was through Ian that Patrick knew the Pur, the peaceful, dedicated side of the Weir race.

"For so long, I believed in Richard and his vision for the company," Carlene continued. "I thought he would save lives, not find more efficient ways to kill them."

Patrick gripped the steering wheel. If only he could tell her that the darker side of the Weir, the Duach, had chosen to break Weir tradition centuries ago. Richard's choice to use whatever connection he'd inherited for self gain had been hard-wired into him, long before he'd met his wife.

"I want Daddy," Bryant mumbled while playing with a toy dinosaur.

Carlene's chest heaved. Her eyes glistened with moisture. She leaned in and kissed his head. "We're not going to see Daddy for a while, remember?" She scooted to the edge of her seat and leaned closer to Patrick. "Everything is happening so fast. I haven't known what to say. How can I make him understand?" Carlene gazed at Bryant in silence for a few minutes. "Where are we going?"

"I'm taking you back to the hotel." He found her shocked expression in the mirror. "It's part of Ian's greater plan. You'll see."

"What greater plan?" she asked.

"Ian doesn't want you running for the rest of your life, looking over your shoulder. The first stage was to get you and Bryant safe and out of Richard's reach. Part two is about to commence."

{34}

Tara's hospital exit was timed perfectly. She'd switched out the black wig for one that matched Carlene's color and style, put on sunglasses, and left the hospital still wearing the nurse's smock. Donovan's Mercedes sat idling at the entrance to the parking garage while he waited for traffic to open up. Tara walked to the rental car parked a few feet from the emergency room doors, in plain view, and slipped inside. She pulled out of the lot. The Mercedes's blinker switched from left, to right. Donovan settled two cars behind her.

Once Tara hit the highway, her adrenaline rush took over and she relished in the acceleration. If she didn't have to keep the latest silly wig on, she would have preferred to open the convertible and allow the surge of air to rob her of her breath. Fast enough and it would be almost as good as skydiving—almost.

Donovan was hardly a match. The man wouldn't get off his cell phone.

Mara had been the better driver, but Tara, too, had been well trained by Marcus's Pur guards. This leg of Ian's elaborate plan reminded her of the old gangster movies she and

Patrick occasionally watched late at night. For the first time, she pondered if that's where Ian got the idea.

"Come on, make some kind of effort," she pouted, but swallowed the rest when a sedan pulled alongside Donovan's car. He gestured, and the second car pulled ahead picking up speed. The sedan maneuvered its way closer . . . closer. She slammed on the accelerator and swerved between two SUVs, but when another car switched lanes, the sedan pulled alongside Tara. A large gorilla of a man was behind the wheel. He glanced in her car, then said something to the hooded man in the backseat. The gorilla brought a cell up to his ear and let up on the gas. The sedan dropped back. Donovan's car took the next off-ramp and disappeared.

Tara held her breath. Had they gotten a good enough look at her to know she wasn't Carlene? When the sedan settled three car lengths behind, Tara held out hope that her disguise had held up.

She contemplated calling Ian about the new glitch, that someone other than Donovan was following her. This part of Ian's plan needed an eyewitness. Did it matter if it was Donovan, or a couple of his men? She decided to play it out.

A few minutes later, Tara exited the highway and pulled into the seldom-used wharf area. The towering storage units cast foreboding shadows across everything they touched. Her final scene couldn't have a better movie set.

Adrenaline licked her spine. The best part was coming up.

Tara verified that the second sedan pulled into the wharf. Forced to keep her speed at a minimum, she steered the car between tight rows of rusting shipping crates.

A core blast slammed into a crate beside her.

"What the hell?" She found an opening between stacks and stomped on the accelerator, headed for the water's edge. She pushed the rental from fifteen to sixty in a heartbeat. A crimson core blast struck the trunk.

Chills coursed in her veins. Her furtive glances in the rearview mirror were more hindering than helpful. Keep your eyes on the road, she chastised herself, and gripped the wheel with both hands.

Her target loomed ahead—a straight shot—fifty feet to go.

A hooded figure ran to the edge of the pier. He pushed back his hoodie. Flaming tattoos covered his bald head. His smile spread. Tara could never forget those teeth. Ning! Mara's murderer. A swirling core blast appeared in his open palm. Tara twisted the steering wheel. The car swerved—too sharp—too fast.

To her horror, the car rolled—how many times became a blur before it came to rest on its side against a warehouse wall. Tara coughed and opened her eyes. Thoughts swirled and she fought to keep her wits. Ning's laugh, straight from her nightmares, off in the distance. She groped to release her seat belt.

Warmth. Tara reached for the button. Flames raced alongside the carriage outside the window. Soothing warmth gave way to sweltering heat. The explosion consumed everything.

Jaered's cell tickled his thigh. He paused at the caller. Why was Yannis calling him? He was supposed to be overseeing the serum production at the lab. "What?" Jaered said.

"I just heard from Donovan's man, Kurt. Your deal is off with Donovan. The wife is dead."

"What are you talking about?" Jaered pulled into a nearby parking lot and sat idling in the truck. "When?"

"I just hung up with him," Yannis said.

The buzz in Jaered's head grew louder, drowning out the throb at his temples. He'd failed to get what Eve had commissioned out of the CEO. Jaered dropped his head and ran his fingers through his hair. "Do you know where Donovan is?" he hissed through gritted teeth.

"The police station. You've got to admit, the guy has balls. Donovan's filing a missing person's report." Yannis said.

Jaered's core sizzled in the center of his chest. "Find out which precinct."

Donovan headed for his Mercedes. The second he settled in the driver's seat and closed the car door, Jaered appeared behind him and grabbed his shoulders.

They reappeared in the vacant office building. Jaered let go. Donovan jerked, then collapsed on the floor with a shriek. A few chipped desks, broken chairs and bits of trash were scattered about. Yannis had found the dilapidated building and had given Jaered the coordinates.

No one would hear Donovan's screams.

It took the CEO a few seconds to recover from the effects of the shyft. He rose on shaky legs. "What do you want?"

"What you promised me," Jaered snarled. "You squeezed me out of the equation."

"You were dragging your feet. I liked Ning's terms better," Donovan said. He brushed himself off. "Once she tells me where my son is, he'll finish her off and I won't have to hand over my serum to you ahead of time."

Jaered paused. "You didn't sic him on her?"

"I put him on her tail. That's all."

Yannis pushed away from the wall. "Your man Kurt called. Ning killed her."

"What are you talking about?" Donovan said.

"That's what happens when you make a deal with the devil," Jaered snarled.

"You lie. You're trying to trick me."

Yannis swiped at his cell phone screen. He turned it around. A video played. Firemen working on a blazing car.

Donovan's smug expression transformed to rage. "Where's my son?"

"I don't know, and I don't care," Jaered said. He drew power into his core and swiped his hand, lifting Donovan off his feet and toppling over the chair. Jaered was on him before he could rise. "You have no one to blame but yourself," Jaered hissed and grabbed Donovan by his collar. "You're going to give me that formula, including the key ingredient. Now!"

"Not until we find my son!"

"That wasn't the deal. Your wife is dead, whether by another's bloody deed or mine no longer matters. Hand it over, or you will join her." Jaered got off him and walked away.

Donovan made the mistake of sucker-punching him.

Jaered spun around and grabbed the man by the throat. He pressed him against the wall and lifted him off his feet.

"You still need me," Donovan rasped. "The serum is being manufactured in two different locations."

"Yannis," Jaered hissed between gritted teeth. "What is he talking about?"

"I only know about the ones at his lab," Yannis said. "Those have been on schedule ever since I arrived last week.

"The key ingredient. It's being produced at another site. Combine the two and you have your deadly Pur cocktail."

Jaered thought back to Donovan's phone call outside the children's boutique. He wasn't trying to keep up with the shipment at his facility. He must have been worried about the second one, off-site.

Donovan struggled. His face turned a sickening shade of purple. Yannis grasped Jaered's arm. "Kill him before we know for sure, and your father will come after us both."

Jaered gathered his wits. He let go. Donovan slumped to the floor and grabbed his throat, coughing while sputtering bits of stomach contents across the carpet.

Jaered bent down next to him. "Don't ever make the mistake of touching me again. You mess with me"—he leaned in—"you mess with Aeros." He rose to his feet. Yannis stared at Jaered without a lick of emotion. No doubt, the man had seen his father do much worse. "I want the key to the serum. Where is it?"

"The second I give up the other location." Donovan rolled onto his back. "I'm a dead man."

"All I want is a single, viable dose of the serum, to test it on a powerful Sar. To reassure my father. That is, if you want to get paid." Jaered avoided looking at Yannis. Jaered cautioned himself to limit what he said in the man's presence. "Where do we go to get a usable sample?" Jaered hissed.

"My office safe," Donovan said and glared at Jaered with seething hatred.

"Get cleaned up. I expect to get past the front gate with nothing more than a nod and a smile." Jaered left them and went into an adjoining office. He leaned against the wall and breathed deep. The heat in his core took its time to soothe. He hadn't lost his temper like that in forever. He unzipped his jacket in a feeble attempt to cool his core, along with his mind.

Try as he might, Jaered couldn't shake what had been weighing him down for the past several months. The longer he fought what his father was, the more he became his father.

{36}

Ian paused at the edge of the stage and stared at Patrick's text as if he'd read it wrong.

Tara hasn't checked in.

Rayne closed the storage room door and locked it. "That's the last of the equipment," she said. When he didn't respond, she walked over and peered out between the thick, heavy curtains at center stage. "Your auditorium is creepy when it's empty and the lights are off."

"Ian!" Marcus bellowed. He approached from backstage. "God damn you. What were you thinking, sneaking away from the estate? You've been gone for hours. You're in enough trouble as it is!"

"He had a performance at the Children's Hospital today. He couldn't disappoint them," Rayne said with the perfect amount of innocence.

"He didn't get permission to leave," Marcus said.

"Would you have granted it?" she shot back. "He's practically a prisoner in his own home."

"He needs to at least appear as if he is honoring the Primary's orders."

What's happened to Tara, Ian wondered, as his racing thoughts took him away from their conversation. Had he expected too much of her? Did he misjudge her skills?

"Ian, get your face out of that cell phone and convince me that covering for you is worth the Primary's wrath."

"Ian?" Rayne asked. "What's wrong?"

"It's Tara. Something's happened. I need to find her."

Marcus grew rigid. The former general kicked into combat mode. "Not without me," he said.

Saxon! The wolf leapt up onto the stage. He brushed up against Ian. *I need your help, it's Tara,* he channeled.

"What do you want me to do?" Rayne asked.

"Keep trying to reach Tara." He tossed Rayne the car keys.

"Zoe still isn't returning my messages," Rayne said. "Maybe I should run by the house, too."

"No, it's not safe. I'll meet you at the hotel. Keep out of sight, don't go up to the room."

"Why not?"

"I'll explain later." Ian stepped into the vortex stream at center stage and gripped Saxon's fur. Marcus grabbed Ian's shoulder. He shyfted.

They appeared at the edge of the wharf. Saxon snapped at a nearby startled seagull. It swooped into the air, protesting the intrusion.

"What was Tara doing here?" Marcus said.

Ian ran over to the edge and peered into the lapping waves. A few struck the pillars below. *Find her,* he channeled. Saxon disappeared between the stacked storage units.

The volcanic odor brought a tidal wave of nausea. Ian fought to stop the churning bile.

"Sulfur," Marcus said. "A Duach Sar was after her?"

"I have reason to believe that Ning might still be alive." Ian ran along the edge of the pier. No tire marks, no heated surface, nothing. She hadn't gone into the water as planned. He turned around. Burning rubber and gasoline hit like a gale force wind. He took off for the back lot.

He rounded the corner of stacked storage units but Marcus pulled him back, out of sight. Two massive fire trucks were on the scene. Uniformed men gathered a high pressure hose. The surroundings were drenched. A charred car lay on its side, propped against a warehouse with its burnt undercarriage exposed. One of the tires was spinning, kept in motion by the dousing stream from a second hose. Spurts of flame spit and rose. A small crowd of dock workers stood with their backs to Ian and Marcus. One of the men was arguing with a coworker.

"I swear, a ball of fire was in his hand and he flung it right at the car."

His friend shook his head and waved him off. "What did you smoke at lunch?"

"I know what I saw." The man stuck his hands in his pockets and turned back toward the wreck.

A couple of news crews were gathered around a uniformed fire chief. They lobbed questions.

Ball of fire. A Duach core blast. Ian leaned against the storage unit and gazed up at Marcus. A fine mist blew in and swirled around them. It floated toward the crowd like an advancing fog.

"She's not dead!" the old general roared and gripped Ian's shoulders. "You don't know that she was in there when it crashed." Marcus stuck his head out from behind the storage unit. His shoulders slumped, and he leaned against the edge. "We aren't losing her, too. Do you hear me?" It came out hushed, desperate.

A blur of white. Saxon used the units as cover to slip around the crowd and the fire trucks unnoticed. He headed for the warehouse on the opposite side of the crash.

Ian closed his eyes. Marcus was right. She might have bailed, she might be near. *Tara,* his thoughts groped for her. *Where are you?*

Silence. He opened his eyes to find Marcus staring at him.

"Keep trying." He stole a peek at the crowd. "It's Saxon, he's become Mara's missing link, hasn't he?" Marcus laid a gentle hand on Ian's shoulder. "Dr. Orr used the twins DNA in his wolf experiments. All this time . . . I had hoped."

Saxon? Ian channeled. *Here,* entered his thoughts. A milky image appeared. Ian grabbed Marcus and shyfted to Saxon's broadcast location. They appeared at an entrance to a warehouse. Splotches of red peeked through slits in the warehouse walls. The fire trucks were just outside.

Saxon's tail was in hyperdrive. He alternated between licking Tara's face and nuzzling her neck. She sat propped against a huge tire. Her face was smeared with soot. She favored her left arm in her lap.

Ian embraced her. It took a few seconds to find his voice. "You fool. You weren't supposed to end up on dry land." Marcus tossed Ian a dark, questioning glare from beneath scrunched eyebrows.

"It was Ning. Ian, how did he know it was me? I was disguised as Carlene."

"What's she talking about?" Marcus said. "Who's Carlene?"

"Someone we're trying to rescue from a Duach," Ian said. He wiped the smudge on her cheek and fought to keep his emotions suppressed. The last thing they needed was a severe shift in the weather outside. Too many witnesses. Cameras.

"I thought Ning was dead," Marcus said.

"Saxon said that whoever attacked him the other night at the mansion was the Duach from QualSton. I didn't want to believe that it was Ning. I had no proof," Ian said.

"He was laughing, taking his time," Tara said. "Setting parts of the car on fire, bit by bit. The smoke. I was lucky I had the oxygen tank and mask. But Ning's fun bought me time to find that." She indicated an opening at the base of the far wall. A screened grate lay on the concrete next to it. "The fuel tank must have caught. I don't know what happened to him after that."

Tara winced when Ian helped her to her feet. She pressed her wrist against her chest. They faced Marcus with Ian's arm around her shoulders.

The fire hose spray ceased on the other side of the warehouse wall. A shout. "There's no one in here. The car is empty."

"Time to go," Marcus said. "But I expect answers to questions I don't even know to ask yet."

Ian nodded and steeled himself for what was to come. Tara was supposed to end up in the harbor. A missing body shouldn't have been discovered for another couple of hours. Speculation that it had washed away, was to buy him several more.

Donovan would soon discover his wife was every bit alive.

Marcus gripped Ian's shoulder. The time for cover-ups and lies was long past. Ian shyfted them without a stitch of remorse, prepared to share everything. The old general wouldn't stay mad for long.

{37}

Ian approached the last elevator. A sign posted on the wall next to it read, Penthouse Suite. JoAnna had insisted that Ian spare no expense. The bottomless funds had allowed him to create the most elaborate illusion of his career. His ego had fed upon it.

He'd nearly gotten Tara killed. When he had called Patrick with the update, his friend had summed it up. Ian's plan had crashed and burned.

Ian hesitated with his finger hovering over the button. He'd forgotten a lesson he'd learned long ago. Any semblance of control, was the greatest illusion of all. He pressed the button. The elevator doors opened. He gestured for Tara to step inside. When Rayne made to follow, he put his arm up to block her. "We're not going up," he said. "We have to rendezvous with Drion Marcus in a few minutes." He eyed the splint on Tara's wrist and clenched his jaw. "Get some sleep," he said. "Then check on the rest."

Tara nodded. The elevator doors *swished* shut.

"Check on what?" Rayne asked.

Ian didn't answer. He led her through the hotel lobby. "With Ning in the middle of this, I'm in way over my head. I won't risk anyone else. No Duach is worth it."

Rayne made to grab his hand, but caught herself and pulled back. "Tara survived. This time Ning walked away empty-handed."

"That Duach assassin murdered Mara and Galen. I can't bear to lose anyone else to him," he said. Sympathy poured from her eyes and leaked into his heart. Ian's core ignited, and he pressed a fist to his chest. Emotional baggage swirled and twisted inside him like a smoldering volcanic cauldron.

Hanging crystal beads in the massive overhead chandelier clinked together. The floor beneath Ian's feet vibrated. He looked at the large digital numbers over the penthouse and other elevators. They blinked on and off, their numbers raising or lowering in typical fashion, the quake too subtle to lock the elevators down. The low, muted tremor stilled as suddenly as it had begun. A few voices edged with concern rang about the busy lobby. Others never flinched at the planet's shifting plates, common in the San Francisco area. Had Ian triggered it with his emotional upheaval, or was it part of what plagued the earth's crust these past few weeks?

"The first time we encountered him," Rayne whispered, "we didn't know what we were up against. You're stronger. As a team, we can fight him."

Thoughts of the scholars sapped his conviction. There had been too much blood shed, too much loss already. Ian led her outside, focused on suppressing what ailed him. The atmospheric pressure brought on by his emotions settled by the time they reached the car. A fine mist, laden with moisture and cool against his skin, filled the air.

"I thought I could bring Donovan down once I got Carlene and Bryant to safety," he said. "But Ning's involvement changes everything."

"You told Marcus what we're doing?" Rayne asked.

"I confessed that I'd uncovered a Duach facility here in town." Ian pulled the car away from the curb and fell into the ebb and flow of traffic.

"Did he blow a gasket?" Rayne asked.

"He just smiled." Ian pressed on the accelerator. The car picked up speed. "He smells an opportunity as much as I do."

{38}

Jaered finished his call to Eve and leaned back. He closed his eyes and focused on the steady pulse of his core to ease the lingering tension of the day. By nightfall, this clusterfuck would be over. Donovan would need to be taken care of once Jaered got his hands on a viable serum for Eve. Sabotaging the shipment without Yannis discovering it was the greater challenge. If Aeros's spy turned up missing, there'd be hell to pay.

Jaered walked into the outer room. Yannis was sprawled facedown on the floor, moaning. He reached for the back of his head.

The room was otherwise empty. Jaered threw open the door and ran down the hall, banging on doors, opening others. Donovan was gone. Jaered returned and pulled Yannis to his feet.

It took some time for the man to stop teetering. Jaered had been in the other office for a while. "What happened?" Jaered focused on suppressing the plume of heat rising from his core.

"Donovan got a call and started screaming at Kurt about killing his wife. Then he quieted and looked out the window, listening. He mumbled something and hung up. He just stared out the window, unmoving for minutes on end. I thought he'd wacked out on me. Then, some flaming tattooed Sar shyfted right behind him. The guy knocked me out before I could react." Yannis shook his head. "I didn't know Donovan had a Sar on the payroll!"

The man looked frightened out of his wits. Aeros would strike the man down for his incompetence, but Jaered couldn't blame Yannis. Jaered's head had been on getting the serum. The fault was his. "Ahhh!" Jaered punched a hole in the wall. Donovan was using his new ally to the fullest.

Yannis flinched. "What, now?"

"Donovan has proven too cunning. I no longer trust the shipment as it stands. I need to get a viable serum sample," Jaered said.

"Agreed," Yannis said. "Stepping in as Donovan's new executive assistant last week forced him to upgrade my status. I can get us onto the executive floor," he said. "I've discovered where the safe is, but it isn't going to be easy getting inside. I'm not a Sar. Will your power get us past a retinal scan?"

"No," Jaered said. "I can draw tremendous amounts of energy, but it would short out a safe's electrical system."

"Is that how you can shyft without a vortex?" Yannis asked. Jaered threw him a glare full of warning. "This building is more than half a mile from the police station where you grabbed Donovan. I was only wondering."

Like most Weir, born powerless, Yannis's curiosity about those who wielded power was commonplace. Jaered wasn't about to reveal all that his unique power offered. When he didn't answer, Yannis knew better not to pry.

Jaered knew a Sar with the necessary power to get them into Donovan's safe, but every fiber of his being told him not to go there. The Sar was Pur, not Duach. Yannis was more attuned than Jaered had given him credit for. This next step could place him in the middle of a minefield.

"There's someone we need to find, and fast," Jaered said.

o

{39}

Vael wasn't at his apartment when Jaered and Yannis arrived. Thanks to enough money changing hands with the slimy landlord, they found the Pur Sar at the local dive.

Rock Solid was a dive in the truest sense of the word. The stench alone could have flattened a stampede. Yannis hung back as Jaered combed through the main floor, weaving in and out of drunken revelers and scantily clad women. Jaered ended up in the balcony where he found Vael surrounded by a trio of women. They were engaged in activity that lent a whole new meaning to the term groping.

Jaered's friend hadn't changed much in the year or so since Jaered had taken off without a word. Vael's southern charm and youthful looks had made him the perfect con man. The two of them achieved a lot in the short time they'd hung together. He didn't approach Vael at first, and took another moment to run through his options outside of using his friend to break into Donovan's safe. A growl rumbled in his throat when nothing else presented itself. No matter how much Jaered wanted, there was no avoiding placing his friend in danger. *For the greater good,* his thoughts echoed.

Jaered approached with the attitude that Vael's declining the upcoming request was not an option. He planted himself directly in front of Vael and his entourage, picked up the full glass of beer on the table and flung it on Vael. From the shrieks and scrambling bodies, the collateral damage extended to the ladies.

That got Vael's attention, but his blasphemous choice of words were lost on the rest of the bar crowd. The girls vacated the couch with halfhearted protests and a few colorful words of their own. Vael jumped up and got in Jaered's face as if challenged to a fight.

"What the hell was that for?" Vael hollered, wielding fists.

Jaered didn't respond. Their staring contest lasted a full five seconds before Vael broke into laughter. He grabbed Jaered around the back of his neck and cupped his chin in the other hand. "God, you're a sight for sore eyes. Where the hell did you come from?"

"I need your unique talents," Jaered said without a hint of pretense.

Vael pulled back and studied him for a second as his smile relaxed. He sat down in the pooling beer on the vinyl couch, threw his foot up on the edge of the coffee table, and wiped his dripping face with his hand. His jolly persona faded.

Jaered tossed him a couple of the cocktail napkins from under the girls' drinks.

"I don't see you for what, a year or more, and you come calling with business." Vael stared at Jaered when he offered up nothing in response. He drained the nearly empty beer in a quick swig. "You owe me a drink."

"You owe me a favor, and according to my score sheet, it's a big one," Jaered said.

"You must be pretty desperate, showing up like this to collect." Vael wiped his neck then wadded up the napkins and dropped them on the table. Yannis sat nearby not paying heed, but he caught Vael's attention just the same.

"Since when do you need a bodyguard?"

"An associate with a shared agenda," Jaered said. He scraped a chair over and sat down across from Vael. "I wouldn't be here unless I specifically needed you."

"You're making me blush."

"No joke," Yannis piped up from across the way.

Jaered clenched his jaw in regret at not coaching Yannis to keep his mouth shut before they arrived. This would be tricky enough without appearing like they were groveling. "Your particular skills for what will amount to a half hour, no more than an hour, of your time."

"What's the payout?"

"In this case, nothing of value."

"You've got some nerve."

"We'll be even," Jaered said. "Straight across."

Vael stared at him as if he wasn't all there. "What's your deal? You disappeared from the face of the earth over twelve months ago." He scoffed. "I thought you were dead."

"That last job went from bad to fucked up. You wouldn't have made it out of the bank alive if I hadn't taken a bullet for you." Jaered clenched his jaw and refrained from pulling back his shirt to show Vael the scar. He was coming across as desperate enough already.

"The last time I saw you, you were falling to your death. I still can't wrap my head around how you managed to shyft," Vael said.

"I wasn't in the best of shape for a while. By the time I recovered, I figured you had moved on to other jobs and were better off."

Vael got to his feet and stretched. He leaned against the railing and peered down at the pathetic crowd, as if deep in thought.

Jaered hadn't wanted Vael to know he was alive and back. He and Eve had used Vael for his skills, and when the jobs were done, had taken advantage of Jaered's near-death experience to cut ties permanently. More than anything, Jaered didn't want to ask this of Vael, the lost sheep of the Pur, who took out his daddy issues in the most self-destructive ways. He'd latched onto Jaered as a surrogate family.

Jaered wouldn't be able to disappear on Vael as easily as last time—if they all got out of that building tonight in one piece.

"What the hell. I'm not missing anything I can't get any other night," Vael said. "It'll be worth finding out what happened to you after all this time."

"I'm not sure you'd believe me if I told you."

"There's no if in this buddy. You're not disappearing again until you spill. Even if I have to hog-tie you." He leaned against the railing. "When?"

"We'll stop by your place so you can clean up, but we need to leave immediately from there."

"That soon, what the hell?" Vael said. Jaered tossed some money down on the table. Vael grabbed his jacket off the back of the couch. "Good thing you showed up. I've been bored out of my mind. What am I breaking into?"

"A three-inch-thick steel wall safe with retina and print scan. Can you handle it?" Yannis said.

"Does the Pope piss holy water?" Vael laughed. He grabbed the scruff of Yannis's neck, jerking it around in jest. "Oh ye of little faith."

Jaered followed them down the stairs. He knew what Vael was capable of.

{40}

Marcus appeared every bit the general while standing near the truck and directing the handful of Pur guards.

"Did you bring it?" Marcus asked.

Ian tossed him the handheld jam. "I know it's supposed to prevent powers up to five hundred feet, but it's more like a hundred to ensure full shutdown. Farther away from there, the Sar's powers are likely to just become weak or glitchy. At best you'll have ten, fifteen minutes max before the jam begins to fade or shuts down altogether."

"How does it work?" Rayne asked.

"It's based on your father's acoustic jam technology," Marcus said. "What we installed on a larger scale at the estate, after the raid on QualSton."

"At least something of my father's work has been used for good," Rayne said.

"But the estate jam gets its power from the solar utilities on the property. This portable power source needs work," Ian said. "It's far from reliable." Ian watched Marcus's hand-picked team prepping their equipment. "How soon?"

"If we're going to coordinate our arrival with the facility's shift change at midnight, we're cutting it close," Marcus said.

A wide phosphorescent glow grew in the center of the vortex. "Looks like my two secret weapons have arrived."

A Pur guard appeared, flanked by two boys no older than fifteen or sixteen. The teens stepped out with satchels slung over their shoulders. They approached the general with attitudes of indifference. Ian was intrigued. These were Marcus's famous geeks.

"Hey, Pops, what's crackin'?" the freckled one said. In spite of dusk muting the colors of the day, Ian swore his flaming hair was a perfect match to the red licorice stick waving between his lips.

The other one's bleached hair bordered on pure white, heightened by his dark complexion. He blew a huge bubble. It popped, loud enough to be heard over the swishing blades of the nearby helicopter. He stared at Rayne like a dog in heat.

"Pur Heir, Ms. Bevan, I'd like to introduce Parker—" Licorice cleared his throat like an angry parent and gave the general a sideways glare. Marcus rolled his eyes. "*Pacman* and Xander."

Ian reached out but the formality of the introduction was lost on them. They flicked their hands in the air, clarifying which was which with a fleeting glance.

"Pacman," licorice said.

"Xander," gum said.

Marcus let loose a deep growl and peered at the boys with warning. "Take this mission seriously, you two. We're infiltrating a Duach research facility. I need you at the top of your game."

"Game we got," they said in unison. They held their hands out in front and moved their fingers as if handling a game controller.

"This isn't a video game!" Marcus roared. "Get focused, or I'm grounding you from this mission before you get us all killed."

The boys sobered with downcast eyes. "Sorry, General," Pacman said with a cursory salute.

"We're just excited for the challenge, *sir!*" Xander said. After professing his "undying devotion to mother earth" and "all that is Weir," Xander turned his attention to Rayne. He invaded her space and his one-sided staring contest kept her eyes averted.

"Stow your gear in the helicopter," Marcus ordered.

"Blades!" Pacman said and stuck out a fist at his friend.

"Sweet!" Xander said. They took part in some ritualistic hand game that ended in a knuckle punch. It was so fast; Ian could barely keep up. He secretly hoped they'd have a chance to teach him later.

Xander smiled at Rayne. He pocketed his gum in his cheek and lowered his voice at least an octave. "We've got official Weir business to attend to. Still my beating heart and promise me you'll be here when we get back."

By the look on Rayne's face, she was cooking up the mother-of-all remarks.

Ian stepped between them. "Sorry, we have our own official business elsewhere."

"Keep it in your pants and let's go you hormonal time bombs." Marcus gripped the boys by their shoulders and ushered them to the helicopter. They didn't stop waving goodbye until Rayne acknowledged them, in spite of a lieutenant's best efforts to shove them inside.

"Anyone who goes on a mission with those two is taking their life into their hands," Rayne said. "Does the Pur Weir army have the Purple Heart?"

"Marcus says they're undisciplined as hell, but put them in front of a computer and they're all business."

She leaned closer. "I'm shocked that Marcus isn't informing the Primary of this," Rayne shouted as the helicopter blades rotated faster and faster.

"Neither of us appreciates being kept out of the search for the book. Marcus is a soldier, not a politician. He'd rather go into battle any day than enforce an order he finds unreasonable."

"He still has to answer to the Primary," Rayne said. "You may have gotten him in this as deep as you."

"Then pray those two geniuses uncover something at Donovan's company, or we're all screwed."

Yannis's ID got them through the front gate and into the building without as much as a second glance from security. All the same, Jaered and Vael turned their faces from the cameras when Yannis signed them in at the front desk.

Vael turned around and leaned in toward Jaered. "Pharmaceutical company. I'm guessing corporate espionage. I like where this is headed," he said under his breath. "I've always wanted to play in the big leagues."

Jaered let Vael think what he wanted. The less his friend knew what he was walking into, the better.

The security guard looked up at the clock. "Will you be here long, sir?" the guard asked.

"We shouldn't be," Yannis said.

"It's just that we change shifts in thirty," the man said. "If you're not out by then, I'll let the night crew know."

With their backs to the security cameras, the three men waited for the elevator. Jaered checked his watch. "Are there security cameras on all the floors and in every wing?"

"Everywhere but the stairwells and elevators," Yannis said.

"Why not there?" Vael asked.

"I heard rumors that Donovan preferred banging his secretary in private."

They stepped inside and the doors swished shut. The elevator rose, headed for the eighteenth floor. They passed the third floor when Vael slammed his hand on the stop button. The elevator stopped with a jerk. "To hell with you not paying me. This swanky building? I want to know what's in the safe and what my cut's going to be."

"And I want us to walk out of here in one piece," Jaered snapped. "Don't play games, Vael, not tonight."

"I'm renegotiating terms. I have a right to know what I'm sticking my neck out for," Vael said, not removing his hand in spite of Jaered going for the button. "Who's this Donovan?"

"CEO of this place. It's his safe we're breaking into," Yannis said.

Jaered glared at Vael. "Once you open the safe, I'll answer all your questions."

Vael stared at Jaered for a few seconds longer, then punched the button and the elevator moved. "My bonus will be two cases of beer," he grumbled.

If we make it out alive, Jaered thought, I'll buy you the whole damn store. When the doors opened, Jaered drew a greater amount of electromagnetic energy into his core, enough to cause static in the video feed.

They stared at mahogany paneling and brass fixtures. Nothing spared for the corporate elite.

"This way." Yannis led them to the end of the hall. He inserted a card key and punched in a five-digit code.

The doors opened onto a private reception area with an office door beyond. Yannis led them into the large executive office with sweeping views of the city's lights.

"That's the cleanest desk I've ever seen," Vael quipped.

"I've been snooping around in his files and records, but he's no fool and is good at hiding things. Either that or he does most of his work at home or at another site." Yannis opened a door. "The safe is in here."

They entered a small adjoining conference room. The executive assistant removed a large portrait of a distinguished-looking man. "Donovan's Dad?" Jaered said, noticing a strong resemblance to the CEO.

"From what I've surmised, a Duach Sar," Yannis said.

Vael dropped a small statue that he'd been checking out. He threw a panicked look at Jaered.

Jaered grabbed Yannis and turned him back toward Donovan's office. "You can open Donovan's secure files, right?" Jaered asked.

Yannis nodded. "It's where I've been spending all my time since I got here. My mission was to find proof of rebel interests in the company."

"But you haven't found anything about the serum, or the rebels?" Jaered asked in hushed tones. Movement out of the corner of his eye. Across the room, Vael squirmed like he was about to pee in his pants.

"No," Yannis admitted. "I need more time."

"We're out of time." Jaered handed the man a thumb drive. "Go out to Donovan's desk and insert this. The virus will attach itself to the mainframe system and wipe anything that ties the facility to my father. It's going to take a few minutes."

Yannis didn't move. He looked skeptical. "Unless you're questioning my father's orders," Jaered said. Yannis left and sat at Donovan's desk.

When Yannis inserted the thumb drive, Jaered closed the door to the conference room, rested his forehead against the door and gave in to a sigh of relief. The second Yannis inserted the thumb drive, the virus swept in to wipe out everything. Eve's rebel involvement with Lux Pharmaceuticals would soon be nothing but whispers. Once he got his hands on the sample, Jaered would silence the pain-in-the-ass CEO for good.

"What the hell did you get me into?" Vael hissed. "A *Duach* facility? Are you insane?"

"Donovan isn't a Sar, neither is Yannis. We'll be fine as long as you keep your cool," Jaered said.

"What's really in the safe?" Vael asked. "What could possibly be worth risking our lives like this?"

"Nothing less than Earth's survival," Jaered said.

Stunned, Vael drew back. "What are you talking about?"

"Donovan created a serum that will wipe out all Weir Sars. He's working with Aeros to mass-produce it and inject everyone that stands in his way." Jaered pulled off his jacket and rolled it up, then placed it at the base of the door. The last thing they needed was for Vael's Pur power to give him away. It would escape under the door in an emerald glow. There'd be no hiding it from Yannis.

"How do you know this?" Vael said. "How did you get in the middle of it?"

"Suffice it to say, I work for someone who is trying to save this planet."

"But—"

"No more talk, Vael. Get inside that safe before we're both discovered." Jaered gripped Vael's shoulder when he looked like he might bail. "We both know you can do this. Just do it fast."

Vael's fist turned translucent. It took on an emerald glow that sparkled and lit up the dim room with dancing light. Jaered hovered over it, concerned that Yannis might still notice the green light around the edges of the office door. Vael pressed the swirling molecules against the steel door. The metal became a twisting gray soup.

"Watch the tumblers," Jaered urged.

"Like I've never done this before." Vael's gleaming fist disappeared inside the door.

Jaered listened. *Click-Click.* Vael hadn't lost his touch.

Vael tugged and the door swung wide. He slowly drew back his arm. A horrific scream.

Jaered grabbed the back of his head and pressed a hand over Vael's mouth. "Shuuush!" Confused at the pain etched into his friend's face, he looked at Vael's hand. The safe's metal had fused with his living tissue. Vael was trapped in the door.

Shocked, it took a few seconds for Jaered to realize that the center of his chest hadn't just cooled. Jaered's core was numb.

"Do something!" Vael cried out. His eyes fluttered. Jaered feared he would pass out at any minute. His friend's legs gave way under him. The safe door swung.

Jaered wedged himself between the door and the opening. He groped around inside. The safe was empty.

Marcus paused next to the door that read Mainframe and signaled for his guards to spread out and keep watch. He couldn't shyft the boys inside the computer room without knowing the lay of the room. He removed the zippered pouch from a pocket inside his vest.

"What's that?" Xander asked.

"He's got lock picks," Pacman said. He leaned in close. Marcus elbowed his shoulder to get out of the way.

"Where'd you learn to do that?" Xander asked, blowing a bubble and popping it.

"Before I joined the Weir guard, I served in the United States Army," Marcus said, listening as much as feeling the gears.

"Does the Pur army teach that?" Pacman said.

"Don't be lame," Xander said. "Powers, duh."

A muted metallic *scrape* and Marcus ushered the boys inside and closed the door.

Pacman and Xander chose positions across the room from each other and before long, clicking echoed in the room as their fingers flew over the keys.

"I'll breech the firewall before you," Pacman taunted.

"In your dreams," Xander countered.

"Quiet, both of you," Marcus warned. He stood still. Something had his sixth sense tingling and he studied every nook, every potential hiding space, unsure of what his sub-conscious had picked up on. A muted beep and an intermittently flashing red light on a wall console drew him closer. An amber bar was sliding down toward a reading of zero.

"Xander, here, quick," Marcus barked in a hushed sort of way.

The young prodigy rushed over and without missing a beat, pushed a button. A panel flipped open and a keyboard sprang out. He worked his fingers across it.

"How'd you know a keyboard was in there?" Marcus asked.

"I could build most of this in my garage," he said.

"Only better," Pacman said from across the room. "This stuff's like, old."

"How old?" Marcus asked.

"At least three years," Xander said. He pushed a button in the digital display column beside them. A touch screen appeared. He tapped and ran his finger across it. "They're deleting something," Xander said. He attacked the keys and pressed combinations of strokes. "It hasn't been running very long. It's only wiped out forty-eight percent."

"Forty-eight percent of what?" Marcus said.

"From what I can tell, everything. At this rate, there won't be anything to copy in ten minutes."

"Then stop it!" Marcus said. "Could this have been started remotely?"

"Unlikely," Pacman said. "This kind of virus needs direct access or the system's firewalls can inhibit it."

"Someone with clearance. Top-floor kind of clearance," Xander said.

Marcus pressed his earbud. "Lieutenant, any sign of company in the executive suites?"

"We've just finished sweeping the sixteenth floor. Heading back to you on seventeenth."

"Stay sharp. I think we have company. I'm turning on the jam. Hardware use only in extreme circumstances. Understood?"

"Roger that." The intercom went silent.

Marcus pulled the jam out of his pocket. He flipped the switch.

A cry reserved for the mortally wounded came from directly overhead.

Xander flinched and looked up at the ceiling. "What the fuck."

"Stay focused. Stop that delete!" Marcus shouted. "Get me what they didn't want found." He activated the intercom at his ear. "Lieutenant, get to the eighteenth floor, west wing near the stairwell. There's a Sar in one of the upper offices. I want him alive."

{42}

Yannis stood at the threshold to the conference room. He didn't utter a sound, but stared with wide eyes and a slack jaw.

"It's not here," Jaered shouted over Vael's cries. "Donovan got to the safe first."

"Or he lied. Kept us distracted so he could skip town," Yannis said. He didn't peel his attention from Vael's wrist. "What about your—"

"Whatever it is shut me down. I can't shyft us out of here." Jaered reached deeper into the safe. He touched what felt like a small vial that had rolled to the back. "Wait, I got something." He withdrew his arm.

"Oh, like hell!" Vael shouted. He pinned Jaered with the door.

Yannis rushed in and punched Vael. He lost his footing and dangled by his wrist. A bloody scream filled the room. Bile spurted out of Vael's mouth.

"Leave him!" Jaered shouted and shoved Yannis toward the door. "Get to the stairwell."

"The program's not done," Yannis said.

"The virus will do the rest." Jaered clutched the vial. "Go!" He propped Vael against the wall, sickened by his discolored arm and the unimaginable pain his friend endured.

"Don't leave me," Vael muttered.

The man's whimper thrust a knife into Jaered's gut. The vial held a clear liquid. The date and inscription confirmed it was from the first trial, the one that Jaered had witnessed. The day Donovan had burned a man from the inside out. It was a bitter consolation. He checked the outer office. Yannis had left. Jaered held up the serum. "This is the Angel of Death for all Weir Sars." Jaered grabbed the back of Vael's neck. "This is bigger than you and me. Hell, it's bigger than the universe. You've got to believe me, Vael."

He scoffed. "They'll only make more."

"I won't stop until I know they can't," Jaered said.

Vael closed his eyes and dropped his head back.

Purple streaks snaked down his friend's arm. Jaered stared at it. "Pray that whoever shut down our powers, finds you before the humans." Horror overshadowed Vael's confusion. "They might be the only ones who can save your hand."

"You planned this—you did this to me!" Vael cried as rage purged his despair.

"I didn't." Jaered backed up, bracing himself for what he had to do. "I'm sorry." He rushed out of the office.

"Jaaaaered!"

Vael's anguish shoved Jaered out into the hall and didn't stop until the stairwell door clanged shut behind him.

"Now what?" Yannis said. He had a gun in his hand.

"Put that away. If we're seen, we're two employees spooked by all the confusion."

Yannis didn't look like he shared Jaered's optimism, but he holstered the gun.

Jaered started down the stairs. Voices rose from below. He raised his hand for Yannis to stop. From the amount of noise filling the corridor, there were more men than they could deal with. "Up is good." He turned and rushed past Yannis, taking the steps two at a time, then burst through the unlocked, unguarded roof door.

"See if there's a way down," Jaered said. They separated and ran along the parapet, checking over the side of the twenty-story building. They met back up at the far end of the roofline with a shared conclusion. They were trapped.

"You really can't shyft us?" Yannis asked.

"No." There was something familiar about the pressing numb in the center of Jaered's chest. Like it had happened before. Jaered searched his memories. Oregon. The warehouse rooftop at Qualston. Jaered's core couldn't draw energy then either, not until he shot the wooden box and the speaker housed inside exploded.

He rushed to the center of the roof, searching. Did Donovan get his hands on the technology? Was it triggered when they opened the safe?

"What are you looking for?" Yannis asked.

"Something large enough to hold a sizable speaker." Together, they combed the roof. Nothing.

Marcus met up with his lieutenant in the hallway. "Where's everyone else?" he asked.

"On the way," his lieutenant said.

The stairwell door clanged shut. Pacman and Xander joined them. "I told you two to stay put and keep working," Marcus said.

"We got what we could," Xander said. "Kudos to whoever designed the virus."

"Voracious appetite," Pacman said.

"Mother lode of appetites," Xander added. They bumped knuckles.

Marcus stepped into the office waiting area. "Who'd we snare?"

The lieutenant indicated the office beyond. "I'll give you some privacy, sir. He's not going anywhere," the lieutenant said. "Orders?"

"Get everyone up to the roof and signal for our pickup from there," Marcus said.

The lieutenant saluted, then left, dragging the boys with him.

His man's reserved behavior left Marcus cautious. He locked the door to the hall, then followed groans to a room beyond the executive office. The prisoner glanced over his shoulder at Marcus's approach.

"Goddamn it!" Vael looked away. "Anyone, *anyone* but you."

His hand had conjoined with the safe's door and his arm hung limp. Marcus had never seen anything like it. "That's gotta hurt."

"Fuck you." He slumped against the wall.

Marcus wandered into the executive office, unable to shake the daze of landing in the middle of an emotional flood. He leaned against the desk and hung his head.

"Hey, old man," Vael shouted from the other room. "Get me the hell out of here."

"I don't care how long it's been," Marcus growled. "You either address me as General . . . or Dad."

The hall doorknob jiggled. Muffled voices at the waiting room door. "I could have sworn I heard someone." A second later. "Security check. The monitors went down in this hall. We're checking all offices on this floor."

Marcus shut the conference room door without a sound. "Your friends have deserted you."

"Right. I'm such a failure, I couldn't possibly do something like this on my own."

"What were you stealing, an empty safe?" Marcus took a step back. "Of course, if you want to deal with this by yourself . . ."

"You wouldn't!" Vael hissed.

Marcus held the jam up in his hand, but covered the red blinking light with his thumb. The battery life was about to die on the jam. His son's power would return at any second. Desperate not to lose the boy, he measured his next words carefully. "Take your chances with the Duach, or *cooperate* and come with me," Marcus said.

"Ahhh!" He grasped Marcus's arm. "Now I remember why I hate you."

Marcus pressed the button just as the scarlet light held steady. Vael's hand glowed.

At the sound of rusty hinges, Jaered pulled Yannis behind the vent. Footsteps crept across the pebbled rooftop, the crunch tracing the men's approach.

Click. Static interrupted the night's calm. "Squad ready for pickup in two . . . roof top location . . . use stealth, over."

The numb thawed. Tingling. A subtle warmth spread, deep in Jaered's chest. He grabbed Yannis. "Do you trust me?" he whispered.

"What?"

"Do you trust me," Jaered hissed.

It took a full second before Yannis nodded.

"Don't resist what I'm about to do." Jaered took off for the edge of the roof with a tight grip on Yannis. Shouts. A volley of shots. Bullets whizzed past his shoulder.

Jaered twisted back, wrapping his arms around Yannis. They fell over the side.

{43}

They reappeared in the middle of a field. Jaered collapsed to his knees. He hadn't made it all the way to the car, but he had to stop the shyft when he did. Keep moving, he urged, but his legs refused to cooperate, and at the moment, they were the ones in control.

"Oh my god!" Yannis cried while pacing in front of Jaered. "If you were able to shyft, why did we go over the edge?"

"My core wasn't at full strength. I had to buy us a few seconds," Jaered said.

"And leaping to our deaths was the answer!"

The tingling cold of the shyft gave way to a fiery spasm in his back. He groaned.

Yannis stared at him. "What's wrong?"

"I've been shot." Jaered tried to push the pain away, but his body had other plans.

"How bad?" Yannis bent down and his fingers probed Jaered's back. They stopped at his lower shoulder.

Jaered clenched his jaw and he held his breath to stifle a wail. His nostrils flared. Breaths came in rapid succession. Nothing helped.

"It appears to have gone in at an angle and missed your shoulder blade. It's too high for vital organs, but you're losing a lot of blood."

"It's worse than that." Jaered collapsed on the ground. The crisp, cool earth felt invigorating. His head cleared. "I need my cell."

Yannis patted him down and pulled it out.

Jaered grabbed the phone with a shaky hand and pressed the code. Two rings. Eve answered.

"Report."

"Code Red," came out barely above a whisper. Jaered caught his breath and closed his eyes, conserving everything he had left.

"Location?"

"Outskirts of town."

"Are you alone?"

"No."

"One of ours?"

Jaered hesitated. "No."

"Transportation?"

"Yes."

"I'll send coordinates to your cell and alert the doctor you're on the way. Do you have the package?"

"I think so."

"Viable for use?"

Her question gave him pause. His suspicions at Eve's true motives surfaced. "It needs to be tested to confirm."

"Get there as fast as you can, and Jaered?"

"Huh."

"Don't die. I need you."

The line went dead. A few seconds later, his cell vibrated in his hand. He turned the screen toward Yannis. "Get me to this address."

"What's there?"

"Help." Mistrust clouded Yannis's face and he didn't move. "I'm sure Aeros will understand, his son bleeding to death on your watch." Jaered moaned.

Yannis threw Jaered's arm over his shoulder and heaved him up.

Jaered's outcry was cut short by the grunts it took to stay on his feet. By the time Yannis stuffed him in the car and the engine turned over, his thoughts were lost in a gray, swirling fog. He slumped against the side of the car door and focused on something, anything to stay conscious. "Kill the lights."

Yannis flicked the switch. Stars lit up the dark sky like spilt salt.

The *thump, thump, thump* of helicopter blades passed over them a few minutes later. "Make sure we're not followed," Jaered said, but his voice was louder in his head than what reached his ears.

Yannis stole a peek from over his shoulder. "I don't see anything but pitch black behind us."

"Make sure," drifted off as Jaered slid into nothingness.

{44}

Ian slouched on the sofa. The night receptionist went about her duties across the hotel lobby. Her acrylic nails clicked against the keyboard. The occasional guest returned and the ding of the elevators signaled they were lucky enough to settle in for the night.

His thoughts had stilled and his muscles melted for the first time in days as exhaustion kicked in. Marcus and his squad had the pharmaceutical facility in hand. Ian welcomed the temporary reprieve.

"Why don't we just join the others upstairs?" Rayne asked from the chair beside him.

"Everyone's asleep." Ian yawned. "I want us to be ready for when Marcus calls."

Rayne's cell buzzed in her pocket. She answered it. "Zoe, where have you been? Why haven't you returned my calls?"

She gasped. Ian opened his eyes and sat up with a start. He strained to hear, but Rayne hit the speaker on her phone and held it out for him.

". . . been tied up," a male voice said. Color drained from Rayne's face. They both knew that voice. "As much as I've enjoyed my plaything, Donovan wants his son. Time for a trade," Ning said.

Rayne shot to her feet. She gripped the phone so tight, her knuckles turned white. "Don't hurt her," she said, loud enough that it earned a glance from the receptionist on the other side of the room.

"Too late for that." Ning chuckled. "But you're welcome to what's left."

"The zoo," Ian said. "Meet us near the Big Cat House, an hour from now." He looked at the ornate clock on the wall.

"No Pur troops, and we might all walk out of there alive," Ning said. "Rayne, you'll be the one handing over the boy." The line went dead.

Rayne headed for the elevators. She pressed the penthouse button and stood, waiting with clenched fists.

"Rayne, we can't go up there," Ian said.

"An hour is no time at all, Ian. We need to gather everyone together and make a plan."

The penthouse elevator doors opened. She stepped in. Ian grabbed her wrist to stop her. Spikes of pain ripped through his body. Her power drain gripped his core and threatened to tear it out of his chest. He let go and chose the button for the mezzanine level. The doors closed on his groan.

She pressed into the corner of the elevator and looked at him like he was insane. "You heard him. Ning's already had his twisted fun with Zoe." Rayne covered her face with her hands. A primal scream, muffled and riddled with despair, spilled from beneath.

Ian's core throbbed. Air took its time to refill his lungs. "We'll get her back, I swear we'll get her back," he rasped.

Rayne's chest heaved. "It's Ning, Ian. What's left of her?"

Ian stepped out onto the mezzanine floor. Rayne hesitated, then followed him. A brilliant blue shone from the hotel pool beyond glass walls. "Outside," he said and led her through the pool area and onto an outdoor patio.

Rayne gripped the railing and stared at the city lights. "Maybe if I can get close enough, I can drain Ning and keep Bryant safe. You can finish him off if you need to. Tara can take care of Donovan."

"I want you to return to the mansion," Ian said.

"What?" She turned on him. "You heard him. Ning expects me to be there. To hand over the boy."

"There's something you don't know. Hell, I'm not sure myself. It's only been a theory," Ian said. He'd kept her at a distance, but with this latest snag, he couldn't keep her in the dark. Not now.

"What aren't you telling me, Ian?" His lack of response didn't bode well. "I'm tired of secrets!" she shouted. "Protecting someone, doesn't mean locking them out."

In protecting her, was he pushing her away? Rayne deserved the truth, even if it meant dredging up her painful past. "Something didn't make sense, the night of the party."

Rayne turned around and leaned her back against the railing. "What?"

"When the Curse was triggered, why did Donovan carry Bryant around in search of the Pur Sar?"

She shrugged. "He didn't want to take the time to return Bryant to their room. Possibly lose the Pur Sar's—your—trail," she said.

Ian leaned against the edge of a patio table. "Then why didn't he go upstairs to the banquet hall or stay on the same floor as the meeting if he was searching for me? Carlene found out that he took Bryant clear across to the other side of the hotel."

Rayne looked at him with a puzzled expression. "He wasn't going after you."

Ian nodded. "I think he was trying to *avoid* the Pur Sar. And when I looked at it from that angle, I formed a theory. What if Richard wasn't born a Duach Sar, but Bryant . . . was."

Her eyes widened. "But you're—"

"The last Sar born to the Weir. The Prophesied Son." He felt the raised edge of the sun on his left breast through his shirt, as if it kept his reality in check. "Before I killed him, Sebastian claimed I wasn't the only one. That according to the Book of the Weir, there's another."

"You think it's Bryant?" she said. "But do Sars skip generations?"

"Not that I've ever heard of. If the firstborn doesn't have a mark, a core, the powers are lost in the family's gene pool forever."

"If a fluke happened, and Bryant was one in a million, then he'd have the triangle mark of a Sar, or even a sun, like you do."

"I had Tara check when I sent her up to the penthouse earlier. He doesn't have a sun." Ian met her gaze. "He doesn't have a mark *at all*."

Brewing thoughts hung between them. "Who is he?" Rayne asked.

"*What* is he?" Ian said. "It's been twenty years since your father tried to give you an artificial core during your mother's pregnancy."

"You think Donovan succeeded?"

"I'm thinking someone did." He stood. "You can't take Bryant to them, Rayne. We can't risk you—"

"Touching him." She pursed her lips. "That's why you didn't want me hanging out in the room with them. Why you've kept me close to you."

"Neither one of us can go near him," Ian said.

"Ning knows about my power drain, but he can't know about Bryant. Not if he wants me to bring the boy."

"Donovan must be in the dark about why Ning wants you," Ian said. "Proving they don't trust each other. Maybe we can use that to our advantage."

"You heard Ning. If I don't show up with Bryant, Zoe's dead for sure." Rayne's heartbeat took on a life of its own. "Ian, if you can't get within thirty feet of him, how are you going to protect either one of us tonight?"

He didn't answer. There wasn't any guarantee that he could.

{ 45 }

Strong hands pulled Jaered out of the car. Yannis supported him and they crossed a small lawn. He propped Jaered against the door and knocked.

Jaered's head bobbed as Yannis took heed of their surroundings. The overhead light was off. The doorway was hidden behind tall bushes. The icy glow of distant headlights inched their way down the residential street. Jaered rested his head against the door and followed their path through the branches. They stopped moving, then shut off. When a car door didn't open and close, Jaered struggled to speak. Nothing came out.

"Where are we?" Yannis said. "This looks like someone's house."

Jaered couldn't give him an answer, even if he somehow managed to find his voice. The door opened, and he fell into someone's arms.

"Shut it," a deep voice said. In spite of his bean-pole build, the man was stronger than he looked. He picked up Jaered and carried him into a back room.

He was laid out on a gurney. A bright light blinded him and he moaned at its glare. Together, they turned him on his side, and he cried out at the searing bolts ripping across his upper torso. Deep in the center of his chest, his core blistered from pain and swelling heat.

"He was shot in the back, right shoulder," Yannis said.

"But he shyfted, after he was shot?"

"Yeah."

The man opened a drawer and removed a long metal wand. He waved it across Jaered's legs.

"What's that?"

"A metal detector. I need to find the bullet."

"It's in his right shoulder."

"No, it's not." The wand moved higher inching its way across Jaered's chest. When it reached his left shoulder, its bleat startled Jaered and his eyes fluttered.

"Bingo." The man handed Yannis the wand. He jammed his fingertips into Jaered's flesh.

"Aaah!" Jaered groaned.

"I can't feel it, it must be deep." The man pressed a hand on Jaered's forehead. "I'm going to give you something for the pain. I'll put you under once the doctor arrives. He'll have to remove it surgically. You're lucky it didn't end up in a vital organ."

"I don't get it," Yannis said. "How did it get there?"

"Our body's molecules know where they belong. But if you shyft with a foreign object inside you, there's no telling where it will end up. Like playing Russian roulette."

Yannis gave Jaered a curious stare. "Where did the one from the bank job end up?"

"My hip." Jaered coughed rough and deep.

A hand pressed against Jaered's forehead. "You're burning up. The sepsis is developing fast."

"Sepsis?" Yannis said.

"Gunshot wounds are full of bacteria. Shyfting spreads it like wildfire. It almost always gets into the bloodstream." He grabbed a bag of clear liquid out of a small refrigerator and wheeled over an IV pole. He hooked it up, then set up a port in Jaered's hand. He connected the bag's tube.

The man filled a hypodermic needle with fluid from a vial. "I've got the antibiotics going. This will help with the pain."

Jaered closed his eyes and focused on breathing, drifting wherever the tide of memories took him. The first time he was shot. Falling . . . weightless. His groggy thoughts touched upon Vael. Guilt swirled around his friend's feet and Vael sank, kicking and screaming, into the crimson quicksand.

Vael's father dragged him inside the mansion, but jerked him to a stop in the middle of the foyer. Vael cradled his sore hand and twisted about taking in the size of the place. I could get used to this, he thought, but the realization of where he was—who lived there—put a damper on his musings.

"Let go." Vael tried to pull out of his dad's grasp. "I won't escape."

"I've heard that one before." Marcus clutched Vael's arm tighter than ever. "Milo!"

A portly man strolled out from a back hall. He wore an apron and held a wooden spoon dripping red. "What? I'm in the middle of my marinara sauce."

"Where's Ian and the others?"

"They haven't returned yet. As far as I know, they're still dealing with the psycho Duach."

The guards let themselves in and stood waiting for orders. Two teenagers yawned and rubbed their heads.

"Get those computer sticks plugged in and tell me what we found," Marcus barked from over his shoulder.

"They're called flash drives, old man." Vael snickered.

Marcus let loose a throaty growl. "Milo, I need a secure room."

Milo sized Vael up. "Is he a shyftor?"

"No, but he has a way with locks. I'm keeping the jam on and one of my men will be on guard duty."

"I've got a place," Milo said.

From the look in the old geezer's eye, the comforts of home were not in Vael's future.

{46}

Ian sat on the rock. Maajida lay at his feet. The massive Bengal tiger purred as he stroked her pelt of burnt orange with lightning bolts of the deepest black and pure white running through.

Rayne chose to remain a spectator, keeping the deep trench and viewing wall between them. "Other than Saxon, animals don't seem to like me, Ian."

"All living things have their own energy," Ian said. "Perhaps they sense your drain and are skittish."

"That explains my houseplant disasters." Rayne sighed. "You've never mentioned your frequent visits to the zoo."

There was so much about his Weir upbringing that he'd kept from her and Patrick, Ian realized. "Not all my trips were pleasant," he said. "The first time Milo brought me to the zoo, I was expected to wander and connect with the creatures. It didn't take long to recognize which ones were bred in captivity and which ones had been transferred from their natural habitats."

Maajida's tiger cub appeared from between the rocks. At spying Ian, it paused with a squealing yawn. "Oh, she has a baby?" Rayne smiled and leaned over the barrier for a closer look.

"Even the elderly and weak animals of the wild know the difference," Ian continued. "I can't help but be affected by their angst at the walls, windows, and trenches that keep them confined. After that first visit, I had to run free in the woods around the mansion for a few hours. It was the only way I could shed the claustrophobic sensation that followed me home."

"Why come at all if it's so painful for you?" Rayne asked.

"Milo. He wouldn't tolerate my resistance to the zoo. Kept bringing me back. Over time, I learned to comfort the animals and to relieve some of their anguish. They calm in my presence, and I've discovered how to tune into their different characteristics and quirks. I've made some friends. Maajida is one of my favorites." Often his first stop whenever he'd visit in the wee hours of the night, he would stroke her for minutes on end, eliciting her purrs and snuggles while relishing in her body's warmth and strength.

Ian perused the tiger's aura and was comforted to know that she was content. "Maajida, this is Rayne," he said. The tiger stared at her.

"She's magnificent, Ian."

He got up from the rock and crouched in front of Maajida, meeting her intense gaze. Their connection strengthened, the emotional bond eliciting a sensation of savagery and igniting Ian's senses. His calf muscles tensed as if prepared to take off at a full run.

"Maajida finds you intriguing," Ian said. "She isn't threatened by you, Rayne."

"You can communicate with her?" Rayne asked.

"Not like Saxon." Ian stood and rubbed Maajida behind the ears. "But we have an understanding, just the same." He looked beyond Rayne, down the path. "Call Tara. If they don't get here soon, we'll be cutting it close."

"She's not happy with the plan." Rayne pulled out her cell.

"*I'm* not happy with the plan. But it's all we've got," he said.

A second later, Rayne's cell chimed. "She's been casing the zoo, making sure they didn't get here early."

"Patrick?"

"He's with Bryant." Rayne paused. "Uh, oh."

"What uh, oh?" Ian said.

"Carlene is with him."

"Shit!" The one person who couldn't get a glimpse of his powers was in the middle of an already haphazard plan. "He was supposed to—"

"He claims she woke up when he was tying her to the bed. He spilled everything."

Ian stepped away from Maajida and took a second to verify where the cub had wandered. He didn't want to spook either one. "Tell him to get Bryant ready and that Carlene is his responsibility." Ian shyfted next to Rayne.

"Where to now?" she asked while typing in her cell.

"I have a couple more friends I want to introduce," Ian said.

He led her across the grounds to the spider monkey cage. Saxon stood watch where Ian had left the wolf. Ian opened the cage and found her slumbering in her hammock. He conjured a peach and bit into it then held it near the monkey's nose. Her eyes flew open at her favorite treat and she leapt into his arms with a squawk.

"Rayne, this is Coco, short for Coconut." He played keep away with the fruit. She wrapped her tail around his eyes and snatched it from his grasp. Rustling inside the cage. The other primates stirred.

When Ian turned down the path leading to the large apes, Saxon came to a halt. *Not him,* the wolf channeled

He's part of the plan, Ian responded. A deep, throaty growl came from the wolf. When Ian didn't acknowledge it, Saxon's paws dragged a few steps behind.

"What's wrong with Saxon?" Rayne asked.

"Buster likes to dump buckets of water on everyone. Saxon is his favorite target." Ian brushed Coco's arm away when the spider monkey tried to stick the peach pit in his ear.

"Who's Buster?" Rayne asked.

Ian smiled. Saxon snorted.

{47}

A crimson flash. Sulfur. The odor of burning flesh. Jaered's lids fluttered, then opened at another burst. Across the room, Yannis held his fist against a blackened chest. The gun drooped, then slipped out of his grasp. He looked at Jaered, and collapsed on top of the bean-pole man.

A dark figure. Ning approached. He held Jaered's arm down. Riiiip. An adrenaline rush diluted Jaered's haze. Pain shot through both shoulders when he pushed to sit. "Ahh!" A nylon tie bound one of his wrists to the gurney's rail.

"Insurance you don't show up and mess with our plans." Ning's gloat distorted the flaming tattoos on his cheeks. "I know how attached you are to our little girl."

"How?" Jaered gulped air and fought to focus.

"Me." Donovan stood in the doorway. "Your father's spy never questioned the added bulk to the passkey I gave him for the executive offices. Thanks to my little bug, I've known Yannis's whereabouts, and stayed one step ahead of his inquiries into my affairs." Donovan patted Jaered's pockets. He withdrew the vial they'd stolen from his safe. "We need this for our little rendezvous tonight. Once my son and I are out of the country, I'll send you half the coordinates to the other serum plant. You'll get the rest of what you need to find the deadly Pur cocktail the second I get paid."

"Do you think Rayne will enjoy South America?" Ning regarded Jaered like a meal simmering on a stove. "Of course, if your father comes through, she won't have to for long."

"You can't get close to her, not while she's with the Heir," Jaered hissed.

"He's bringing her to me." Ning licked his lips.

Jaered stilled. What could possibly motivate the Heir to put her in such danger?

"I'd feel better in a crowd," Donovan said. "If we could find such a place at three o'clock in the morning. He'd be less likely to use his powers in front of humans."

"I stopped worrying about Weir law long ago." Ning snickered. "I'm betting the Heir won't upset the animals. Besides, their tranquilizer guns will come in handy if he brings that bastard, Marcus, as backup." Ning regarded the vial in Donovan's hand.

Jaered groped for Ning with a limp arm. The assassin deflected his feeble attempts with a laugh. A slammed door snuffed it out. The assassin's taunt rang in Jaered's ears long after their footsteps died.

The tie cut deep into his wrist and he soon gave up trying to wedge a finger under it. He searched the room. Surgical instruments lay in neat rows on a tray at the far counter. Jaered focused on drawing pure magnetic energy into his core. The metal tray shook as Jaered turned his chest into a powerful magnet.

The stainless steel instruments bounced across the tray as if reacting to an earthquake tremor. He clenched his jaw at the strain and increased the energy's pull. Screeching metal sang in the room. Steel cabinets creaked and tilted from stressed hinges. The IV pole toppled on him. Just when he feared he couldn't draw enough, the surgical instruments took flight, aimed at Jaered's chest. He caught one of the scalpels with his free hand and deflected others with a twist of his torso. One of the scalpels left a deep, bloody streak in his forearm that stung like hell. The instruments' metal tray slammed into his chest and stuck to him like glue. He sliced the nylon tie. Jaered rolled off the gurney and used the tray to dodge the onslaught of all things metal while he reversed his core energy. The last of the objects settled and fell to the floor. The room silenced.

He refused to give in to the darkness filling his head. A cry that could wake the neighborhood helped him to focus. He collapsed into a nearby chair and tore open his shirt. He dug a finger into his upper chest, desperate to locate the bullet that had gouged a path toward his core.

He used his teeth to free a hypodermic of adrenaline from its bag, set it aside, then stuffed a wad of rolled gauze in his mouth. Jaered held the blade to the spot, then paused to find his courage. The smell of antiseptic snaked up his nose. With a vow to take revenge on the gods themselves if he should pass out, he wailed as the blade cut deep.

{48}

Donovan approached the Big Cat House with frequent glances over his shoulder. Ian wondered if it was from fear or to verify his ally was nearby. Their union had turned Ian's greatest fear into a living nightmare. The narcissistic Sar had lowered himself to work with a powerless Duach like Donovan for one reason only. Ning couldn't snatch her. He needed someone without a core to do it for him.

"I don't see Ning," Patrick's voice spurt into Ian's earpiece.

"Tara?" Ian said.

"It's a big zoo, Ian. Nothing so far."

Ian drew out of the shadows when Donovan was still several feet away. He counted on Ning keeping his distance to avoid setting off the Curse.

"Where's my son?" Donovan came to a halt.

"He's here." Ian looked around. "Where's your partner?"

"With your end of the bargain." Donovan looked sheepish and gazed at his feet. "For the record, I had nothing to do with her . . . condition."

Ian's stomach lurched, and he silently vowed that Ning would stay dead this time. "I'll show mine if you show me yours."

"Behind you," Donovan said and looked up.

Ian turned. Ning had Zoe, what was left of Rayne's roommate, dangling over the faux cliff above the outdoor pen where Ian had shared a tranquil moment with Maajida earlier. Blood dripped from deep gashes in her arm and leg. A dark socket, where one of her eyes had been melted away by a core blast, turned toward him. Her other eye was swollen shut. She whimpered amidst feeble thrashes. From what he could tell, she was barely alive.

"Where's my little energy sucker?" Ning shouted. "She better show up to the party or she might miss her reunion." Ning lowered Zoe a couple of feet when Maajida's mate appeared in the open hatch. "This human doesn't have long before she's manure for the earth."

"Not until they give me my son!" Donovan's bold shout fell on deaf ears. Ning was here for one reason only.

The assassin laughed and set Zoe into a gentle sway. A pungent whiff of blood reached Ian. Another tiger entered the pen with Maajida's cub standing watch at the doorway. Concerned its fretful cries would distract Maajida from her task, Ian took the initiative.

"Neither of you will get what you want if she dies!" Ian yelled. He drew heat from his core into his hands. They glowed. A core blast directed at the tigers might prompt them to run for safety. Another blast at the door hatch would seal them inside.

From that height, Ning could still drop Zoe to her death. Ian could shyft, perhaps catch her. Core blast power swelled in his chest. He directed it into his hands at the same time he prepared to shyft.

"Stop!" Carlene's scream came from the other side of the building. Silent curses rang in Ian's head at Patrick's failure to keep her out of this. His hands cooled in a blink. She ran up and dropped to her knees across from her husband. "Richard, please! Don't do this."

"I'm not leaving here without Bryant," Donovan sneered.

Carlene turned to Ian. "You promised me, Bry would be safe. I trusted you."

"Patrick!" Ian shouted.

"Here," came from the rear of the building, muffled.

"Let Donovan know that Bryant is with you," Ian said.

Bryant called out a moment later. "Mommy?"

Carlene swiped at a tear. "Bry, I'm here!"

"I wanna go home," came out in a mournful pitch.

"So do I, Bry," she whimpered. "Soon, baby, soon."

"How touching." Donovan grabbed Carlene and dragged her toward the building.

"You're not getting him!" The young mother screamed and lashed out at her husband.

The second her back was turned, Ian waved. A tremendous gust of wind picked Zoe up and tore her from Ning's grasp.

With a swoop and jerking dips, it deposited her in the deep trench at the edge of the pen, out of Ning's sight.

"No!" The assassin bolted to his feet. A core blast formed in his open palm. He ran along the edge of the cliff closer to where Zoe had disappeared.

Ian took off, in a race to narrow the distance between him and the assassin. Ning stopped and pulled back to fling a blast down into the trench. Ian reached the threshold before he could release it. Ning clawed at his chest with a wail. Ian collapsed against the railing as the crushing pressure battled within his chest, the Curse dropping them both.

The Curse lifted as quickly as it began. Ian looked up. Ning was gone.

Maajida growled in anticipation. The tigress had a prey in her sights. Ian ran for Carlene. Pressure returned to the center of his chest. An instant later, the Curse dropped him to one knee, and he jammed a fist against his rib cage. "Ugh!"

A child's wail. Maajida leapt out from the side of the building. Bryant was in her jaws.

A deafening scream. Maajida threw Carlene a throaty growl, then rushed toward Ian. Bryant cried out in pain at the same time Ian collapsed on the path, writhing in agony. The animal reached the railing and sprang into the air. She landed at the edge of the outdoor pen, then disappeared through the open hatch. The second the tiger put enough distance between them, the Curse lifted. Ian bolted to his feet.

"Nooo!" Carlene rushed to the building and threw open the door. She disappeared inside.

Ian stepped back and prepared to shyft to the bottom of the trench. A dart struck the trash can next to him.

"You're gonna pay!" Donovan screamed. He aimed a tranquilizer gun at Ian's chest.

Patrick wrapped strong arms around a hysterical Carlene. "He's all right, Bryant is all right," he insisted but didn't let go, unsure if she had processed what he was telling her.

"You swore if I cooperated, Ian would take care of Bry." Carlene turned and pounded on his chest. "A giant tiger crushed him in his mouth!"

"Bryant's in the back, playing with a ball." Patrick said. "See for yourself." He led her through a door marked Zoo Staff Only.

Purring and giggles greeted them when they entered a large room. Bryant was inside a cage. The tiger lay down across from him. The boy kicked a ball and it rolled off to the side, but the tiger stopped the toy with its tail. A swish, and it rolled back toward the giggling child.

"Bry," Carlene gasped. She ran up and wrapped her fingers around the bars.

"Mommy, kitty play ball with me." He turned and tossed the ball in the tiger's direction. It caught the toy in its mouth, then flipped it up in the air. When it bounced on the cement floor, Bryant clapped and ran after it.

"Carlene, this is Maajida," Patrick said. "She and Ian have a very special bond. Ian knew she would never have harmed Bryant."

"What is he wearing?" Carlene stared at Bryant while the color took its time returning to her face.

"A padded suit that Ian created," Patrick said. "He wanted Maajida to be able to grab Bryant without harming him in any way. The tiger has a baby. Ian covered Bryant's suit with her cub's scent. They played back here and got comfortable with each other before their performance outside." Patrick pushed against a hinged section of the cage. "Here, Bry, come crawl through the tunnel."

"I wanna play with kitty."

"No!" Carlene crouched down at the opening, her voice softened, "It's time to go, I promise we'll come back and visit the tiger again, soon."

"Bye-bye kitty." Bryant tossed the ball at Maajida, then crawled out of the opening.

Carlene scooped him up and buried her face in his neck. "Why put him through that?"

"Richard would never stop trying to get Bryant back," Patrick said. "This way, he thinks his son is dead."

{49}

Rayne's pacing formed a path down the center of the Large Primate House while Buster, the gigantic orangutan that Ian insisted keep her company, mimicked her every move. When Rayne came to a halt and told him to stop, he bent down his lower lip and chattered like he was scolding her.

She plopped down on the bench. He sat on the concrete floor next to her and fidgeted with the laces on her sneaker.

For so long she'd resigned herself to living life with Ian at a distance. The feather, as promising as it had been, only proved that their relationship would always be based on compromise. Being kept out of this might have been Ian's definition of compromise, but it was far from Rayne's. "I hate not knowing what's happening," she said. Buster laid his head in her lap. She stroked his back and found an odd sort of peace.

The revelation that there was a Sar child that she could never touch triggered an avalanche of childhood memories, and of the short life she lived with a father who could never hold her. Thoughts touched upon her mother and eventually came full circle to Carlene. Did the young mother even know what her son was? Ian swore that Carlene was human, that she didn't display any signs of being Weir. How could they help her learn about the magical beings that had cared for Earth for centuries, and appreciate that her son was a ray of hope for their dying race?

A knock at the door. Rayne opened it to find Dr. Mac standing in the dim light of the Primate House entrance. "What are you doing here?" she said.

He lifted his old, worn medical bag. "Ian sent word to meet him at the zoo and to come to this building. That I might be needed for triage." He glanced over his shoulder. "What does he think I am, a veterinarian?"

"You're here for Zoe, my roommate." The realization that Ian called the doctor confirmed that he was prepared for the worst. Seeing Dr. Mac standing there, clutching his bag, brought a tidal wave of reality. If Rayne didn't lose her best friend tonight, she still lost the life they'd shared. She stepped to the side. "He's trying to rescue her and save a mother and child from a Duach."

Shock grooved deep creases in Dr. Mac's face. "Where's Marcus? Why isn't he taking care of this?"

She thought fast. "He and his squad infiltrated the Duach's lab," she said. Ian hadn't told Marcus what they were doing. The Drion might have triggered the Curse with Bryant. It dawned on Rayne that she would have to keep Dr. Mac on this side of the zoo.

"Where're Ian and the others?"

"They're on the opposite side of the grounds," Rayne said. "Ian insisted I wait here."

"Are you alone?" he asked.

"Not exactly." Rayne looked at Buster. The orangutan was stretched out on the bench, one arm dangled over the side while he picked at his butt.

"Let's find the surgical offices," Dr. Mac said. "I passed a map on my way here."

Rayne closed the door behind her and together, she and Dr. Mac found the medical building.

"It's locked," she whispered. "Can your power get us inside?"

"No," Dr. Mac said, peering down the path. "But my ingenuity shouldn't be discounted." He gripped the doorknob tight and jerked it. Nothing. He gestured for her to stay put and walked out onto the path, grabbed a large rock, and threw it at the window. It bounced off but hit with enough force that it set off an alarm.

"Why'd you do that?" Rayne asked.

"So someone will let us in," Dr. Mac said matter-of-factly.

A couple of minutes later, running footsteps approached. They slowed. "Stay where you are!" A security guard stood at the edge of the path with a gun pointed at them. "Who are you?"

Dr. Mac cleared his throat. "Young man, I am a doctor." He held up his bag. "I was called to tend to an injury. I was told someone would be here. I'm afraid I accidently triggered an alarm when I tried the door."

The security guard lifted a walkie-talkie to his ear. "Luis, come in." Spitting static. The guard stepped toward them. The tip of the gun pointed toward the ground. "Where's your ID?" he asked.

Dr. Mac shook his head. "The vet on duty couldn't come. He called me to cover."

"Larry. Do you know if someone called in an outside vet tonight? Respond." Sizzle. The guard grunted and approached. "Is it about the cat that got loose? The other guards took off to check on that," the man said. "I'll need to call and confirm this."

"Of course, but in the meantime, would you be so kind as to let us in? We have to familiarize ourselves with the place. My assistant and I have to prepare for surgery."

Rayne conjured her best veterinary assistant smile.

"Sorry Doc, but I can't admit you until I verify this."

"Of course." Dr. Mac touched the guard's forehead with his index finger. The man went limp and Dr. Mac caught him. He grunted. "He's heavier than he looks. Rayne, be a dear and open the door."

She grabbed the passkey hanging from the guard's lanyard and swiped it. The red, steady dot turned to green. A metallic click and she swung the door wide. "What was that?" Rayne propped it open and helped Dr. Mac drag the unconscious guard inside, careful not to come in contact with the Pur Sar doctor.

"I have the Somex power." Dr. Mac removed the guard's lanyard from around his neck and unlocked a door at the far end of the room. He turned on the lights. "I trust you to keep my secret."

"How long will he be out?" she asked. The man looked like he was sleeping peacefully.

"I can revive him with another touch, or he'll wake up within two to three hours on his own." Dr. Mac said. He opened a door and turned on the light. "The surgery is in here. I'll get prepared. What of the other security guards?"

"Ian was taking care of them," Rayne said.

Dr. Mac looked at the slumbering guard. "He missed one," came out gruff and full of gravel.

Rayne grabbed the walkie-talkie and handed it to Dr. Mac. "When Ian secured the other guards, he may have hung onto one of these." She headed for the door. "Use it if you need to connect. Don't go looking for him. You might mess up his plan."

"Where are you going?" he asked.

"I've got a job to do," she said. She slipped out of the building, but took her time returning to the Primate House. Tara was to leave clues for Ning to head there, but Dr. Mac's unconventional entry made his location vulnerable. Rayne had to keep Ning away from the medical building.

A few furtive glances over her shoulder at the quiet surroundings failed to reassure her that the coast was clear. Had something happened to Ian or the others? Where was Tara?

A laugh from the depths of Rayne's nightmares came from the bushes. A core blast slammed onto the concrete at her feet.

Sulfur snaked up Rayne's nose. The sickening odor lit her muscles on fire. She ran toward the Primate House and slammed the door. *Bump.* The metal door grew warm. Smoke peeked through the cracks. Buster jumped to his feet and let loose a deafening screech.

Memories of Ning chasing her and Patrick through a snowy forest sent shivers down her spine. Ning liked to have fun with his prey. He enjoyed the hunt.

She rushed to the door marked for zoo personnel, but the piece of wood Ian used as a doorstop was missing, and she was locked out. Perplexed at what could have happened to it, she spied it balancing it on the orangutan's upper lip like a mustache. He gave her a wide, toothy smile and chattered. Rayne let loose a curse. She'd left the guard's passkey with Dr. Mac.

"You did this," Rayne yelled and slapped the locked door. "How are we supposed to get inside?"

Buster rushed over and knocked on the door. "No one's home, Buster," Rayne snapped. He grabbed her hand. The orangutan dragged her through the winding hallway. He pounded on the far door marked Exit. She opened it and he shoved her outside. The door banged shut behind them. The outdoor exercise pens would have offered ideal places to hide, but they were covered in wire mesh attached to a network of steel bars. Rayne looked for a ground level entrance. There wasn't anything she could squeeze through. The orangutan climbed the bars like a jungle gym. He slipped through an opening at the top and dangled from a beam. He waved as if wanting her to follow.

The lowest steel bars were too high and out of her reach. She grasped the wire mesh and pulled, but it cut into her fingers and she let go, rubbing her stinging hands. Buster climbed down and peered at her from the inside.

"I can't follow you," she said. She looked around. The tree canopies were wide and thick on this side of the Primate House and they blocked out much of the moonlight. She couldn't see but a few yards down the path.

Ian stared at the barrel of the tranquilizer gun and raised his hands. "Calm down, Donovan, and we might all just walk out of here tonight."

"My son is dead because of you!"

"You're the one who brought the Duach head case into this," Ian said. His pulse quickened. His heartbeat revved. Ian drew upon the only weapon that Donovan wouldn't see coming. The weather's reaction to Ian's emotional upheaval.

Nearby birds squawked. Their voices rose to a deafening pitch and mixed with lion roars and elephant trumpets. Shrieking monkeys filled the gaps between. Ian dropped to one knee and pressed a hand to the ground. This wasn't his doing.

With a screech, Coco leapt onto Donovan.

"Get off!" Donovan groped for the spider monkey with his free hand but managed to keep one eye, and the gun, on Ian.

"Donovan, a quake is com—" A low rumble cut off Ian's words.

The ground shook with a subtle vibration under Ian's hand. It intensified with every heartbeat. The building moaned, windows creaked. An overhead glass pane crackled into an ornate spider web.

Coco reached up and grabbed the overhead eave. She swung away and scampered toward Ian. Donovan fell against the door.

A blur of white. Saxon leapt at the CEO. The wolf's powerful jaws clamped down on Donovan's wrist. "Ahhh!" The tranquilizer gun slipped out of his weakened grasp. In his struggles with Saxon, he kicked the gun. It spun away.

The quake wasn't easing. The front eave at the entrance to the Big Cat House buckled. The large concrete lion and tiger statues at the entrance rattled. One spun around, then tumbled toward the ground.

"Run!" Ian yelled. Saxon let go and took off. Donovan fell to his knees. Ian swept his arm and sent a hurricane wind toward the man, but the giant lion statue crushed him before the gust could sweep him out of harm's way.

The animals ceased their protests. The earthquake's grinding mantle settled.

{50}

The trembling ground knocked Rayne to her knees. A crimson core blast struck the viewing wall beside her. A dry bush transformed into a fiery torch.

She tried to remain upright, but the ground tossed her about like a pebble on a freeway. She grabbed for the wire mesh to stop from falling into the blaze, but it cut deep into her fingers and she let go with a yelp. The tip of her ponytail sizzled when it swung close to the flame.

The exercise compound wall cracked and split open a few feet away. Rayne scrambled for the opening and fell through with a face-plant against the cool grass inside the compound. The trembling ceased. Rayne got to her feet and took off for the nearest tree.

She pressed up against the wide trunk. Silence. In spite of burning lungs, Rayne held her breath. It didn't ease the pounding in her ears.

"You do have the sweetest, most pungent fear." Ning's voice came from the other side of the wide tree. He'd followed her inside.

Grunts came from the branches. Something landed on the ground. Rayne stole a peek. Buster had left the tree and was confronting Ning.

"Do you know what happens to the brain when a concentrated blast hits it?" Ning said.

Rayne shrieked, "Don't!" She lurched and grabbed him by the ankles. The core blast snuffed out in his hand, her drain extinguishing whatever energy he could draw upon. He tried to kick free, but she held on with a grip that shocked even her. Buster jumped about chattering as if cheering her on.

The blow struck Rayne across the temple. She fell against a picnic table bench. Its corner dug into her side and robbed her of breath. She gasped for air.

Buster cried out and swung at Ning. The assassin dropped and rolled away. He rose to one knee and sent a core blast at the orangutan just as it grabbed a branch and swung up into the tree. The blast clipped the animal's arm, setting its fur on fire.

Buster disappeared in the thick foliage. Branches creaked overhead. The animal's cries ripped apart Rayne's heart. The smell of burnt hair blended with sulfur and floated down.

Ning looked at her with a piercing madness. The assassin's scuffle with the animal had at least erased his gloat.

"You're going to die for that," he snarled.

"You don't dare kill her. She's not worth anything to you dead, is she?" Tara had crawled inside the exercise compound and stood next to the crack in the wall. A bucket sat at her feet. She was backlit by the blaze. She held a large knife.

A core blast swirled in Ning's hand. It lit his face in a bloody glow. He laughed. "You brought a knife to a core blast fight. You must be dumber than your sister."

"You went after the book the other night," Tara said. "But I'm guessing you left empty-handed. Otherwise you wouldn't be so intent on kidnapping Rayne."

"I was supposed to kill the Duach's wife on her way down in the elevator, but I saw all of you arrive at the hotel. The opportunity to go after the book was too good to pass up.

"You're not a shyftor, how did you get there so fast?" Tara asked.

"There was a vortex in the alley across the street from the hotel. It made it so easy to slip away."

"Saxon recognized your scent," Tara said. "He spoiled your plan."

"I handled the wolf." Ning sneered. "It was the Pur Guards storming the place and slaughtering the old monks that sent me shyfting back to the party. But by then, I'd missed my chance with the wife. You surrounded her after that."

"The Pur Guards didn't murder them," Rayne shouted. It came out raspy. It hurt to draw a deep breath.

His laugh rang about the exercise compound. "Naïvety suits you, suckling. You still believe the Primary can be trusted."

"Rayne, you okay?" Tara asked.

"Yeah," she said and gulped air to refill her lungs. She got to her feet. "Zoe?"

Tara didn't answer. She took a few steps toward Ning while flipping the knife around in one hand. "If you're waiting for Donovan, he's not coming."

"That complicates things." Ning raised his hand, and the core blast swirled. He took a step toward Tara. "But I can be quite persuasive. Either Rayne cooperates, or I'll reunite you with your sister."

Tara tossed the knife high above her. "I do miss her." She caught the handle on the way down and in one swift motion, threw the knife at Ning. The blade sliced through his raised hand, nailing the core blast to his shoulder. He screamed.

The fireball swelled as if his core continued to feed the unspent blast. The swirling ball of sizzling energy engulfed the assassin's shoulder. Ning stumbled back with a shriek as the melting steel blade dripped down his chest.

Tara grabbed the bucket handle.

Buster swung out of the tree and landed solidly in front of Tara. He grabbed at the bucket.

"Sorry, but this one's mine, Buster," Tara said. She approached and tossed the contents at the screaming assassin.

He burst into flames, engulfed in a blinding funeral pyre. The overwhelming odor of gasoline and burning flesh choked Rayne. Ning's screams ceased. The assassin collapsed onto the ground. Flames licked at the damp grass.

The empty bucket slipped from Tara's grasp. "Are you sure you're all right?" She didn't look at Rayne, as if unable to peel herself from her twin's executioner.

Rayne didn't know what to expect from Tara, but this cold reaction unnerved her. Relief at no longer looking over her shoulder, made Rayne almost giddy. Not Tara. Revenge wouldn't resurrect her sister.

Tara approached the dying flames. "Dr. Mac said you know where to find him." She grabbed Rayne's arm. "It's not good. Ning had his way with Zoe before they even brought her tonight. I'm sorry."

Rayne took off and crawled through the opening in the wall. When she looked over her shoulder, Tara stood stock-still, staring at the inferno.

Movement out of the corner of Rayne's eye. Someone with a bent back stumbled, farther down the path. A muted groan, and the man grabbed his arm. She ran toward him, frightened that Tara held something back. Had Ian or Patrick gotten injured? Rayne ran to catch up, then pulled ahead to intercept. She froze.

It was Jaered. Blood covered the front of his shirt.

"You," she whispered and glanced about. "What are you doing here?"

"I found out Ning was coming after you." He clutched his arm tight against his chest. He swayed like he was drunk. "The Channel can really throw a knife."

"Tara, her name is Tara." Rayne scrutinized him closely. "You need a doctor."

"I *need* to get out of here." His head lobbed like he couldn't keep it upright.

She stepped to the side. He took another step, but collapsed against the nearby lamppost. He hissed and clenched his jaw.

"Stop being so stubborn and let me help you," she hushed.

"What are you going to do, carry me?" He gave her a grimace that in the dark could have been a smirk.

"Follow me," she said. Rayne led him to the rear of the medical building, pausing long enough for him to catch up to her with dragging steps. She found a sturdy crate next to a large Dumpster and gestured for him to sit. The surrounding trash reeked of blood and antiseptic. Jaered rested his head back against the cool brick and closed his eyes.

"I'll be gone in a few minutes," he said in a feeble voice.

"What happened? Was it Ning?" she asked.

Jaered shook his head but didn't offer anything more. "I have to get inside," she said. "But I promise I'll bring help as soon as I can."

He waved her off. She stepped around the Dumpster and knocked on the back door. Ian answered. He had his cell phone to his ear. "She's here. Leave the body. Marcus is sending a clean-up crew." He held the door open and stepped to the side. "Tara told me what happened. Are you sure you're all right?"

"Thanks to Buster and Tara." Rayne hesitated, then stepped inside. The surgical room smelled of disinfectant and soap, but the body covered in a white cloth stilled her heart.

"Rayne, I'm so sorry. She didn't make it. Dr. Mac did everything he could," Ian said gently. The pain at his inability to wrap his arms around her was so clearly written on his face. Would she have welcomed his comfort if it could have been given? Memories bombarded her. Identifying her mother's body in the morgue. Her father's dying words on the balcony in Oregon. How cruel the brain is, that what we'd choose to forget, is what we remember with the most vivid detail.

Rayne walked over and touched the edge of the cloth. Smooth plastic, cool, crisp. Did Dr. Mac carry it in his bag? Was death as much a way of life for the Weir as nurturing the planet's life?

"Patrick took Carlene and Bryant back to the hotel. He wanted me to tell you how sorry he is," Ian said.

"Donovan?" Rayne asked.

"Dead."

She looked up at him.

He gave a muted shake of his head. "The earthquake claimed him. Dr. Mac is going to stay long enough to get Zoe's body prepared, and then I'll shyft her to the mansion. Marcus is dispatching a squad to cover up what they can."

"She has family, Ian. What am I supposed to tell them?"

"Marcus will find a way for her body to be discovered based on the . . . injuries." Ian's gaze fell to his feet. Rayne lifted the corner of the cloth. "Don't," Ian's whisper stilled her hand. "Don't remember her this way."

"I want to remember," Rayne said, anger flushing her despair. "To be reminded of what we're all fighting for. Why you and I sacrifice happiness and intimacy for something bigger than ourselves. Why I have no choice but to live a life less ordinary." Rayne pulled back the sheet. A scream as primal as any found in the animal kingdom lodged in her throat. She dashed to the sink and retched until she had nothing left.

{51}

Jaered propped himself up on his elbow and stared at his wife. The blistering sun's scarlet rays entwined themselves in Kyre's golden hair. She opened her eyes and found him watching her. His wife's smile ignited his core. "How long have you been awake?" She ran her finger across the stubble at his chin.

He wrapped his lips around the tip of her finger and his tongue played with it. She smiled. "Awhile." He rolled onto his back and pressed her hand against his beating chest.

"You never sleep anymore."

"There's not enough time with you as it is," he said. "I'll take what I can."

"Don't go," Kyre said. "Let someone else transport the rebels this time." A tear found its way down her cheek.

Jaered brushed it away before it dripped from her jaw and into his heart. "No one else can take so many at once. Only my power is strong enough."

"There have been too many trips to Earth." She sat up on the bed and turned her back to him. "Your father will soon discover what you've been doing, if he hasn't already."

"Earth is a pristine beauty, Kyre, unmarred and plentiful." Jaered placed a gentle hand on her belly. "Once you bear our son, we'll live out our days on that amazing planet."

"Living there won't stop what you're doing."

She was right. He wouldn't stop until the last man, woman, and child had been brought to Earth. He gazed into her eyes, the color of Earth's oceans, and wrapped what he hoped were reassuring arms around his wife. Jaered pressed his lips against hers and tasted her sweetness. The rhythm of their heartbeats fell into sync and they touched in favored ways. He kissed her abdomen and reeled back his lust, until her tender voice pressed him to continue while her hands made sure of it.

Once they satiated each other's desires, Jaered gathered her up in his arms and held her tight with his face buried deep in her silky hair. He swam in her scent with thoughts drifting on the rising heat of the day.

"I love you," Kyre whispered, the peaceful moment enriched by her words of devotion. She grabbed his hand and locked their fingers, gripping tight.

An invisible finger pressed hard against Jaered's forehead.

His wife's image splintered outward like a drop disturbing the surface of a pond. He gasped. "Kyre!" His desperate plea was silenced by the pitch that enveloped their surroundings and erased her memory. His world turned black and cold, an eternal void.

"Are they groggy when they wake up? Do they dream when you put them under? Can Ian do it?" Rayne asked, each question louder, crisper than the one before.

"I'd teach him if I could," a man said. "To hell with Weir law. The Primary's insistence at nondisclosure is poppycock. That boy needs training, not indifference."

Jaered struggled to open his eyes. He lay on his back against a cold metal surface. Something soft beneath his head. The butchered shoulder felt numb. Creaks rose from Jaered's parched vocal cords when he attempted to speak. He blinked.

A familiar face cast a hardened and cautious expression. "Angus?" Jaered croaked. The man's eyes widened in shock.

"You know him?" Rayne said.

"No," the old man said.

"But isn't Angus your first name?"

"I've never gone by that, not even as a child."

"Why did you call him that?" Rayne asked Jaered.

Jaered remained mute. He didn't dare look in her direction, at his wife in another life, from another universe. He closed his eyes. The dreams and memories that followed him back into this reality were still vivid and fresh. He wasn't ready to let them go. A heartfelt sigh escaped before he could stifle it.

"Who do I thank?" Jaered said.

"Dr. Mac," Rayne offered when the old man didn't reply. The short, stout doctor pressed two fingers to Jaered's wrist and looked at his pocket watch. A growl cleared the doctor's throat.

A knock came at the door. Rayne paused with her hand on the knob. The old man wheeled the gurney out of view of the door and then tossed a sheet over Jaered.

"Ready?" It was the Heir's voice.

"Ready," she said. "Thank you, Dr. Mac. For everything."

"So you keep saying." The old doctor grunted. "Go."

"Tara says you have about ten minutes at the most."

"I'll be out in five," Dr. Mac said. "Don't worry about me, Ian."

The door shut. A second later, the sheet pulled back. The old doctor peered at Jaered with a touch of irritation. "You were supposed to be at the safe house."

Jaered blinked. Safehouse? It seemed like a lifetime ago that Yannis delivered him to the run-down shack. "What do you know—"

"Eve contacted me. They were to keep you stable until I could get there," Dr. Mac said.

"Ning slaughtered everyone. I followed him here."

"You make a better butcher than a surgeon. I stopped counting the stitches." The man wiped his hands on a blood-stained towel. "You are from Thrae. You know my paral. He goes by Angus."

Adrenaline flushed the last of Jaered's drowsy state and he pushed to sit up, but spikes drove into his chest and shoulders. He propped himself up on one elbow and waited for the shuddering pain to ease.

Dr. Mac didn't move to help. A clear message for Jaered to stay put. The old man pulled the edge of the bandage back, revealing a portion of Jaered's sun on his right breast. "The second I pulled off your blood-soaked bandage, I knew who you were."

His thoughts stopped cold. Not another breathing soul on Earth knew of his birthright besides Eve—and his father. He gave into the weights pulling at his muscles, and he collapsed against the pillow.

"You're Thrae's Prophesied Son, the counterpart to our Ian, here on Earth," Dr. Mac said.

Jaered gritted his teeth and steeled himself to the truth. Born too late—or not soon enough—forever destined as the one to fail his planet. "Did she see it?"

"No, I told her to keep watch at the front door while I treated you back here." Dr. Mac wiped down the rest of his instruments and closed his bag. "I have a couple of questions," the doctor said.

"I'm not one for answers." Jaered said.

"Is he a healer, like me?"

His question gave Jaered pause. So much he could have asked, and yet, all he wanted to know was if his mirror image in the parallel universe had something in common. "Yes, he is."

"Is he married? Are they happy?" Moisture veiled the old man's eyes. He looked over Jaered's shoulder and drifted into memories, painful or pleasant, Jaered couldn't tell.

"Very happy," Jaered responded truthfully.

Dr. Mac nodded as though satisfied. He laid a gentle hand on Jaered's arm. "I've contacted Eve. She'll send help to wherever home is for you. She said that you're like Ian, that you don't need a vortex to shyft, but I gave you a shot to boost your core just to be sure. You should be able to draw enough energy for a local shyft." He grabbed Jaered's arm and helped him to sit up. "At least wait until the room stops spinning. You lost a lot of blood." The doctor shuffled over to the sink in soiled bunny slippers, washed his hands, then wiped down the surfaces. "Seeing how reckless you can be, I suspect our paths will cross again."

"Thank you," Jaered said.

"For the greater good." Dr. Mac recited the rebel litany with more emotion than Jaered had heard in a while. The old man turned off the light and left Jaered sitting in darkness.

"For the greater good," Jaered whispered to no one in particular. He'd known for some time that Eve's rebels were numerous and stretched across Earth. Jaered had brought most of them from Thrae. But not all.

Jaered slid off the gurney. He drew energy into his core and a second later, shyfted into the bushes across from the Big Cat House building. He stifled a cough. Once he verified the coast was clear, he snuck up to the entrance. Blood seeped out from beneath the crumbled lion statue. The Pur clean-up crew had left Donovan where he died. How would the news speculate and spin the CEO's demise? A twilight drug deal gone awry?

After shyfting to the zoo, it had taken the last of Jaered's core energy to fling a concentrated energy blast at the statue. It toppled down on Donovan without the Heir any wiser, thanks to the quake. Jaered told himself he'd been saving the Heir from certain death, sparing the earth from premature genocide in the process. He knew better.

Jaered felt for the dead man's pockets under the statue, careful not to disturb the blood. He found Donovan's cell phone. It took a few seconds longer to locate the tranquilizer gun. In the scuffle with the wolf, Donovan had kicked it into the nearby bushes. The Pur clean-up crew hadn't stumbled upon it. Jaered checked the chamber. One dart remained, still intact. The fool had wasted half the serum on the trash can. A partial dose was better than nothing.

{52}

A growling stomach roused Jaered from a dreamless sleep. The aroma of baking bread was overshadowed by garlic and onions.

Humming came from the opposite side of the room. A clatter as dishes collided in the sink.

At first, Jaered's lids refused to cooperate, but with some effort he succeeded in opening his eyes. Eve stood at the kitchen counter with her back to him. Her hips shimmied while she scrubbed, splattering sudsy water into the air.

"You shouldn't be here. It's dangerous for us both." He cleared his throat when his words came out raspy.

"After the safe house, I wasn't about to trust anyone else," she said without turning around.

"It was Ning." Jaered tilted his head to get a better look at something that dangled overhead. It was an IV bag, suspended from a wire hanger hung with a bent nail.

"A trick from my nursing days." She hummed while stirring something in a pot at the stove. "This place was quite the mess. You're all male, you know that, don't you?"

"Whatever that means." A deep inhale inflated his lungs, but it triggered a spasm in his upper chest where the doctor had repaired Jaered's butchering. "There's a cell phone on the table."

Steps. A second later, a beep. "Donovan's?" she said.

"Trace who he was talking to on Sunday, around one thirty in the afternoon." He licked his parched lips and swallowed. "Whoever it was, knows about the serum's key ingredient being manufactured off-site. You can track it down and make sure it's destroyed."

"Making whatever Aeros gets his hands on, useless." She pocketed it. "Good work. My men found a tablet in Yannis's car when they cleaned up at the safe house. My people cracked his password. We now have the shipment addresses."

"You know where my father's legions are?" This was huge. If Jaered had any spare energy, he'd have jumped out of bed. As it was, he compromised on a smile. "How many?"

"A little more than a thousand." She resumed her stirring, her humming more lively than before.

Jaered rubbed his eyes. Beyond the IV bag, Eve had tacked several photos to the wall. They were from the batch he collected at the Duach warehouse and sent to Eve a few months earlier. Rayne was in most of them. The Heir in the rest.

He stared at them and fought to keep his breaths steady and even. "What is this, a test?"

"No." She wiped her hands on a towel, then dragged a chair over from the dinette table. She sat down and pressed a gentle hand to his forehead, while at the same time she checked his pulse at his wrist. Her rose-pink nail polish clashed with her apron's bright yellow and green stripes. "I get it now, why you can't stay away from her. She's a re-minder of why you're here," Eve said.

"And the Heir is up there to remind me that it isn't her," he said. Eve kissed his forehead, then returned to the sink. Jaered closed his eyes. She moved around the kitchenette, cleaning up, turning on and off the water. The sounds of normal life dumped emotional drawers that had been stuffed with painful memories. "She was pregnant," he blurted, compelled to voice what his heartache could no longer ignore.

Eve stilled. "That's why you didn't bring her to Earth with the others. She couldn't parashyft."

"I lost them both because I wasn't willing to risk it."

"You lost her because your father found out you were bringing his enemies here and hiding them among the popu-lace."

He clenched his eyes against the flaming memories that consumed what little happiness he'd found in the universe. He had stopped trying to drown out her screams long ago. His father's message loud and clear. Aeros couldn't kill Jaered. But everything, everyone else, was fair game.

"How far along?" Eve asked.

"Five months." Jaered stared at the pictures. Eve had opened the door, encouraging—expecting him to rid himself of what made him weak. A racking sob drove painful spikes into his chest and shoulders. He welcomed it. The floodgates burst open, and he gave Eve what she wanted. What they both knew he needed.

Jaered opened his eyes to find Aeros standing over him in the darkened room. He grabbed Jaered's arm. They reappeared at the base of a rocky cliff. His father let go. Gale force winds slammed Jaered into a boulder, and he slunk to his knees with a groan. He grabbed his arm and pressed hard into the boulder against the painful jabs radiating from his shoulders.

Aeros crouched down and sized Jaered up. "You look like hell."

"I was shot trying to cover your butt."

Aeros shyfted to the top of the boulder a split second before the surf's spray swept in. It doused Jaered. He spit saline out of his mouth and shivered from the icy chill. Salt water seeped into his wounds, christening them with a fiery ache.

"The shipment, where is it, Jaered?" Aeros shouted from his perch. "If you want to be spared my wrath, you had best tell me it's en route."

"Donovan double-crossed us. He tried to use it as a bargaining tool."

"For what?"

"His wife's murder."

"And you had issue with that, no doubt."

Jaered's core turned into a searing cauldron and it took deep breaths just to control his voice. He was thankful the latest wave doused his temper before his father had the satisfaction of witnessing it. "He separated the formula into two parts. One half was being manufactured at his facility. The other half at a secret location. Unless they're combined, the drug is no better than water. Somehow the Pur got wind of it. They didn't waste any time infiltrating the company. We had no choice but to delete anything that could be traced back to you and cover your ass. Yannis and I barely made it out of there with our lives."

"Ah, Yannis. Where is he?"

"I was wounded. He took me to get help. Ning showed up. Yannis died trying to protect me."

His father scoffed. "Why would Ning waste his energy on you?"

"Donovan had us in a race to kill his wife. The winner would get everything."

"What interest would Ning have in the serum?"

"We didn't stop fighting long enough to make chitchat. But you saw what the serum did to a Sar's core."

"He'd administer it just to watch Sars burn," Aeros said. "Where's my little pyro, now?"

"I wish I knew. I have unfinished business with that asshole." Jaered wondered what the Heir's group had done with the body.

Aeros's silence was never a good sign. Failure was hardly tolerated, much less betrayal. The unknown fallout kept Jaered's nerves raw. His shivering masked his tightly wound nerves.

"I have a job for you," Aeros said.

Someone's fate was decided. "Are you blind? I'm injured!"

"Richard Donovan is dead and therefore out of my reach."

"So, send flowers."

"Before he is placed in the ground, I require a package."

"What?"

"His son."

Jaered gave his father a puzzled stare. "Why?"

"There's a rumor about the child's . . . origins. I want to see for myself exactly what he's made of." A gust of wind. His father was gone.

{53}

They'd settled on the patio, but the sun's energy did little to revive the group. The drawn faces and slumped figures seated at the round table resembled the aftermath of a frat party. Ian ran on adrenaline in spite of his restless night. Sorrow at the loss of Zoe had given rise to their newest nightmare.

"You think someone baked Bryant this way?" Patrick shook his head.

"If he was genetically bred," Tara said, "that would explain a lot."

"QualSton couldn't have been the only Weir facility dabbling in genetic engineering," Ian said. "Galen told me that the Weir turned to science decades ago in search of answers to our extinction."

"I can't see Carlene agreeing to something like that," Patrick said.

Ian shrugged. "I doubt she knows."

Patrick scraped his chair back with a nervous laugh.

"What part of this is funny?" Tara said.

"You've got to love the irony. My mother had no idea what she got us in the middle of." Patrick peered at Ian with concern. "If he's a Duach Sar. What are you going to do?"

Ian had spent several sleepless nights wondering. He looked at Tara. "Protocol would be to either confront the Sar or inform Marcus about his existence."

"You wouldn't—"

"No, Patrick, he wouldn't." Rayne crossed her arms and stared at Ian.

"That doesn't erase the problem," Ian said. "It only stalls it."

"Who's going to inform Carlene about Bryant's heritage?" Tara said. "And who is going to guarantee Bryant's anonymity and protection from both the Pur and Duach?"

"Nature eventually kicks in. Playful lion cubs grow up to be formidable foes," Ian said. "If Bryant isn't raised to understand and control whatever power he's inherited, he could pose a threat."

"To himself, Carlene—" Tara looked at Patrick, "—humans."

"What if he's raised as a happy, well-adjusted child?" Rayne looked at Patrick. "Like one of us. Doesn't nurture play a part in his nature?"

"Especially now that Daddy Dearest is out of the picture," Patrick said. "He's barely three years old. He hasn't exactly been tainted yet, has he?"

"This is virgin territory," Ian said. "Unprecedented." Movement inside the kitchen. Marcus gestured at Ian through the patio door. Ian lowered his voice. "For now we only trust each other. Have faith that I'll come up with something we can all live with."

Marcus opened the door. "Ian, a word?" The old general's disgruntled expression twisted the throb at Ian's temples into hyperdrive. What had they uncovered at Lux Pharmaceuticals? The others excused themselves and scattered.

"What happened last night?" Ian leaned against the railing.

"Others got there before us. Most of the data was erased, but the boys were able to salvage enough for us to begin piecing together some information."

"Worth giving to the Primary?"

"I'm hoping it will provide a trail to Duach enterprises and where their money is tied to." Marcus signaled to his guard on the lawn. "Maybe give us some insight into tracking down this Eve who has the Primary so riled." The Pur guard escorted a twenty-something man onto the patio.

"Pur Heir, this is Vael," Marcus announced formally. "My son."

Ian extended his hand. "Ian, please."

Vael hesitated before he accepted Ian's hand. The shake was brief, his greeting indifferent. The young man's cold shoulder piqued Ian's curiosity. "Are you visiting your father?" Ian asked.

Vael glanced in the direction of the nearby guard. "Does it look like it?"

"I found Vael at the facility, literally with his hand in the safe."

"That's me. Wayward son and all around pain-in-the-ass." Vael plopped down in a patio chair and put his feet up on the table between them.

Marcus swiped Vael's boots off. "Behave," his father growled.

"You were robbing the place?" Ian asked.

Vael shrugged. "These two guys cornered me at my favorite hangout last night and told me they needed me to get them into a safe." He held up his hands. "It's my power."

"Whoever Vael was helping had a delete virus. We only got the tail end of that data." Marcus rubbed the back of his neck. "Ian, whatever their research was, at least a piece of it involved you. My boys unearthed copies of your medical records."

Ian leaned against the railing. What could Donovan have possibly wanted with his medical information?

"But that's where they made their mistake," Marcus continued. "There was only one location where we kept that information. The Primary's bank in Belgium. I'm confident we can trace how it was compromised."

Vael's breath sucked in like a black hole and he grew stiff. Ian stared at him. "You know something about that?"

Marcus startled. He glared at Vael. "What is he talking about?"

Vael crossed his arms. "No clue," he said, but wilted in the chair.

Ian focused on the beat of the man's heart. "You were there, but your accomplices kept you in the dark."

"It wasn't like that. It was just the two of us."

"I knew it," Marcus said. "The company you've chosen to keep has you at odds with the Heir." He smashed a fist onto the patio table. "With me."

"It was a bank job. We grabbed money . . ." Vael hesitated.

"You were separated, at some time or another," Ian prodded.

Vael nodded. "For about five minutes."

"Was he a shyftor?" Marcus said. Vael's downcast eyes confirmed it. "He returned to the vault to grab the Heir's records and God knows what else." Marcus glanced in the direction of the guards standing at the base of the patio steps. He lowered his voice but kept its edge. "As if you weren't foolish enough to get yourself involved, you had to do it in the one place connected to the Primary. I've already set men on reviewing the videotapes. How am I going to keep this from him?"

Vael's heartbeat came to a standstill. "The Belgium bank job wasn't the only one, was it?" Ian guessed. "How many others?"

Vael shot Ian an irritated glance. "What are you, some kind of lie detector?"

"Spill it, Vael," Marcus said.

"His name's Jaered. We did half a dozen jobs together, maybe more. The bank was the last one. He was injured trying to escape from the rooftop that day. I thought he died. I never saw him again until he showed up yesterday."

"Ian, something to write with, please."

Ian touched the patio table. A tablet and pencil appeared.

Vael stared at it. "What's that for?"

"You're going to write down everything that you remember about the jobs. What you took, when they occurred, and where." Marcus shoved the pad and pencil at Vael. "And I mean everything."

"Was it always Jaered?" Ian asked.

"Yeah, only him, no one else." Vael hunched over the pad and started writing. "I didn't know, dad, honest." From the beat of Vael's heart, that part was true.

"I need to be able to trust you, son," Marcus said. "But it's impossible with the choices you make." Marcus stormed across the patio, headed for the back door. "Ian, keep an eye on him. I'm getting my laptop to check the sites on his list."

Ian stood by as Vael added robbery after robbery to the list. "How did you and Jaered connect in the first place?"

Vael paused and leaned back in the chair. He tapped the end of the pencil against the pad. "I wasn't in a good place. Strung out on drugs, I'd spend whatever I made on some bad shit. Jaered found me on the street, cleaned me up, and gave me jobs. You're wrong about him. He's not bad."

"He taught you to steal, and by the sound of it, deserted you when it suited him."

"The guy saved my life!" Vael shouted. "That's more than you or my dad ever did for me."

"Cleaning you up to do his dirty work isn't the same thing," Ian said.

"I was cornered on the bank rooftop. The guard had an itchy trigger finger and a hero complex. When Jaered shyfted nearby, he didn't even hesitate."

"He took a bullet for you?" Ian said.

Vael scoffed. "You with your cushy life, a mansion, an army at your beck and call. What do you know about the rest of the world?" Vael hunched over the pad and kept writing. "I'll give you what you want, but you gotta give me something."

"What?" Ian asked.

"A get out of jail card. I want nothing to do with the Syndrion, you, or my dad."

{54}

Tara rang the bell. A couple of minutes later, the door opened. Patrick froze. "Mother!"

JoAnna smiled wide. "I'm so glad you're here." She ushered them all into Carlene Donovan's house.

Rayne peered past her. "Where's Carlene and Bryant?"

"They're in the backyard." JoAnna shook her head. "I thought Ian was coming?"

"He had to run an errand. He should be here soon," Rayne said.

"Carlene was touched that you called to see how they were holding up."

"She was sweet to invite us for the day," Tara said.

"Mother, what are you doing here?" Patrick swiped his palms on his slacks.

"Of course I flew here as soon as I heard." She pressed a fist to her chest and lowered her voice. "I feel somewhat responsible, as tragic as it is, what happened to Richard and all," she said. "But I can only hope that Carlene and Bryant will have a happy life together once this tragedy is behind them." She brightened up. "But enough about the ills of the past few days. I'll play hostess and get everyone some refreshments. Carlene has been slaving away in the kitchen. She's planning on all of you staying through dinner." She linked arms with Tara and led them through the house.

Rayne's steps dragged as JoAnna herded them toward the back of the house and opened the rear French doors. Carlene was pushing Bryant on a swing at the far edge of the lawn.

Two tables had been pushed together with a long table-cloth spread across them. Folding chairs surrounded the banquet table waiting to accommodate their large group.

Patrick held up next to Rayne. "This turned into a cluster-fuck."

"His funeral is in two days. Who knows when we'll get another chance to search for Donovan's safe."

"Ian should reconsider my idea," Patrick said. "We would have had the house to ourselves for a month. No pressure. Plenty of time to search," Patrick muttered. "But hell, I only think like a human."

Rayne gave him a sideways glance. "Rigging a contest and having her win an expense-paid trip to Europe wasn't a sure thing, Patrick. In spite of everything he did, Carlene and Bryant are still mourning the loss of a husband and father."

"Who is this Eve, anyway?" Patrick said.

"If we can crack the safe, we might be one step closer to finding out." Rayne chewed on her lower lip and watched Carlene pick up Bryant. When the young mother took him to greet Tara, he held out his arms to give her a hug. Rayne sighed and pulled out her cell. "I'll give Ian a heads up."

Patrick looked around. "The grounds might be spacious enough, and the mansion's extending wings are a plus. Ian's plan just might work."

She pressed his number and held the phone to her ear. "It better, for Bryant's sake." And mine, she kept to herself.

"Fuck!" Jaered lowered the binoculars and rubbed his hand across the tree branch in a feeble attempt to erase the needle-like tingling that had set in once the pain meds wore off.

He had counted on the widow to seek solitude in her time of grief. When he woke up that morning, he'd decided to get in and out before the mansion became overrun with acquaintances offering condolences.

When the Heir's group arrived, Jaered's plan tanked.

From the tree's vantage point, he had a clear view of the office and a portion of the backyard. The child tossed a ball at Patrick, then raced to get it. Tara sat on the patio with the mother.

Rayne stepped outside. Jaered lifted the binoculars. The longer he studied her, the more intrigued he became. When the mother brought the child over to say hi, Rayne tickled the boy's nose with a peacock feather she had been twirling in her fingers, but she leaned back when he reached toward her.

Jared lowered the binoculars. Sweat broke out along the back of his neck in spite of a cool breeze sifting through the tree. His cell buzzed. It was Eve.

"I don't see any way around this. Kidnap the child as planned."

"Do you know why Aeros wants the kid?" Jaered said.

Silence. He slumped against the trunk. Jaered needed to trust her. Lately, there'd been too many reasons not to.

"By the end of the day," she said. "And there's one more thing. I need you to bring me everything you find in Donovan's safe."

A crucial puzzle piece slipped into place and revealed the unknown that had plagued Jaered for days. "Your history with Donovan. It concerned the boy." Jaered's thoughts sped up when she didn't deny it. "Donovan didn't have the knowledge, the background to create his kid. But you did."

"Building our rebel force hasn't been the only step I've taken to save this planet, Jaered. I've also worked tirelessly to save the Weir race." A moment of silence passed between them. "Are you good for this?"

The squealing child ran across the lawn chasing Patrick with a stick. Memories of Kyre's screams drowned out the sounds of innocent delight. "For the greater good," he said and hung up. A moment later, a text arrived with intel on the safe. The location wasn't going to be a challenge. The obstacle was getting inside.

Rayne knocked on the walls at the back of the built-in bookshelves. Ian stood in the center of the office and turned a keen eye on everything else. Between knocks, he listened for any sound of gears or other mechanical lock mechanisms working on a preordained schedule. Except for the tinny strikes of an antique mantel clock, all was quiet.

A loud knock came from the office door. Ian leapt onto the couch and tossed one of the throw pillows under his head. Rayne covered him with the quilt, then answered the door.

Carlene entered carrying a silver tray with a steaming teapot and mugs. "Are you feeling any better?"

"I'm afraid not," he said and sat up. He gave her a weak smile.

Carlene set the tray on the desk. "I was hoping you could join us for dinner. It'll be ready in a few minutes."

"I'll see," he said and accepted the steaming mug. "If the queasiness doesn't settle soon, I may just head back. I'd hate for anyone else to come down with this."

"Are you sure you don't want to lie down in one of the guest bedrooms?" Carlene glanced about her husband's office with a pained expression.

"It's quiet and comfortable enough here," Ian said. "But thank you."

"Well, come find me if you need anything else." She let herself out.

Rayne listened at the door and then gently pulled the dead bolt until it locked.

Ian sat in Donovan's desk chair and studied the surface while he sipped the herbal tea. Pictures and mementos of Bryant littered the desk.

Rayne stood next to him. "There aren't any of Carlene."

"It's not her absence, but Bryant's prevalence that's significant," Ian said. "Born without a core, Richard was the one to bring their family's Weir power to a grinding halt."

"Donovan's childhood couldn't have been easy," Rayne said.

Ian set the mug on the desk. "Bryant would have been Donovan's chance to follow in his father's Duach legacy."

Rayne picked up one of the pictures. "Carlene mentioned that he often brought Bryant in here behind locked doors."

Intrigued, Ian glanced about the room with a different set of eyes. "He may have needed Bryant for the safe," he said.

"Why?"

"Carlene said the mansion has been in Richard's family for the last three, maybe four generations. That means Bryant's grandfather and his great-grandfather also lived here. Before Richard, the Sar power would have been passed down through their generations. What if it takes core power to trigger the safe?"

Rayne brightened. "Start touching things."

Ian swept his hand on the walls and behind the books at the back of the built-in shelves. He pulled back the rug and brushed his palm across the floor. The furniture in the room was modern, but he swiped his hand over it anyway. Except for earning a dirt-smudged palm, he found nothing that reacted to his touch. He ended up at the French doors leading onto an attached patio.

"Rayne, what did your research say about Richard's father, something about his hobby?"

"He was into horticulture. Crossbreeding plants was a passion of his."

Ian stepped onto the outside deck facing a dense wooded area. He paused and studied the thickness of the exterior wall. When he checked, the opposite wall wasn't nearly as wide. Ian touched the surface of the wall, but stopped when he came to a plant growing out of a sizeable pot. It trailed large fernlike leaves up the surface. Over time, the vine's stems had fused themselves into cracks and ridges.

Rayne kept watch from the open patio doors.

Ian stroked one of the feathery leaves. It shriveled to his touch.

She joined him. "What did you do?"

"It reacts to touch, much like the Shame-Old-Lady plant in Jamaica. But that species is quite small and it grows along the ground."

She brushed a leaf with her finger. It didn't respond. "I don't have the magic touch."

He swept his hand across several leaves. Each one shriveled and closed upon itself. Ian stood back. Similar to its Jamaican cousin, the leaves spread open a moment later. "It reacts to my core." Ian worked furiously, beginning at its base. At shoulder height, one of the closed leaves revealed a metal corner. "Here." He touched the area surrounding it. Behind the branches, a metal plate, a little more than a foot square, was embedded in the wall. To Ian's dismay, its surface was smooth.

"Where's the handle?" Rayne asked, pushing in for a closer look. "There's no hinges."

Ian pressed at the sides and corners, then in the middle of the panel, but he was greeted with solid resistance. He shut other leaves within arm's length searching for a lever or a switch, but found none. He pressed a palm against the plate and summoned a variety of natural energies. Nothing. Fed up, he stepped back and allowed the plant to conceal its mysterious treasure.

"Maybe it isn't a safe at all," Rayne said.

Ian pondered his next step. He pulled out his cell. "If it is the safe, and we can get inside, it might lead us to Jaered, or maybe even Eve." He swiped the screen, scrolling through the list of numbers although he knew Marcus's code by heart.

"But what about Bryant?" she said.

"Donovan had my medical records, Rayne. Bryant has a core. Are you betting they aren't connected?" Ian pressed the screen.

{55}

Entertained by their futile search, Jaered's amusement vanished the second the Heir stumbled upon the safe.

Sitting in the tree taxed his already strained muscles. He dropped down and stood behind the thick trunk, flexing his better shoulder. The butchered one offered lightning strikes of pain whenever he lifted his arm above his chest. The thought of wearing a sling hadn't occurred to him when he woke up that morning.

When he looked back at the house, two people had joined the Heir on the patio. Jaered raised his binoculars, then pulled away with a start.

A large man held onto Vael.

Jaered's head reeled. The Heir led them to the hidden safe. Jaered tightened his grip on the binoculars. Vael's arrival wasn't a coincidence.

A knock at the door. Rayne rushed in and opened it a crack.

"Dinner's ready," Carlene announced from the hallway. "Is Ian joining us?"

"I'm afraid not," Rayne said. She glanced at Ian from over her shoulder.

"Go," he whispered. "Buy us as much time as you can." Rayne slipped out, and Ian locked the door when their footsteps faded. He returned to the patio.

Marcus stepped away from the plate. "How can you be sure it's a safe at all?"

"I can't." Ian regarded Vael. "Can you get inside?"

Vael shrugged. "Getting in isn't the problem. But without any obvious gears or levers, I have no idea what to do once I'm inside. Do you know how thick this is? I lose feeling in my hands and arm when I use my power. I could go all the way through and not know it."

"We'll judge by the thickness of the outside wall," Marcus said.

"But how thick are the safe's walls, one inch, two, three?" Vael regarded Ian. "Do you have X-ray vision along with that lie detector?"

Ian shook his head.

Vael plopped down in a patio chair. "I'll do this for you, but I have to know how far to reach and what to do once I'm in there."

Marcus pulled his cell out of his pocket. "I'll connect with the boys. Maybe they can research the type of safe it is and get some specs." He left them on the patio and settled in the desk chair.

Ian sat down across from Vael and rubbed his face. Weariness gripped him, and he leaned back absorbing energy from the elements.

"Guess the almighty Pur Heir isn't so mighty after all," Vael mumbled. "Or just want the fuck-up to do your dirty work? How are you any different from Jaered?"

Ian dropped his head. It pained him to admit that Vael had a point. "What's with you and your dad?"

Vael scoffed. He leaned forward and rested his forearms on his thighs. "I was the first Pur Sar to be born in almost twenty years. I didn't have the mark of the sun, but at least one Pur Sar held out hope." Vael regarded Marcus through the open door. "Then you came along . . . suddenly, I didn't exist anymore."

Knuckles rapped on the office door. "Ian?"

He bolted from the chair, mindful of his steps as he hurried through the office. He gestured for Marcus to stay back. Ian opened the door a couple of inches.

JoAnna gave him a concerned grimace. "Are you sure you can't join us, even if just to meet Bryant? Carlene was so hoping."

Ian slipped out into the hall and closed the door behind him. "I don't want to risk getting anyone else sick. He headed for the foyer and withdrew his car keys. "I think I'll just slip out quietly. Please give Carlene my regrets. We'll make plans to get together again when I'm feeling better.

JoAnna squeezed his arm. "Drive safe. I'll call before I leave town to see how you're doing."

Jaered shyfted behind the large man. When he made to turn, Jaered struck him with a heavy bronze statue from the bookcase. He slumped to the floor.

"What the fuck!" came from the doorway. Vael stared at him with a slack jaw.

"Am I glad to see you," Jaered said and headed toward him. Vael slugged him, hard. It knocked Jaered on his butt. "Ugh!" He grabbed his arm.

"You son of a bitch! You have some nerve showing up here," Vael hissed.

"I guess you're still sore about how we parted."

"What, the other day?" Vael snorted. "Try all last year when you used me like you did. What are you in the middle of, Jaered? Who did you get me to do your dirty work for?"

"What are you talking about?" Jaered grabbed the edge of the desk and pulled himself to his feet.

"Don't play the dumbass. I'm talking about that Belgium bank job. You returned to the vault and stole the Heir's records."

Jaered froze. "How did you—"

"There's more to it, isn't there?" Vael stepped out onto the patio.

Jaered followed. "It's a long story, Vael. We don't have time at the moment." Vael's gaze fell to the growing red patch at his shoulder. "A nasty by-product of getting shot," Jaered said.

Vael shook his head. "I overheard the guards say they grazed someone during the raid at the pharmaceutical building. Were you really shot saving my life in Belgium, or was it all an act?"

Jaered unbuttoned his shirt far enough to reveal the scar. Vael's furrowed brow softened.

"Can you get into the safe?" Jaered said.

"It is a safe?"

"Yeah, but only the kid can open it, and that's not going to happen in the next thirty seconds." Jaered touched the plant. The leaves shriveled. "It's an inch thick and the left side corners are spring activated."

Vael hesitated. "Why should I help you? What's going on?"

"Not now, Vael, there isn't time."

"*Make* the time, Jaered."

"Remember what I said at Donovan's office?"

"The crap about saving the universe?" Vael said.

"I'm not exaggerating." He touched the leaves. They shriveled under his hand. "I'm working with rebels trying to stop Aeros from ripping this planet in two. The egomaniac who created that serum, had ties to our rebel leader. There could be records in this safe that, if found, might expose her and the rest of us."

Vael scrutinized Jaered. He released a tremendous sigh. "Then why knock out my dad? He might have been able to help."

Jaered weighed his next words carefully. "Not all of the rebels . . . are Pur."

"The Duach from the other night?" Vael asked.

"The Pur aren't alone in caring for this planet. Not all Duach are bad. Eve is trying to unite the Weir—*all* Weir— and put an end to the feud before it's too late."

"They can't be trusted," Vael hissed.

"There's plenty of Pur that can't be, either. Your Primary among them," Jaered said. He looked over his shoulder toward the office. "Your father may be in more danger than he realizes."

Vael stared at Jaered as if weighing more than his words. Jaered may not have shattered Vael's beliefs in what he'd been raised to believe about the Pur and Duach, but from the look on his face, Vael was willing to question it. "We're running out of time," Jaered said. "Are you going to help me, or not?"

Vael's hand transformed into a swirling light show. "This isn't over . . ."

Jaered swiped across the leaves and exposed the panel. Vael pushed his translucent fist through the metal. "If my hand becomes solid, I swear to god I will find you and beat you to death with my stump."

At a low, muted sound, Jaered glanced over his shoulder. The sound didn't repeat itself. "How was the family reunion?"

"Piss off." *Click. Click.* Vael jerked his hand out. The door popped open.

Jaered withdrew the contents. Two CD's. One wasn't labeled. The other read, Heir. The center of his chest turned frigid. He spun around. Vael's dad held a remote in his hand.

{56}

Ian's core grew numb. He rushed past JoAnna, and burst through the door in time to see a man jump over the patio railing with Vael close on his heels. Ian flipped the dead bolt on the office door at the sound of running footsteps in the hall.

Marcus grabbed a patio chair and pulled himself to his feet, moaning. Ian ran to the railing. The two men disappeared around the corner toward the front of the house.

The doorknob rattled. Knocking. "Ian, if you're going to throw up, the bathroom is two doors down, dear," JoAnna shouted.

"Marcus—" Ian said.

"What are you waiting for, go!"

Ian leapt over the railing and took off in pursuit. When he rounded the corner, he paused. Vael stood on the front patio. Alone. Ian surveyed the area. The front stoop was wide open, it didn't offer any hiding places.

Vael held his hands up as if in surrender. "Jaered showed up."

Ian slowly approached. "Why help him?"

"I figured he's as good an escape plan as any." Vael's chest heaved. Ian couldn't tell if he was gulping air from the dash or if it was from fear. "There's something you've got to know. This isn't about the feud between the Pur and the Duach. This is bigger, scarier than that," Vael said.

"What's worse than the Duach using science experiments against the Pur?" Something jammed into Ian's back. He closed his eyes in defeat. Jaered controlled the remote. Ian had been so intent on Vael, he'd failed to notice the fluctuating changes in his core.

"The Pur aren't as innocent as you think." Jaered leaned in from behind. "The Weir's war is going to be the end of this planet. It's been the perfect distraction, blinding all of you to the greater threat. What you should all be uniting against."

Ian held his hands up and slowly turned. The man's bruised lip struck a nerve. Jaered was Rayne's stalker. He held the remote. Ian made to grab it, but Jaered jerked it out of reach. A spreading pond of bright blood stained the man's shirt at one shoulder. "You were the one the Pur guards shot the other night," Ian said. The breeze carried a scent that scraped across Ian's memories. His stomach lurched at recognizing the odor. He'd passed it on his way to find Tara. Jaered had been at the zoo.

"Wake up before it's too late," Jaered said. "The Weir should be focusing on Aeros, not each other. What he's begun to do to this planet may already be irreversible."

A plume of heat rose from Ian's core and burned his throat. "Who are you?"

"An ally, protecting this planet," Jaered said.

"Bullshit." Ian clenched his fists to control his blistering chest. His hands glowed. "Who do you work for? Aeros?" Jaered's expression never changed, but the beat of his heart and the set of his jaw told Ian that Jaered had likely crossed paths with the Duach leader, and not in a good way. Warm. He ventured another guess. "You work for Eve." Shock flitted across Jaered's features. His heartbeat soared. Warmer, Ian decided. Much warmer.

Jaered jerked his chin at Vael. "Come on, we need to go."

"Like hell." Ian slammed his sizzling hand against Jaered's bleeding shoulder.

Jaered wailed and dropped the remote. He knocked Ian's hand away and stumbled back. It was a feint. A swift kick and Jaered nailed Ian in the center of his chest. He crashed into the concrete railing with such force that it punched the breath out of him. Ian pushed off and lunged. The two men landed on the floor of the front stoop. A fist as solid as a bowling ball connected with Ian's jaw and sparks sizzled behind his eyes. He rolled to the side, then twisted around and caught Jaered's head in a crushing vice between his thighs.

"I want the contents of that safe," Ian snarled. When Jaered didn't comply, Ian squeezed harder. Jaered's face grew a deep crimson. He groped at Ian's legs and tried to pull free, but Ian grabbed the railing and hung on tight.

Jaered stopped resisting and reached into his pocket. He withdrew a CD case and dropped it. Thousands of needles penetrated Ian's hand. He cried out. Vael stepped away from the railing with a glowing hand.

Ian released Jaered with a growl and groped at his hand, fused to the railing. Vael pulled Jaered to his feet. "Wake up, or Earth will succumb to the same fate as Thrae," Jaered said and grabbed Vael's arm. The air shimmered around them.

"No!" Ian screamed and scrambled to his feet. White sparks surrounded the two men, and their images faded. Ian froze. Jaered's corona boasted no hint of color. It wasn't emerald of the Pur, nor crimson of the Duach. He strained to break free, desperate to jump into the man's corona and not lose him. But Ian remained cemented to the railing. A second later, Jaered and Vael were gone.

"Shit!" Ian stared dumbfounded at the chunks of concrete blended with his living tissue. Without knowing how to control Vael's power, he couldn't undo it.

"There you are."

Ian swallowed a wail full of pain and frustration. He glanced over his shoulder. JoAnna stood at the front door.

He kept his back to her. Vael hadn't told Ian how his power worked, but Ian had asked a few questions that morning at breakfast. He had seconds to put the pieces together.

Ian concentrated on drawing pure electrical energy. Static cling sucked his clothes tight to his skin and puffed up his hair. It filled his core. Ian directed it into his hand.

"Is everything all right?" JoAnna asked. "When you didn't answer earlier, I went to find the girls. They're searching for you inside."

"It felt like I was about to throw up. I wasn't going to make it to the bathroom. I couldn't do that in front of you." His fist didn't change. The needles stung worse than ever.

"Ian, I raised an anxious child," JoAnna said with a glint of amusement in her voice. "I'm hardly affected by a little throw-up."

He switched his strategy and drew only electromagnetic energy. His fist chilled to the bone. "The fresh air is helping it to pass."

"Is there anything I can get you?" JoAnna's voice grew closer.

His hand transformed into a swirling orb, resplendent with sparkling light. He turned, keeping it behind him.

She grabbed the crook of his loose arm. He stiffened. "Come inside. We'll get you another cup of tea."

Ian took a deep breath to ease his heart back in his chest. He gently lifted her hand from his arm and ushered her toward the door. "I'll be another minute. I think it best that I say my good-byes and leave soon." He stepped away from the railing and stuck his sore, but intact hand into his pocket. Rayne and Tara approached from the side yard. They held up at JoAnna on the patio with Ian.

"I'll let Carlene know," JoAnna said. "We'll throw together a to-go bag for you. You can at least sample her wonderful meal once you can keep it down." JoAnna took a step. Scuffling. Her foot knocked the CD case and sent it scooting across the front stoop. She picked it up. "Music bands have such silly names, don't they? Who would ever call themselves the Heir?"

Ian took it from her. "It's mine. I must have dropped it."

"Don't leave without meeting Bryant. Carlene really had her heart set on you two connecting." JoAnna let herself into the house.

The girls met up with Ian on the steps. "What happened?" Tara asked. Rayne grabbed the remote from the top step.

"Jaered showed up." A racing pulse wasn't the only thing that gave Rayne away. Surprise—something more profound—flooded her crystal-blue eyes at the mention of his name. Heartache squeezed Ian's core and denied him breath.

"I'll get Patrick." Rayne rushed off. "He's with Bryant."

"Rayne!" Ian shouted.

"I'll be careful," she tossed over her shoulder. Thanks to the Curse, she retreated to the one place he couldn't follow.

Tara stared at him. "Ian, what's wrong?"

The setting sun cast the surroundings in a warm glow. Nature's dying, brilliant burst as the day shed its radiance before draining into the grays of night. He rubbed the center of his chest with his fist, but it didn't dispel the throbbing ache.

Ian's core ignited. He didn't suppress the blistering heat as it seared something as precious to him as her love. Trust.

{57}

Jaered led Vael into the apartment and shut the door.

Vael wagged his head. "I can't believe we got the best of the Heir."

"I'm weaker than I want to admit." Jaered grabbed his arm and held on tight as the ache took its time to ease into a stuttering throb. "He's used to using his head, not his powers. That's the only reason you got the slip on him." Jaered grabbed a fresh shirt from his packed duffle and stepped into the bathroom, then locked the door. He perused his shoulder. The fight had torn several stitches. He slapped on a fresh bandage and changed out of his bloody shirt. He removed the back panel to the medicine cabinet and verified that the serum vial was where he'd left it. He returned to the outer room. Vael took a swig from a beer he'd found in the refrigerator and handed Jaered one.

Jaered took a generous gulp. "You're sure the Heir doesn't have your power?"

"He can't, otherwise, why would they have called me in to help?"

"Lie low here for a couple of days." Jaered cradled the beer under his arm and pulled a wad of bills from the bottom of the pack. He tossed them on the kitchen table. "When you're sure the coast is clear, get as far away as you can before the Pur track you down. I have to go."

Vael spurt beer. "I'm sticking with you."

"You can't, Vael. What I'm in the middle of, it's too dangerous."

"I want in, all the way."

Jaered turned to go, but Vael was as good as a wall. "You're a lost puppy looking for a home," Jaered snapped. "I'm not the master you want, believe me."

"After this, my dad won't stop hunting me down. He'll toss me in a Pur prison, or worse," Vael said. "Sticking with you is the only option I have left. What part of that don't you get?"

"Friends don't use you for your talents and then desert you. Hell, I've murdered people closer to me," Jaered said.

Vael snorted. "You're not a murderer, Jaered."

He drove his fist through the wall. The jarring pain rippled through both injured shoulders. Pain was all Jaered knew, the only thing left to him in the world. "People around me end up dead, Vael. Don't be one of them."

"After this afternoon, you owe me." Vael leaned against the door. "I'm one favor ahead, and it's a big one."

Jaered stepped away and concentrated on steadying the throb in his neck. He still had a job to do. "I have a loose end to take care of," Jaered said. "Then I have to meet about a package. If you're still here when I get back, we'll talk."

Vael scrutinized Jaered closely, then stepped away from the door. Jaered paused with his hand on the knob. "You don't know what you're getting into. If I bring you into this, there won't ever be the option of getting out."

"It's about saving the world, you said so yourself."

"But you won't like the means we're taking to get there." Jaered shyfted.

Jaered reappeared in the bushes at the edge of Donovan's backyard. The last of the sun's rays set at the horizon and the welcoming shadows grew plentiful. A fine mist blanketed the lawn.

From the direction of the garage, a man's laugh coincided with a child's giggles. They emerged from the side door. The child perched on Patrick's shoulders as he walked toward the short rock wall that separated the back lawn from the steep slope of the hill.

"More rocks," the boy said, hanging on to Patrick's ears.

"As if we don't have enough already." He tilted his face up toward the boy. "Your mom won't be able to get the car out of the garage if we put any more in there."

"Pleeeze." The child giggled and kicked.

"Ouch, all right already." Patrick stopped at the wall and set the child down on the lawn. He ran, trailing giggles behind him.

Movement. Rayne hurried toward them.

A slew of curses were buried in Jaered's shoulder. He'd counted on a couple of them trying to free the Heir at the front of the house while the rest focused on distracting the other women. If these two were here, where was the Heir? Where were the others?

"Did you find Ian?" Patrick kicked a ball.

It landed a yard from where Jaered hid in the bushes. The child ran toward him.

The boy reached for the ball but his shoe got there first. The toy rolled inches from Jaered's boot at the base of the bush.

Patrick had his back turned, talking to Rayne. Jaered leapt from the foliage. The child took one look at Jaered, and let out a shriek. Jaered grabbed him but the boy fought back. A punch from his tiny fist found Jaered's injured shoulder. Splintering pain erupted. "Ugh!" His grip on the child weakened.

"Put me down." The boy kicked and thrashed.

Jaered ignited his core, but he couldn't shyft. His chest was numb.

"Bryant!" Rayne ran toward them. The remote was in her grasp.

"I'm taking the child. Don't try and stop me," Jaered warned. He eyed the remote. "Turn it off!"

"Let him go!" She reached for Bryant.

Jaered took a step back. "Are you sure you want to do that?"

She froze. "Don't . . . he's just a baby."

Jaered hesitated. He turned from the woe in her crystal-blue eyes before he lost his nerve altogether. Patrick tackled him from behind. His legs buckled. The child broke free and dashed through the open door into the garage.

Patrick straddled Jaered and held down his arms. He had no more fight in him. His shoulders were dead in the water. Jaered dropped his head back in defeat.

"I've got this," Rayne said, standing guard over Jaered with the remote in her hand and fury burning in her eyes. Patrick took off after Bryant. "Ever since Oregon, I thought you were a Pur. Ian's guardian angel." Her hand sagged. "Mine—" It was more than disappointment that cut off her words. Pain flushed her anger. He wasn't who she wanted him to be, who she needed him to be. "Who are you working with? You owe me that much."

"A rebel force fighting to stop Aeros." He searched her eyes for the slimmest of signs that she believed him. Her face scrunched, as if her emotions and thoughts were jockeying for dominance. "If Aeros finds out that I'm helping them, I'm a dead man and Earth, everything you know and care about, won't be far behind."

"I've had it with your secrets. You ask too much!" she cried. "How can I trust you after everything you've done? What you're about to do?"

"You trusted me with the Heir's life in Oregon." Jaered got to his feet. "You didn't expose me the night of the party." He took a step back, then another. "I'm begging you to trust me, one last time." At her hesitation, he took off for the garage and locked the side door a second ahead of her.

He tuned out her pounding from the other side and listened. Women's voices joined the ruckus at the door. "What's wrong? Where's Patrick and Bryant?"

Could this get any more fucked up? Jaered thought. He waited for his eyes to adjust to the dim light. In spite of its size, there was very little stored inside the space. Not much lent itself to potential hiding places. Three cars sat side-by-side in the center, each with their own separate garage door. An extended workbench covered the far wall. Its cabinets were the perfect size to hide the child, but not Patrick. Jaered paused next to a Mercedes.

A child's whimper—*click*—came from the SUV at the opposite side of the garage.

He crouched and snaked his way around and between the vehicles. He tried the driver's side latch. It gave, and he slipped behind the wheel. He shut the door and hit the vehicle's master door lock, pulled out his pocketknife and fell to one side. When he found the necessary wires from under the dash, he made a decision. "Feel free to exit the car in the next two seconds, Langtree, but the boy stays."

Silence. Jaered swiped the two sliced wires and a spark sizzled. The engine turned over. He twisted them together, then pushed up with a groan when his shoulder reminded him who was in charge. He shifted into neutral, pressed down on the brake and stomped on the accelerator. The engine revved up to a deafening pitch. "Last chance!" Jaered yelled.

"I'm not leaving him." Movement in the rearview mirror. Patrick rose from the rear bed of the SUV with his arms around the boy.

"Then get in the middle seat and strap both of you in tight." Jaered winced when he threw his arm over the bucket seat. "And hold on."

Patrick did as ordered. "Why are you doing this?"

"For the greater good," Jaered roared over the engine noise. The car lurched before it sped backward on squealing tires. A jarring impact. Bent, strained metal. Jaered threw the car in drive and sped forward. The particleboard cabinets collapsed under the front grill. Assorted tools rained onto the SUV's hood. He shifted into reverse and slammed on the accelerator. The impact ripped the garage door off its hinges. The vehicle skidded sideways, smashing into trash cans. Two cars blocked the driveway.

Jaered pumped the brake and controlled the slide. The top-heavy vehicle skidded to a stop inches from the parked cars. He spun the steering wheel in one hand while shifting with the other. Shouts from the backyard. A woman screamed.

The boy moaned and clutched his chest in the backseat. The Heir appeared on the back patio. He leaned heavily on the railing.

"You're trapped," Patrick said.

Jaered swerved off the driveway and into the backyard, cutting a path across the expansive lawn. It would be tight. He fought to remember the yard at the far side of the mansion. Was it wide enough?

The boy reeled back and screamed. Patrick held him tight. "Stop, you're hurting him."

"Not me." The car sped past alongside the patio deck. Jaered rolled down the driver's side window and swerved the vehicle within inches of the steps. The Heir yelped and tumbled down the steps onto the lawn. He rolled onto his side. His face contorted with pain but turned a hateful glare at Jaered.

Jaered gave the Heir a smug grin and a two-finger salute. He twisted the wheel and headed for the open side yard. The tires spewed chunks of turf and mud when Jaered slammed the accelerator into the floor. The SUV's back end fishtailed across the lawn before correcting.

A tickle deep in his chest. Jaered headed for the low, stacked rock wall at the opposite end of the estate.

From the edge of the elevated patio, Tara tossed folding chairs onto the lawn, directly in the car's path. They were mowed down by the SUV, but the rear tire sent one sailing toward Rayne. It slammed into her and knocked her to the ground. The remote flew out of her grasp. Jaered pulled his eyes from the rearview mirror in time to see a long tablecloth flying toward him. It swept across the windshield like a curtain.

Blinded, Jaered let up on the accelerator. A jolt. The SUV smashed through the low rock wall and soared into the air, rising ever higher above the steep slope. The nose of the car tilted downward.

{58}

The Curse lifted. Ian bolted to his feet and ran for the opening in the wall.

"Who was that driving the car?" JoAnna shouted as she ran toward Ian.

"Where's Bryant? They're not here!" Carlene screamed from the wrecked garage.

"Oh dear god." JoAnna's steps slowed. Tell me they weren't inside . . ."

Ian peered over the wall. The SUV had left the hill airborne, landed upright a distance down the slope, and gouged a path in the shrubs before slamming into a cluster of small boulders. From what Ian could tell, it somersaulted over the boulders and came to rest on its roof.

"Are they all right?" JoAnna asked. "I can't see a thing in the dark."

Ian vaulted over the low rock wall. The hill was steeper than he'd judged, but he managed to stay on his feet with dirt and rocks carrying him along. He reached the wreck and grasped the bumper to stop his slide.

The front and side airbags had deployed. Ian smashed out what was left of the rear passenger window and pushed the bag out of the way. A quick glance confirmed what he had hoped and prayed since the moment the car burst through the wall.

The jam's battery had died. The vehicle was empty.

The lawn and hillside were ablaze in floodlights and chaos. The local police were in a heated battle with the recently ar-rived FBI who were claiming that a kidnapped child gave them jurisdiction. Ian returned to the ambulance and leaned against the open door while the paramedic treated Rayne.

"I really think it's broken," the paramedic said, slipping her bound forearm into a sling. "Let me take you to the hospi-tal."

"I'm not going anywhere until I find out what's happened to my friends," she said in a tone that snapped off further ar-gument.

The paramedic grabbed a red bag and turned to Ian. "I'll be back. Talk some sense into her."

"As if that's possible," Ian said.

The second the paramedic was out of earshot, Rayne sniffed and her hand pressed against her lips. Whatever held her together threatened to crumble. He leaned against the open door, weakened further by his failure to protect any of them.

"Why?" he said on rising anger that had nothing to do with her, and yet, everything.

"I was trying to help. He was getting away."

"That's not what I meant," he said and stared at her, reluc-tant to press further, fearful of what he'd find.

A tear moistened her cheek. "As far as I know, Jaered's been near, for weeks, maybe longer."

"Why didn't you tell me?"

"He swore me to secrecy," she whispered. "It was his price for saving your life."

"What are you talking about? When?"

"On the cliff, overlooking QualSton. You were dying, I couldn't do anything. I couldn't touch you."

Galen had questioned how Ian had been able to make it home. His injuries were too severe for such an unprecedented shyft, yet somehow he'd made it. At the time, Ian had no explanation for what he couldn't remember. "He would have been trapped in the northern vortex building."

"I don't know how he does what he does. He appeared that day on the cliff and saved your life. I didn't see him again until the night of the party. When Patrick and I stepped into the conference room."

"And never said anything." Was omission the same as a lie? Ian's swallow lodged in his throat, cutting off a wail of torment. "You've protected him. Why?"

"Until now, I thought he was an ally."

"He helped Donovan—"

"We don't know that for certain," she said.

"—probably Ning," Ian added. "He was at the zoo!" She stilled, her heart stopped dead in her chest. Ian went to grab her shoulders, but pulled back at the last second. His hands balled into tight fists. "You knew he was there."

"He discovered Ning was coming after me." Rayne turned and grabbed her jacket from the back of the ambulance. "He came to help, in spite of being seriously injured."

"How can he possibly justify kidnapping Bryant and Patrick?"

She closed her eyes and shook her head.

"If there's anything you know, something that would lead to where he might have taken them—"

"He told me that he wasn't born on Earth. How can that be?"

"I think he's from Thrae," Ian said. It was the only explanation for not having a corona.

"Where's Thrae?" Rayne asked.

"It's Earth's mirror universe. Shyftors can get there, but they need a powerful vortex stream or field. Thrae is forbidden territory. Crossing dimensions, parashyfting, is punishable by death."

Rayne slid off the back of the ambulance and stood on wobbly legs. "You have no way to follow them?" she asked with genuine concern.

"They could be anywhere in the world by now," he said. Or beyond, Ian realized. Earth was vast enough. If Jaered moved between dimensions, Bryant and Patrick could be lost to them forever.

Saxon lurked behind the tree line at the edge of the forest. Tara stepped out onto the office patio a few feet away.

How is she? Tara channeled to Ian.

Broken forearm, scrapes and bruises. He watched Rayne struggle to put her jacket on. Even now after everything, it pained him that he couldn't do it for her. *Confused.*

Don't be too quick to judge, Ian. Withholding knowledge from loved ones is never easy, especially when it's done in the name of good, Tara channeled.

Ian's thoughts reached out to Saxon, combing the grounds for any clues. No response. The wolf had nothing to share. If the safe contents had been Jaered's primary objective, why come back for the child? Did he know about Bryant? Ian fingered the CD case in his jacket pocket. He'd chosen not to reveal the miniscule victory to Marcus. The Drion had left for Germany. He'd called an emergency meeting with the Syndrion. If Ian was honest, Rayne wasn't the only one guilty of withholding key information.

Ian and Rayne found the others on the back patio. Carlene sat in a daze and appeared oblivious to the swarm of bodies that invaded her house. JoAnna stood watch as agents scurried nearby with indifference to the woman's pain, focused on their assigned roles.

"We won't know what's really going on until they make contact," an FBI agent said, walking up the steps. "But until the kidnappers make the next move, all we can do is wait."

There was a haggard look about Patrick's mother as she hugged herself, staring toward the wrecked wall, into the darkness. Her fingers tapped against her arms, as if her thoughts were racing under the weary exterior. Ian was at a loss for how to comfort JoAnna. It was his fault that her son had been put in harm's way.

{59}

Jaered watched Patrick through the cracked window in the abandoned office. The man's wrists were bright pink and chafed from fighting the handcuffs. Patrick's face drooped with defeat while his head rested back against the dented metal file cabinet. Jaered entered and shut the door. He turned back and glanced through the cracked window to guarantee Cyphir hadn't followed.

Patrick came alive and tried to stand, but didn't get far. Jaered had handcuffed him to one of the lower, exposed pipes in the room.

"Where's Bryant?" Patrick hissed. "What have you done to him?"

Jaered dropped to one knee in front of him, but kept an arm's distance between them. "I need you to listen with an open mind to what I'm going to tell you."

"Fuck you," Patrick slumped to the office floor. "Why would I believe anything you tell me?"

Time was running out. Jaered's rendezvous was within the hour. "The Pur believe that the Heir is Earth's savior. The Primary instilled that belief for—" Jaered caught himself and paused. "—a very long time."

"Who do you work for?" Patrick said. "Did you have anything to do with murdering the scholars?"

"Our people got there too late to save them. We lost one of our own protecting the caretaker and the Drion."

Patrick leaned back against the file cabinet. He raised his knee and rested his arm across it. "So Aeros got the book."

"Aeros didn't go after the book," Jaered snapped. He cautioned himself and measured his next words carefully. "It was the Primary's death squad who murdered the scholars."

Patrick snorted. "Did someone tattoo stupid onto my forehead while I wasn't looking? Why would the Primary have them killed? He's the one who brought them to the mansion."

"But the Primary didn't have the book," Jaered said. "The Heir kept it hidden from everyone. Pur and Duach. He refused to disclose the location unless the Primary could find someone capable of translating the ancient Weir language."

Patrick didn't respond.

Eve had told Jaered that if he dangled enough truth, Patrick couldn't help but listen. "The scholar's abbey was protected and beyond even the Primary's reach," Jaered continued. "He had to lure them away. He used the promise of meeting the Heir after all these years, and the chance to decipher the Book of the Weir, to his advantage. But the Primary had to act fast once they were gathered and had access to the book. He couldn't afford for them to disclose whatever they uncovered." Patrick picked at the loose carpet fiber and didn't look up at Jaered's pause. "If the Pur found out the truth about the

Weir and your so-called savior, they would revolt. The Primary would lose everything he'd built."

"Is this a new kind of torture? Lie me to death?" Patrick dropped his knee and leaned forward. "If you're not going to let me go, at least release the boy."

Jaered clenched his teeth and turned away. He might have pricked Patrick's curiosity, but belief was something else. "The boy was created in a test tube, born with a viable core."

"A homemade Sar," Patrick said. "Tell me something I don't know."

"He wasn't the first." Jaered pulled the scrap of paper out of his back pocket and tossed it at Patrick's feet. He stood and looked out the office window. A hint of light ran along the horizon. Dawn was upon them. Jaered was out of time.

Patrick stared at the paper. "What are you saying?"

"There's a reason the Heir has struggled with developing his powers," Jaered said. "Hell, it's a miracle of science that he has any at all."

Patrick's pallor drained. "I don't believe you," he whispered.

Jaered leaned against the wall and grabbed his arm. The ache emanating from both shoulders had kept him awake. He couldn't remember the last time he'd slept without the benefit of drugs.

"That paper has a name on it. It's the Heir's mother." At the chime, Jaered checked his cell phone screen. Eve sent the preliminary blood test results. He removed the plastic bag he'd been carrying around in his jacket pocket. A teaspoon of water sloshed in the bottom, the ice cube had partially melted. He set it next to Patrick.

"What's that?" Patrick said.

"Before long, you'll be able to extract the key to the hand-cuffs." Jaered turned the knob and opened the office door a crack. He made sure he hadn't been followed. He left the door open on the way out. He couldn't risk Patrick interfering downstairs.

"I'm not leaving without the boy!" Patrick shouted to Jaered's retreating back.

Jaered headed for the door marked Stairs and made his way down the three flights to the ground floor. The slumbering child clutched the dinosaur, still in the manufacturers shrink-wrap, tight against his chest. He sucked his thumb.

Cyphir pushed away from the wall at Jaered's approach. "What did you give him?"

"Benadryl." Jaered rubbed his face. "Even if he wakes up, he'll be drowsy."

"It's time," Cyphir said.

"I know." Jaered crouched down and gathered the boy in his arms.

{60}

Ian found an ideal vantage point in Carlene's upstairs bedroom window and waited with churning emotions. A fleck of white at the distant tree line. Saxon lingered nearby.

A few minutes later, the squad car pulled up with flashing lights, minus the siren. An FBI agent rushed in and opened the back door. Patrick emerged, but drew back at the throng of reporters headed his way. The FBI and police did their best to contain the crowd. One of the agents escorted Carlene and JoAnna down the mansion steps and past the cameras.

Reporters broke through the barricade and headed for the taxi. The FBI agent in charge shouted at everyone to stay back and to let the women through. The authorities got the group under control. When Carlene reached the squad car, Patrick bent down and grabbed Bryant from the backseat. The child didn't lift his face from Patrick's shoulder until he heard his mother's cry. Carlene wrapped her son in arms that no human could penetrate.

JoAnna engulfed Patrick with more emotion than Ian had ever seen between them. For once, Patrick didn't resist. The reporters got their images, and story, in time for the midday news.

Tara pushed in and threw her arms around Patrick. She clung to him and buried her face in his chest.

Why kidnap the child, and then release him?

The question had ricocheted in Ian's thoughts since hearing the news. He leaned on the windowsill. When they got word that Patrick and Bryant were found, unharmed and safe, Ian had used Rayne's broken arm as an excuse to leave. When she was whisked away for an X-ray at the hospital, he slipped into a bathroom stall and shyfted to Carlene's. Ian had to see for himself that they were okay.

Dark clouds rolled in and occluded the sun's warmth. A breeze picked up. Hair fluttered. Shirts flapped.

Patrick looked up and paused at Ian in the window. He touched Tara's shoulder then leaned in and said something.

Patrick says he's okay, Ian, Tara channeled. *Whatever you're struggling with, let it go. The storm has blown over.*

Tell him . . . that I'm sorry, Ian responded.

Tara tilted her head and relayed the message. Patrick laughed.

The clouds dispersed on Ian's sigh.

{61}

The aroma of bacon and sweet breads filled Jaered's head as he stepped into the great room on his father's yacht. Platters of assorted fruit, meats and pastries lined the polished cherrywood counter at the opposite side.

"May I serve you, Master?" the waiter stood with all the patience of a statue, eager to please. The perspiration stain at his collar spoke volumes. The weaker Duach who joined Aeros's army never lasted long. "If you don't see anything to your liking, I can order it special."

"Coffee." Jaered leaned against the counter and plopped a chunk of cantaloupe into his mouth, then crunched on a slice of bacon. It wasn't until the flavors ignited his taste buds and his stomach growled that he realized how long it had been since his last meal. The grinder whirled with a spitting clatter. Jaered accepted the proffered cup and settled on the plush couch. There was no relief in sight for his tightly wound muscles. In all likelihood, this was his last meal.

A few sips and Jaered set the cup on the coffee table. A chill ran across the back of his neck at the change in molecular energy in the room. "Dad," Jaered said. He stood to face his father head on and steeled himself for what was to come.

His father approached the counter without addressing him, giving Jaered no hint to his mood. The waiter silently handed Aeros a cup of coffee. Jaered caught the slight rattle in the man's hand before he released the fine-china saucer with nary a spilled drop.

"Leave us," Aeros said. The man bowed with an audible sigh, then slipped through a back door. Aeros sipped from his cup and regarded Jaered with nothing short of disdain. "You arrived empty-handed."

"You would have killed him."

"Your conscience disgusts me." Aeros flicked his hand.

An invisible elephant stomped on Jaered's chest—the walls pressed in—fireworks behind his eyes. He collapsed on the couch as muscles strained for dominance over the unforgiving force of his father's power. Aeros watched with the indifference of one passing the time at a bulletin board.

Bile surged. Cantaloupe and coffee weren't as satisfying on their return. With the last ounce of free will, Jaered turned his face into the expensive cloth and retched. Acidic chunks filled his mouth and he smeared them from cheek to cheek, euphoric in his final act of defiance. Thoughts of Kyre flitted in and out of what little consciousness remained. He grasped onto them and found peace in her memories as he lay dying on his father's soiled couch.

The squawk of seagulls. Swirling images faded. Jaered opened his eyes. Still on the couch. The odor of stomach acid—gone.

"Explain." His father's voice floated from nearby.

Jaered rolled over but let out a groan at sliding onto his injured shoulder.

Aeros gripped it and dug his thumb into the wound. Spikes of screaming neurons shot out in every direction. Jaered gulped air to stay conscious.

"How does this substitute for a child?" Aeros held up the vial of blood from Jaered's duffle.

"Everything you need for your analysis is right there. You didn't need the child."

"I'm to believe this is him, why?"

"Because Cyphir witnessed the blood draw," Jaered said.

"Report," Aeros commanded without tearing his attention from Jaered.

"I received word that he was ready to hand over the child. When I arrived, he drew the boy's blood," Cyphir said from across the room. "Two vials. He took one, I took the other." The guard stepped forward and held out the second tube. "He said to test them both to verify he didn't swap them."

"I kidnapped the boy as ordered, got what you wanted," Jaered said. "But I'm not you. I don't kill innocent women and children."

"You are as stubborn as your mother," Aeros said. "But you're not as humane as you would have me believe. My blood flows in your veins. My cells make up your tissue. You are a part of me no matter how much you fight it." His father stood and approached the counter. He picked up the pot and breathed deep the coffee's aroma, then poured himself a fresh cup. The Duach waiter burst into the room and stood at the alert. "Take those and have them assessed in my lab immediately," Aeros said. Cyphir handed the Duach the two vials, then approached the couch.

"You should know better than to be presumptuous." His father set down the cup and stepped to the center of the room. "Insolence will cost you every time."

"No!" Jaered screamed. Cyphir held him down by his shoulders.

Aeros shyfted with a deafening clap of thunder that bounced off the walls and rattled the porcelain cups. The shimmering vortex gases swirled, then slowly dissipated.

The corner of Cyphir's mouth curled in a sneer. His father's guard left without a word.

He lay still with the sonic boom echoing in his head long after it died in the room. His father went hunting on Thrae. Jaered slammed his fist on the coffee table and it shattered. Scarlet streaks ran down his forearm. His father couldn't kill Jaered or the Heir—but everyone else was fair game.

{62}

The howling winds and sleet that had racked the area breathed a momentary lull. The lingering moisture blanketed the lake in a swirling mist.

The service was simple, the crowd thin. Yet, those who attended Zoe's funeral served stories and laughter alongside the tears. When her little brother stepped forward and placed a rose on top of her casket, Rayne's resolve crumbled. Patrick threw his arms around her like a shield of armor, cloaking her self-imposed guilt from all but the most discerning. Random, subtle sniffs came from Tara's direction as she stood staring at the grave site, no doubt recalling memories of burying her sister, like a scab ripped off a partially healed wound.

Ian had buried so many, knew of countless more. The fight to protect Earth came at such a steep price.

Back at the mansion, Rayne changed out of her black dress and went in search of a cup of tea. She stepped onto the mansion's back patio to see if Saxon was nearby. Fog rolled toward her and encased the house in premature darkness. The crisp, wet surface bit into her bare feet, and she lifted them in an impromptu dance. She hugged herself and peered through the opaque cloud. The last of the drizzle stopped. A burst of warmth swirled around her while it dried the deck below her feet. Ian's loving gesture brought moisture to her eyes.

"I should have been there," Ian said.

"It was for the best. She kept our relationship secret. You showing up would have been difficult to explain." Rayne turned.

Ian was perched on the railing at the far end of the patio. His clothes and hair were drenched. His haggard despair clawed at her heart. "Milo said you had to deal with a hurricane in the Pacific."

"And now I've been summoned to appear in front of the Syndrion," he said.

"Why?" she asked. When he didn't answer, she gripped her sleeves tight. "After everything that's happened, the Primary still expects you to choose?"

"I promised us that our destinies would be of our own making. But it couldn't be further from the truth." He hopped down from the railing and approached with drooped shoulders.

"You are the earth's soul, Ian. There's no walking away from that. I know that now," Rayne said.

"All others may be my duty, Rayne, but you're the one I choose to . . ." He dropped his head along with his voice. "You know how I feel."

How she longed for his lips to form the words just once. The chasm between them had never felt wider—deeper. "I share you with the world. I knew it wouldn't be easy," Rayne said.

"There will always be somewhere else I need to go. Something that will keep us apart." His heartfelt sigh sent a gust across the patio. "Someone."

Sleet fell. Rayne's cheeks stung. She stood her ground and weathered Ian's heartbreak. She'd given him reason to doubt her. An urge to reassure him never made it to her lips. Rayne's grip on her sleeves turned into tight fists and she urged herself to stay strong for both their sakes.

He took a step back, and then another, retreating before her eyes.

She walked toward him with determined steps. "If I'm to lose you, let it be for the good of the earth." She stopped and bit her quivering lip. She willed the tears not to spill. "But know that you have not lost me. You never will."

His eyes softened. A drop dampened his cheek. She didn't know if it came from the rain or his own making. For Ian, they were often one and the same.

He gave her a soulful look. A green burst. Ian was gone.

His lingering warmth dissipated. The bitter cold left in his wake bit into her and she shivered. Rayne fell to her knees and gave in to the sobs that racked her chest.

Patrick threw open the kitchen door and swept her up into his arms. He half carried, half dragged her into the house, away from the rain and pelting sleet unleashed upon the area.

He dried her off as she sat trembling on the kitchen stool. Winds howled outside. Tree branches struck the sliding glass door and whipped in a scurrying path across the patio. "Where are the others?" she asked through chattering teeth.

"Milo is securing the house," Patrick said. "A freakish storm is about to hit.

Tara appeared in the kitchen archway. The concern on her face was palpable. "Where's Ian, did he return yet?"

Rayne shook her head. "Yes, but he left to meet with the Primary."

"Crap, Milo called Dr. Mac," Tara said. "He's on his way."

"Why?" Rayne asked.

"Ian's energy has been deteriorating. His boost is barely making a dent. Milo thinks the rise in severe weather patterns is taking a toll on him. And now this latest catastrophe."

"What's happened?" Patrick asked.

"A 9.0 earthquake devastated Indonesia. The resulting tidal wave is estimated to reach India's east coast within the hour," Tara said. "I'm going to the study to turn on the news."

"I'll put on a pot of coffee in a minute," Patrick said. He tossed the wet towel on the floor and grabbed a dry one from Milo's clean-laundry basket, wrapped it around Rayne's purple feet, then rubbed them vigorously. Her chattering eased and she clenched her jaw to make it stop. He left her and grabbed Milo's steeping teapot from the stove. Patrick poured her a cup and handed it off. A deep sigh escaped. "Ian's meeting with the Primary isn't about the weather, is it?"

"I don't know." Rayne pursed her lips. A lone tear found its way down her cheek.

Patrick stepped to the kitchen archway and checked the hall. When he returned, he withdrew a piece of scrap paper from his jeans pocket. He hesitated, then unfolded it. "Jaered gave this to me before he released me," he said under his breath. He held it up for her to read.

"Who's that?" Rayne asked.

"According to Jaered, it's Ian's mother." Patrick stared at the name on the paper. "He said that Bryant wasn't the first child with an artificial core."

Her shivering came to a standstill. She took the paper from Patrick and stared at the woman's name. "What else did he say?"

"That it was the Primary who was behind the scholars' murder." Patrick leaned against the kitchen island and crossed his arms. "To keep us from knowing what was in the Book of the Weir."

"Before Tara killed Ning, he swore the Pur guard were the ones who attacked the mansion that night." She flinched when a patio chair crashed against the back door. "I didn't believe him."

"I don't know what to believe anymore," Patrick said. "Rayne, I need a straight answer from you. No bullshit. Do you trust Jaered?"

She nodded, slowly, as if she couldn't believe it herself.

"Ian's overloaded as it is," Patrick said. "But I can't ignore this."

"I'm done with sitting on the sidelines." Rayne set the mug down and slipped off the stool. She wobbled over to the stove and turned on one of the gas burners. She held the paper close. The corner caught and a narrow flame snaked along the edge.

It wasn't until the pain grew unbearable, and she'd committed the name to memory, that she released it. It floated to the floor, crumbling into bits of ash. She rinsed the remnants down the drain and turned on the disposal for good measure.

The only way to earn back Ian's trust was to set out on her own mission to find the truth.

{63}

Jaered released his grip on Vael's shoulder and stepped out of the vortex stream. A blast of moist heat filled his lungs.

"Where are we?" Vael followed Jaered out of the sweatbox structure and into the day. The intense sun reflected off the metal hut. Vael shielded his eyes.

"It doesn't matter," Jaered said. "It's never the same place twice."

"How do you know when and where to meet if it's so random?"

Jaered fingered the burner cell phone in his pocket. "You ask too many questions." His tone reeked of warning. "That's your first weakness."

Jaered walked to the rear of the building. Concrete loomed ahead of them, littered with tufts of burnt grass. The crude airstrip stretched across a barren atoll. The horizon offered no landmarks, no sense of direction with the sun centered overhead. Not a tree or bush to be seen between the single dilapidated structure behind them and the endless ocean beyond.

"Nice place. I think my next vacation will be here," Vael quipped.

Jaered remained silent. He closed his eyes and stood still, waiting. Listening.

"Don't mind me. I'll just absorb a few carcinogens." Vael plopped down on the blistering sand and lit a cigarette.

A couple of minutes later, Jaered opened his eyes to the hum of an engine and tracked the black dot. "It's time." The plane circled low overhead. Jaered gave a cursory wave. One of the wings dipped. The aircraft pulled into approach.

It touched down on the worn surface, spitting gravel and chunks of asphalt in all directions. The private jet taxied around, facing them as a majestic bull confronting a matador. Its long nose cone pointed downward.

In spite of the heat, Vael shuddered. "Looks like a bird of prey."

A door swung open. The short flight of stairs lowered. "This is your last chance to walk away," Jaered said. "Once you get on that plane, you won't ever have the option to leave."

"I'm no quitter."

Jaered had tried to talk Vael out of it for most of the night over a case of beer. But it became clear as time wore on that, other than his mother, there wasn't anything holding Vael to his former life.

Vael started up the steps, but Jaered stopped him and led the way. They entered the opulent interior.

"Wait here," Jaered ordered. He walked between the high-backed cushioned seats.

Eve sat at the back of the plane. She tossed him a wry smile. "You meant to drive off that cliff."

"I needed to shyft. She wouldn't turn off the jam." Jaered settled in the seat across the small table from Eve. "She wasn't about to let them die."

"Rayne didn't turn it off. She dropped it when the chair smashed into her. The only thing that saved you and the others was weak battery power."

"I got the job done."

"Insanely reckless, considering the cargo." She took a sip from her ice tea glass and tapped the screen on a tablet. "All three tests confirm it. The child has a weak core, but no power gene."

"Millions and you still can't recreate your miracle." He leaned forward. "Oh, wait, it wasn't *your* miracle, was it?"

She ran her finger along the condensation on the side of the glass. "You left the name?"

"Patrick might choose to ignore it."

"Not if you've managed to instill doubt. He'll seek an ally."

"Rayne."

"The rest is up to them. If Ian's to join the fight, it's important that he finds his own enlightenment. They will be his beacon."

"Or he'll take his own path, altogether," he said.

Eve gave him a piercing stare. "Where's the serum, Jaered?"

"I might have bought the Nurse Nightingale stunt, if you hadn't cleaned up my place." He settled back and melted into the cushion. A grin tugged at his lips. "It must have irritated the hell out of you when you couldn't find it."

"Let's just say it's a good thing you didn't die on me," she said.

He shrugged. "The important thing is it's out of my father's reach."

"But still *in* reach?" She studied his face.

"I know what you commissioned it for," he said. "When the time comes, I want to be the one who delivers it."

"You still don't trust me."

"Would you trust you?" He stared at the old, weathered book sitting on the table between them and tried not to dwell on the bloodshed of the past few days.

"A child and his mother will live a full life thanks to you," she said.

"It came at a tremendous price," he said.

"Unavoidable whenever your father is in the equation." She glanced at the bandage on his forearm. "And this time?" she asked softly.

She could be so hard one minute, so sympathetic the next. "He went hunting," he said.

Regret flashed in her eyes. "Stay focused on what you have control over, Jaered. The best way to help those who are left on Thrae is to defeat your father on Earth." She lifted her chin and peered over the bucket seats. "Are you sure he can be trusted?"

"As much as anyone born to Earth can be. His skills are useful." Jaered slipped out of the seat and gestured to Vael.

At Vael's approach, Jaered released a sigh of resignation. The look of confusion sealed his friend's fate.

Eve indicated for him to take the seat vacated by Jaered. "Hello, Vael," she said in a voice reserved for running into an old friend.

"You look familiar," Vael said. His face brightened at the same time he snapped his fingers. "You were in a few photographs at the Heir's mansion. You're Patrick's mother."

She gave him a guarded smile and ran her finger across the Book of the Weir. "You can call me Eve."

Glossary

Book of the Weir: A volume of letters and notes kept by the Ancient Weir Counsel. It is rumored to include secrets to the Sars powers and predicts the coming of the Heir.

boost: A device that draws elements from the planet, such as calcium or proteins, to aid in healing. The boost is fueled by the energy stored in a Sar's core.

Channels: A set of identical Weir twins who share a genetic marker with a Sar. The three are able to communicate telepathically or, when standing close enough together, the Sar may receive visions or eavesdrop on the thoughts of others.

core: Sars are born with a core, deep in the center of their chest. It allows them to control, and contain, energy drawn from the planet. Not all cores are alike, and therefore, it dictates what power they yield. If a core extinguishes, the Sar dies.

core blast: Known as the Dragon's Breath during the Dark Ages. A core power that enables a Sar to draw and manipulate energy from below the surface of the planet. Scholars believe, from the center of the Earth.

corona: A colorful gas that's created when a Sar uses a vortex. If a Pur steps into a vortex field and draws energy into their core, the gases turn green. When a Duach uses the field, the gases turn red.

Curse: An unpleasant, often excruciating reaction when a Pur Sar and a Duach Sar come in close proximity to each other. Developed by the Ancients, it prevents the Duach and the Pur from stealing each other's powers, a barbaric practice which often results in death.

Duach: \dū-ôk\ A rebellious group of Weir who use their powers for self gain. They are considered the black sheep of the Weir and are despised by the Pur for their narcissistic ways.

Heir: The Ancients predicted the eventual decline of the Weir race and predicted the coming of the Heir, the last Sar born to the Weir. Prophesy stated that he would be born with the most powerful of cores, and thus, inherit all of the combined powers of the Weir Sars that came before him. Since the Weir keep the energies of Earth in harmony, the planet would continue to survive.

mark: In ancient times, known as a Seal. A triangular image of raised skin found on the left breast of Sars. Only the Heir's mark is a triangle that houses a sun. Weir males born without a mark are powerless.

paral: Someone from Earth and someone from Thrae who are the mirror image of each other.

parashyfting: Crossing into an alternate dimension during a shyft. A powerful vortex stream or field is required. Only Sars born with the shyfting power can parashyft.

Primary: The head of the Syndrion.

Pur: \pūr\ Thought of as the original and longest practicing of the Weir. They continue to work tirelessly for the good of the planet and to lessen man's impact on the world and other living creatures.

Sar: A firstborn Weir male who's inherited a core, granting them control over a single Earthly power. Most Sars control plants or animals. Sars born with rare powers, such as shyfting or core blast powers, are the most revered and sought after.

shyft/shyfting: \shift\ The ability to teleport. The Sar's core allows him to use one of thousands of vortex energy fields or streams found across Earth in order to move around the surface of the planet.

shyftor: \shif-tor\ A Sar born with the shyfting power doesn't need a vortex to shyft over short distances.

somex: \sôm-ex\ A Sar born with the somex power can control neurotransmitters in the brain that affect consciousness.

Syndrion: \sin-drī-un\ The Weir counsel. Ever since the Duach broke away from traditional practices centuries earlier, the current Syndrion is made up of only Pur Sars. Representatives from each continent serve on the counsel.

Thrae: \thrā\ Earth's twin planet in an alternate dimension.

vortex: A specific location where energy fields emanate from the planet surface and circulate on invisible gases.

Weir: \wē-er\ Magical stewards of the Earth who have lived quietly among humans for more than two thousand years. Their purpose is to ensure harmony between Earth's various energies and all living creatures. With each generation, there are fewer Weir Sars born with a connection to the Earth. The

Weirs' power is dwindling, and along with it, their control of Earth's combined energy. As a result, natural disasters are on the rise in frequency and intensity.

I hope you enjoyed reading *Masks and Mirrors, Book Two: The Weir Chronicles*. To get caught up on the series, don't miss *Fade to Black, Book One: The Weir Chronicles* available in paperback (ISBN 978-0-9905628-0-1), hardback (ISBN 978-0-9905628-1-8), on Amazon (ISBN 978-0-9905628-2-5) or through Smashwords, Barnes & Noble, iBooks, Kobo and other ebook sites (978-9905628-3-2).

To receive the latest news about the series, visit my author website at www.sueduff.com. Add your name to the fan email list and receive notices about book events, the latest information on upcoming novels in the series, and more.

Here's a peek at the next exciting adventure in the series, *Sleight of Hand, Book Three: The Weir Chronicles* appearing winter, 2016.

Jaered pulled the Jeep onto the interstate and soon reached the stretch along the ocean cliff. The distinct odor of the city's pollution morphed into the salty sea and he inhaled deep, filling his lungs. The morning's haze had given way to the intense glare of the natural sun. Jaered turned his face toward the heavens and absorbed the energy's warmth, a constant reminder of his mission on Earth.

A remote overlook offered the privacy Jaered sought. He crossed the vacant lot and came to a stop at the concrete barrier separating the overlook from the two-hundred foot drop on the other side. He shut off the engine, then verified he was alone.

Jaered withdrew the cell from his pocket and stared at Eve's early morning text. *It's time.*

He thought of the hundreds of rebels scattered across the globe. Each one received the identical message. How many stared at their screens, wallowing in the significance of those two, simple words?

A gust of wind whipped through the open cab. Jaered grasped the steering wheel to steady himself. At the horizon, a gray blanket rose from the ocean. It billowed and swirled. The dark mass soon obliterated the sun's warmth and transformed the blues of the sky to cement.

Jaered tapped out his response on the cell. *Rec'd.* His finger hovered over the send button. A moment later, he touched the screen. The text turned green.

He got out of the Jeep and approached the edge of the overlook. Jaered threw the cell phone over the side. It tumbled to the surf below, then shattered on the rocks, its pieces exploding outward and scattering into the ocean's spray.

There was no reason to stay in contact with Eve in the days ahead. Jaered, like the other rebels, were well versed in their next assignments.

So much to do, he thought. Retrieve the serum from its hiding place at the back of his medicine cabinet. Close out his affairs and erase any lingering sign he'd ever been in San Francisco. Eve insisted that he cover his tracks. It would be disastrous if Jaered's father discovered his association with the rebel forces, and his hand in the events to follow.

The sun's rays poked through the overcast sky and ignited Jaered's core. He savored the afterburn while his thoughts fell to his assignment.

Kill the Pur Heir.

Acknowledgements

No one is an island and this is especially true when writing a novel. I am blessed to be surrounded by experts, colleagues and loving family and friends.

A shout out to The Tattered Cover writer's group: Mark, Bob, Chad and Tim, for their weekly support and valued critique. Steve Parolini at Novel Doctor, your insight into what my stories need keeps them fresh and believable. Thank you Stephanie Wardach, copyeditor, for catching my numerous mistakes and making me look like I know what I am doing. Karri Klawiter, you take my vision for the book cover and apply your gift to make it your own, artistic achievement. You continue to amaze me.

Heartfelt thanks to Matthew Woolums and Wendy Barnhart Terrien, the best beta readers anyone could hope for.

As always, my family and friends deserve my deepest gratitude for their continued support and contagious excitement. It is your belief in me that gives this series its fuel.

ABOUT THE AUTHOR

When not saving the world one page at a time, Sue works as a speech therapist. She enjoys taking her octogenarian, mini Dachshund and Great Dane puppy for strolls, or stretching her creative juices in the kitchen. A Colorado transplant, she savors the incredible seasons, but appreciates that Mother Nature spares her from shoveling the driveway, too often.

Masks and Mirrors is her second novel in *The Weir Chronicles series.*

Visit her at www.sueduff.com, on Facebook at Sue Duff – Writer and follow her on Twitter @sueduff55.

Book cover designed by Karri Klawiter, Art by Karri

Author photo by Liz Garcia